ADVANCE REVIEWS

"Sagnier takes us to vividly realized, lovesick Montparnasse, weighted with upheaval and rebirth in the aftermath of the first world war. Drawing together intimate lives, period authenticity and lurid twists, Sagnier has composed a must-read for historical fiction buffs, Francophiles and fans of Caleb Carr alike."

> — Taylor Zajonc, Bestselling author of *The Maw* and winner of the 2018 Clive Cussler "Grandmaster" Adventure Writers Competition

"*Montparnasse* is a fascinating, utterly compelling read set in avant-garde Paris, specifically the artists' haven of Monparnasse, just after World War I. Life in Monparnasse, where at this time anything goes and nothing is forbidden, unfolds before the reader in a series of delightful anecdotes held together by two main stories, one of a serial murderer of well-off widows, of whom there were plenty after the trench massacres of the war, and the other seen through the eyes of a pair of mis-matched American newlyweds. Famous artists drink absinthe in the cafés and walk the cobbled streets in a delightful depiction of a city and a land coming back to life after the tragedy of war."

> — Jane Feather, *New York Times* bestselling author of *The Blackwater Brides* series

Montparnasse

Montparnasse

THIERRY SAGNIER

Apprentice
House Press
Loyola University Maryland

First Edition

Casebound ISBN: 978-1-62720-235-0
Paperback ISBN: 978-1-62720-236-7
Ebook ISBN: 978-1-62720-237-4

Printed in the United States of America

Designed, edited, and promotion plan developed by Dani Williams

Published by Apprentice House Press

Apprentice House Press
Loyola University Maryland
4501 N. Charles Street
Baltimore, MD 21210
410.617.5265 • 410.617.2198 (fax)
www.ApprenticeHouse.com
info@ApprenticeHouse.com

PROLOGUE

The little man poked at the flames with a long-handled rake. The wind outside his rented villa ran to the southeast, carrying the greasy black smoke away from the neighbors and dispelling it quickly. The man sniffed at the fire's aroma and wondered how many more days or hours they would let him ply his trade. Turning over a particularly thick hunk of meat and bone, he listened to it sizzle as a vein of fat hit red coals.

They were closing in. The man knew this, had made his peace with it, and longed for a resolution. He'd had an excellent run. The newspapers had spread his fame to the four corners of the country and beyond, and on a daily basis he was receiving letters from war widows and maiden women eager for the company of "a distinguished gentleman, polite, presentable, well-off and well-spoken, looking for a lady of like caliber to share his achievements, love and life." The advertisement ran in the personal sections of 17 newspapers in France, and he had agonized over its composition, every word chosen for sincerity and discretion.

It was searing hot next to the oven. With the tines of the rake, he dragged a mass of backbone and ribs, then turned the rake over and smashed the bones before pushing the pieces under the coals. Next he dragged a pelvic girdle from the giant oven onto the floor where it smoked and emitted an acrid odor. He fetched a large hammer from a corner of the room and hit the bones twice. The girdle split with a cracking sound. A third and fourth blow shattered it completely. Sweeping up the debris with a twig broom, the man shoveled the shards back into the oven.

He had always relished the planning stages; the wording of the advertisements, the culling of letters and proposals, the selection process. The women were unfailingly the same. The older ones protected their assets, the younger ones their virginities. He took both, mostly with gentleness and an occasional harsh word when progress lagged. The meeting and wooing, the financial intricacies, the inevitable resolution, all these interested him far less than the development of a plan, the persuasive arguments of an avid suitor, and of course, the performance. The creation of the character—embodying the role of the would-be lover—was what truly excited him.

Now, it was nearly time for the next act.

He took seasoned oak logs from a stack near the door, threw them into the oven and waited until they burst into flame. Oak burned hot; it was the wood which had been used to burn heretics and Templars a few hundred years earlier. Though the man had no faith or religion, the historical detail pleased him.

He shut the oven's door and removed the blacksmith's apron he wore over his suit. In the upstairs bathroom, he carefully inspected his hands, fingernails, teeth, and hair, then applied a minute amount of wax to his beard and mustache. Satisfied that he could now see himself as the women did, he sat before the stack of letters on the kitchen table.

CHAPTER 1

It had been 16 days. The deck felt slick and dangerous. A hundred feet below, the ship's prow cut through a sullen Atlantic, sending frigid mist into the air.

It's too cold, thought Frederick Cowles. I should return to the cabin. Easter will be wondering where I am.

A spray of icy seawater brushed his face and made him step away from the railing. Far beneath him, *La Savoie's* giant steam engines thrummed dully in the night and the vibrations made his legs tingle.

He had a slight headache; too much Beaujolais. Now, mouth sour from the wine and the meal's peppery entrée, he allowed himself the small satisfaction of discomfort and wondered one more time at the unfairness of life.

It had been 16 days, and they'd made love twice. In the recesses of his mind, Frederick wished he could address the subject as a man should, wished he'd done so earlier. Perhaps he should have been more insistent right from the start and made demands, not requests. Yet it was such a delicate matter of which he knew so little that broaching the subject seemed unbecoming and might make Easter even more hesitant to encourage his advances.

A week before leaving Chicago and 20 hours before he and Easter pronounced their vows, his mother, over lunch near the harbor, had told him he might expect Easter to fulfill the conjugal side of the marriage union once a week, no more, and probably less. His mother had frowned, as if introducing the subject of a dear friend's embarrassing illness. "Once weekly is enough for any man, Frederick. Remember that, as I fear you might have inherited your father's intemperate spirit. And try to be quick about it. Carnality is a sad necessity imposed upon us women, and there is nothing less pleasurable than enduring the onslaught of one's husband. Your father occasionally takes overlong, particularly if he's been imbibing." Mrs. Cowles was a founding member of the local Anti-Saloon Society, and Frederick knew his father's tippling repulsed her. "So when you intend to press yourself upon Easter," she continued, "do so only after a light meal free of drink."

She spooned a bit of orange sherbet into her large, toothy mouth. As an afterthought, she added, "And avoid spicy foods, Frederick; garlic and onions in particular. A foul breath is ungentlemanly, thoughtless, and frankly disgusting."

Frederick had been mortified. It had been the first and only time his mother had ever referred to his father's amatory habits in his presence for, in fact, Mrs. Cowles rarely referred to her husband at all. The exchange had left Frederick unable to eat his dessert.

That night he had been subject to appalling images of his mother and father locked in an obscene embrace. His parents always maintained a cordial distance from one another, two goldfish in a very large bowl. He had, until this moment, always assumed Mother and Father had somehow arisen from the marital bed without ever making physical contact; now he struggled to put the scene out of his mind.

His own physical needs were not that urgent; they never had been, though he participated freely in randy discussions with his friends. Desire was more like an expectation denied, the disappointment of a gift hoped for and not received.

Another spray of icy water washed across the deck. Easter was asleep in their cabin. Or perhaps she had woken and was scribbling in her diary. It was the one thing that brightened her mood. She wrote for hours, hunched over the correspondence table and humming to herself. He admired her neat handwriting and had from the day she'd sent him a thank you note for taking her to lunch after a work interview with his father's company. The roundness of her *l*'s and *w*'s had impressed him, but now he found her devotion to the journal irritating. He was forbidden from reading the entries, and that was vexing. Complaining of a mild headache, he had left her in the cabin a half-hour earlier and now stood on the topmost deck of *La Savoie*. He was the only passenger out in the inclement weather.

The enveloping mist made him shiver. He could dimly hear the strains of music—a waltz full of strings—coming from the formal ball-room one deck below. Their first night aboard, he and Easter had danced to the very same tune.

He considered seeking shelter there; a stiff shot or two at the bar could lighten his mood, but no, it probably wouldn't, and might indeed act to the contrary. He wasn't dressed for the occasion. A guest had spilled a glass of red wine on the trousers of the elegant evening outfit he'd had tailored for the trip and the suit was in the hands of the ship's laundress.

It wasn't all Easter's fault. Who could have known that the slightest movement of the ship, the merest hint of pitch or wallow, would cause her discomfort? When they were courting, she had enjoyed their outings on the lake, sworn a love for the water and not once had he considered that the trip across the Atlantic could be less than a joyful experience. In fact, he had deliberately opted for a slow journey. There were faster ships than *La Savoie* afloat—the *Flandres* traversed the Atlantic in less than a week—but a leisurely 12-day cruise had seemed a splendid way to begin their lives as man and wife.

The voyage, sadly, had become a nightmare for her. In fact, Frederick thought, it was a nightmare for them both.

Easter hardly ate. After the third day, she refused to accompany him to the dining room and asked instead that meals—inconsequential as they were—be brought to the cabin. She survived on toast, tea, an occasional cup of beef broth, lettuce without dressing, and fruit. Her slim form grew leaner; her lips became pale and thin, almost marginal. Her eyes lost their gleam.

They had visited the ship's doctor four times, and the man had finally stopped prescribing larger and larger doses of nostrums to settle Easter's stomach. Now he came by the cabin twice a day, hinting to Frederick that

3

Mrs. Cowles' discomfort might be more than mere seasickness. Perhaps, he hinted darkly, it was *mental*, even *psychological*. The words frightened Frederick.

"The stress of the marriage, I might assume," the physician said, his voice barely a whisper. "The fear of physical intimacy." Giving Frederick a meaningful look, he'd added, "The—how may I put it in acceptable language—*discomfort* associated with certain *marital acts* committed during the honeymoon."

Frederick had nodded, not sure he did understand, fearful of the implications but unwilling to pursue the subject. The man's dress white uniform with galloons and epaulets spoke of authority, but he *was* French, and everyone knew the French thought of sex with disturbing constancy. So of course, physician or not, he would mention *that* first.

Back home in Chicago, men who'd returned from the war were full of tales of the French's sensual indulgences.

The music from the ballroom changed cadence, strains muted by damp and wind, to something jazzy and bouncy, horns, clarinets and slide trombones. The orchestra had four American Negro singers. On the first night the quartet had sung a medley of spirituals. Frederick and Easter had danced to those, too. He had heard Negroes were highly prized in France.

Perhaps the French doctor was right; it was the stress of it all, the harried days before the wedding, the demands made upon a bride, the train trip from Chicago to New York, the wedding night at the Pontchartrain.

Frederick shook his head free of carnal thoughts. That Easter was feeling so poorly was not her fault, and it was only normal she should prefer not to share her bunk. The situation had nothing to do with him; women were that way, their meeker constitutions prey to every affliction.

On the other side of the deck, a couple leaned on the railing and looked out to the sea.

How long had they been there? They both wore long matching raincoats and the man's arm was across the woman's shoulder, pulling her to him. There was a brief flare of light, a match on a cigarette. Something the man said made the woman laugh, and the sound was snatched by the night wind. Her hair whipped about her head. She stretched her neck to kiss the man's cheek. The man turned slightly and their lips met. The band struck up another waltz. Frederick plunged his hands deeper into the pockets of his coat, felt a flash of envy and anger. He watched the couple embrace briefly, then disappear into a doorway.

If he returned to the cabin, Easter might be feeling better by now and could, conceivably, welcome his arrival.

And I could be, Frederick thought, Queen Marie of Romania and Emperor of Rome, as his father was fond of saying.

CHAPTER 2

The diary beckoned. It was in the smaller travel bag, beneath her undergarments. A silly place for a woman to hide anything, she knew, but hiding it was habit, not precaution. Frederick would never dare search her luggage.

Easter wanted to write; she had always kept a journal. Now, *not* writing caused her almost as much discomfort as the movement of the great ship.

Frederick was at the bar—how he could even consider eating or drinking was beyond her understanding—and her nausea was not as acute as it had been earlier in the day. She sat up in the bunk and swung her feet to the floor, then took a moment to breathe deeply and evenly. Opening the travel bag, she gathered journal, pen and ink.

*****

Aboard La Savoie, Sunday, April 6, 1919

So much has happened this year! I feel guilty writing this, but since childhood, I've been led to believe my new status of *wife* would be the culmination of my existence. It isn't. Now that I am *Mrs. Frederick Cowles*, I'm not even certain I like the name. I thought vast secrets would be revealed, but this has not happened. I have put my life as Catherine Easter Beaumont behind me, yet I have not changed at all and frankly do not plan to do so. Does this make me a poor spouse?

We've spent the past four days aboard this dreadful ship, and I do not understand the charms water holds for so many. My stomach is in a constant state of rebellion. I cannot eat, much less drink anything but the mildest infusion. According to the French doctor who visits me twice daily (and whom I do not like; he has hair on his knuckles and an oily complexion. He must be from the south of the Continent), I have not yet found my sea legs, much to Frederick's dismay. I avoid mirrors; I know I look a fright. Plus, of course, "my friend" will soon come to visit, so I suffer from cramps and am irascible. If I believed in omens, I would certainly see all this as an inauspicious beginning to my wedded life.

Shall I write of the wedding night? It was memorable only by the associated revulsion. I will write only in the interest of posterity (How foolish! As if this diary will ever be seen by anyone but me).

*****

Easter put her pen down. In her first entries, she'd avoided the embarrassing, the rude, and the awkward. Nowhere was mentioned her first period, or the painful infection that had laid her low for a month when she was 16, or, a short time later, the perfunctory groping of the boy who lived down the street. As she grew older and began to trust her powers of observation, her descriptions of events became freer and she occasionally reveled in the retelling of gauche moments. However, she was a wedded woman now. Did the same freedoms of expression—even in private—still hold sway?

*****

I prepared as best as I could for this event, minding the endless discussions with Charlotte and Enid. I wonder now if my two best friends lied to me. More likely, they claimed experiences they've never had. Also (and I make this confession for the first time), I did read excerpts from *The Pearl*. Charlotte gave me a tattered copy filched from her brother's room. I found some parts of it mildly arousing and did harbor a measure of curiosity about *the act*.

I was ready for a certain amount of pain and discomfort, but never could I have imagined that my future husband was (I strive to put it delicately) so *endowed*. To be honest, I might have suspected this, that afternoon on the lake when we were caught in a horrendous downpour and both soaked to the skin. Frederick's bathing costume quite clung to him, and I remember thinking he must have something secreted in a front pocket, his wallet or perhaps a set of keys kept in a clever holder. This would explain the unaccountable bulge... but I am getting ahead of myself.

First, the setting: Frederick rented the bridal suite at the Ponchartrain. It had a large bedroom, a bathroom, and a small dressing room, all appointed with dark, polished furniture, damask upholstery and too many mirrors. The rooms bore a faint aroma of cigar smoke, which made me wonder whether smoking cigars might be part of the rites and, if so, whether it was done before or after the act.

There were several garish bouquets of silk roses in vases around the room, and the wedding gifts were piled in a far corner. Frederick tipped the bellboy (the man winked and made a thumbs-up gesture, which was uncalled for), then locked himself in the bathroom. I changed into my new peignoir and got into bed with minor trepidation. My main concern was to fulfill his expectations; I was very much in love with Frederick that night.

*****

Easter nibbled on the end of her pen. All her writing tools had teeth marks, even the expensive ones. After a moment's thought, she bent back over the page.

I heard the water running in the bathroom, and soon Frederick returned, freshly shaven and smelling of cognac. He wore silk pajamas beneath the same bathrobe I saw hanging in his apartment the one time I visited there. We had embraced that night and he had touched my breasts—but only for a moment. He extinguished the light, entered the bed and rolled on top of me, squeezing the very breath from my lungs. He fumbled for my buttocks, ran his hand across them a time or two as if squeezing the stuffing of a chair, all the while gasping into my ear. I could feel his manhood prodding my stomach. It was insistent, like an ill-mannered dog yapping at a door to get in. I found this rude and so kept my legs tightly closed. He tried to kiss me, breathing alcoholic vapors up my nose, and I went quickly from dismayed to disgusted. I don't think he noticed any of this; the lights were off and the entire episode occurred in silence, save for here and there a grunt as Frederick tried to lodge himself.

In the end he managed it, but only after I pushed him off, went to the bathroom, and applied a liberal amount of *Miss Nelly's Smoothing Skin Cream* to the place he so desperately sought. The cream was recommended by Enid, and in this, at least, she was right. It eased the pain somewhat, but not enough that I would want to repeat the act too often in future.

At least it was not dreadfully bloody. I have read that in Sicily, the mother-in-law of a new bride proudly displays the soiled wedding sheets for all to see, and that the greater the stain, the deeper the respect for the groom!

It did hurt a bit, but not as badly as I was led to expect. What I was not ready for, as I mentioned earlier, was the sheer size of Frederick's appendage! I felt *stretched*. I imagined a large and dumb animal attempting to enter a small burrow. I suppose that birthing a child will create even greater distention. This does not give me encouraging thoughts of motherhood.

The episode lasted a minute or two. Frederick ejaculated (another new word from Enid) or at least I believe he did, withdrew, attempted once again to kiss me (by then I had buried my face into the pillow), then rolled over and went to sleep. I did not.

Is this really how the human race pursues its lineage? Where was the pleasure, the ecstasy described at such great length in *The Pearl*? Let me say that I, for one, can only hope science will discover a way to ensure future generations without the performance of this unseemly deed.

Now, I fear Frederick is getting randy again. Luckily, he seems to know that in my sorry state, his advances annoy me. I suppose that once we reach Paris, I shall have to make it up to him. That is what a good wife would do.

Paris! We shall soon be in Paris! *Life* magazine called it the very center of today's artistic expression. Enid, who spent a Parisian summer with her family, told me that the morals there are loose. She spoke of sneaking away while her parents were at the theater, taking a cab to Montparnasse, and eating with artists and writers and such at the Café de Versailles. She says she met Pablo Picasso, the young Spaniard who is causing quite a furor, and that he tried to pinch her bottom. I don't believe her—she does have a tendency to overstate—and I understand from reading the European magazines that Mr. Picasso is now happily married after a tragic love affair that saw his first soulmate die. I have seen a photograph of the woman he wed, Olga Koklova, and she is far more attractive than Enid.

I am as excited as a child in a toy store! I have wanted to go to Paris ever since I was small and Mama took me to the museum where we saw an exhibit of the works of Mr. Matisse (or should I say *Monsieur* Matisse?). As we returned home, I forced Mama to stop at Kresge's, and we bought heavy paper and a box of colored pencils. That was more than a decade ago, and I haven't stopped sketching and painting since.

Frederick sees this "hobby" of mine as charming, not realizing the depth of my commitment. I tried to explain it to him, but could tell from the glazed look in his eyes that his interest in the arts is, at best, cursory. He does admire some watercolors I did of the lake, and had two of them framed. I thought this quite sweet, but in retrospect I also remember that he did this after we had a fight, so it may have been nothing more than an act of apology. I assume his tastes will run to the cabarets I have read about, where women (some of them Negro Americans) dance in various stages of undress. I will tolerate his attending such garish places if, in turn, I have my way.

I expect that by day we will seek out the artists' lairs; by night he can, within reason, do what he wants.

Eight more days before we reach Le Havre, and a brief train ride from there to Paris! I cannot wait to step upon solid ground again!

*****

She put the pen down, blotted the ink, quickly reread what she had written and closed her notebook, then went to the minuscule bathroom to rinse her face with cold water before returning to her bunk. Moments later Frederick returned, slightly disheveled, slightly drunk. He gave her a wan smile, lurched into the bathroom and latched the door. He was in there a long time.

CHAPTER 3

There were times when Landru opened his eyes early in the morning having forgotten who he was. He didn't like the feeling; it implied a weakness easily exploited, so he would lie in the bed and rediscover himself by staring at the woman sleeping close by. Was it his wife of 18 years? His most recent lover? The latest war widow from the personal advertisement in *Le Matin*? It was easier if there was no woman, no middle-aged Dômestic with folds of pale skin beneath her chin and a government pension. Then he could choose who he was that day.

He had worn so many names. His life had been a series of small crimes marred by unforeseen evidence and followed by arrest, prosecution and sentence, parole and release. Then, a new name and a new identity. He was a failed criminal, what the gendarmes called a *petit forban*, rarely showing a profit from his schemes. If there was money, it sifted through his fingers, apportioned to his wife and four children, to his mistress of the moment, to planning the next doubtful adventure. He considered himself an exemplary father and a doting husband. His own father, an honest provider, had been so ashamed of his son's endless skirmishes with the law that one somber day in October 1913 he had hanged himself in the Bois de Boulogne.

Henri Désiré Landru (the "Désiré" reflected his mother's desperate desire to have a boy) hardly noticed his father's suicide. He did not attend the funeral; he did not send flowers or a card expressing his sympathy. He did not tell his children that their grandfather had passed away. He did, though, find and keep the man's identity papers, birth certificate, and bank book, since these might come in handy. Landru's years in jail had been spent with petty thieves, pimps, addicts and suppliers, strong-arm men, bigamists, deserters and other truants. He knew the value of a dead man's personals.

He was dapper if not elegant, with piercing eyes. One woman had called him *"parfaitement proportionné sauf pour ta tête,"* and it was true. His arms, legs, feet, torso, were the stuff of a sculptor's model, but his head was overlarge on a thin neck punctuated by a lump of an Adam's apple. His mustache and beard were perfectly trimmed, his fingernails clean and well cut. He had smooth, taut skin stretched over perfect bones. He neither drank nor smoked, though he had a fondness for dark chocolate from the colonies. At the height of his infamy, he had seen himself declared in print as a student of Franz Mesmer.

In reality, he had been an undecorated soldier, a bicycle mechanic, a brilliant but tragically unappreciated inventor. Still, he was well-spoken, smelled of cologne and ironing starch. If he wished to amuse, he could contort his body like an acrobat and juggle plates and glasses. He could sing the aria of the day's operetta. He had discovered in himself a charm that, nurtured and played properly, provided a steady stream of goods he could sell, and bank accounts he would pilfer.

His attitude toward earning a living had changed over the years. At first, he had abhorred the idea of a steady job, and had searched for easier, quicker roads to profit. He had hoped to be an entrepreneur, manufacturing motorcycles, but had little success. There had been other businesses, other initiatives, endeavors that had worked for a while, then failed. Mostly there had been widows.

In 1915, France was creating 12,000 widows a day and Landru was corresponding with more than 250 of them. They were young, old, seldom well-educated, though he insisted they be able to read and write. When they responded to the small advertisements placed in the personal section of Paris newspapers, they were hopeful, delighted by what he claimed to offer, easily wooed and trusting beyond the norm. They knew him as Monsieur Petit, Monsieur Legrand (a small joke he allowed himself), Monsieur Freymier, Monsieur Dupont. He was an international engineer, the owner of a rubber plantation in Brazil, a secret government

14

agent soon to be sent overseas to promote the war effort, or the next consul to Australia. He wrote charming letters, sent flowers and candy, squired them about town. They found his habit of noting every expense in a small *cahier* charming and responsible. In bed with him, they discovered passions never before explored, and when over a lunch of *pâté et fromage* he held their hands in his, stared deeply into their eyes and proposed, they accepted immediately and with gratitude. Soon, he would suggest they move in together, since they would shortly be going abroad for his next posting. He would volunteer to sell their furniture, and arrange for the banks to open new accounts that could be accessed from wherever they might be assigned.

He was a man of mystery, of taste and refinement. The widows gloried in his company.

CHAPTER 4

On the fifth day of the voyage, *La Savoie* was struck by a gale-force storm that came from nowhere and stayed. Only the hardiest passengers ventured from their cabins, and Frederick watched as seamen from the engine room tied down the first and second-class decks. The men were bare-chested brutes with grimy hands and sullen expressions, unshaven and heavily tattooed. They worked methodically in the driving rain, securing deck chairs and tables, parasols and recreation equipment. They were unconcerned by the weather, and the male passengers gave them wide berth. The females stared covertly and whispered behind their hands.

One of the wealthier passengers, a Texan with three master suites for himself, his mistress and their entourage, took a nasty fall and broke a leg and an arm. A Jewish woman from the Bronx was mildly bruised when a brutal swell threw her against a bulkhead. Dozens took to their bunks, whispering of the *Titanic*. A Portuguese deckhand was crushed when a supply locker accidentally opened and released cylinders of compressed oxygen.

The galleys were shut, and the few passengers capable of eating had cold sandwiches and salads. The captain ordered the liquor supply—wine included—secured and locked, and the bars on every deck were closed. Passengers complained and resorted to their private stocks of spirits. The injured Texan, a hard-drinking man, threw a party in his suites for all first-class passengers. Some 50—mostly men—attended and found no shortage of alcohol, though the canapés were marginal at best. Working in his overwhelmed infirmary, the ship's French physician, aided by two nurses, ran out of bismuth and dispensed white chalk tablets.

In their cabin, Frederick and Easter had surprising reactions to the storm. As his complexion grew sallow, hers took on color. She began to laugh, clapping her hands every time lightning burst. She jumped up and down like a child, and when the wind howled loudest, she insisted on going outside. Frederick forbade it, but she wrapped herself in a shawl and did so anyway. Furious, he chased her, grabbed her elbow, and when she turned to face him, he saw a wild glow in her eyes. She set her jaw, wrested her arm away and resolutely walked to the deck's nearest entry. Frederick, weaving, followed as each swell threatened his balance. When Easter reached the door, it was locked. She turned, marched in the other direction until she found a porthole. That had also been sealed shut, but she unscrewed the four brass wing nuts and fought it open. A blast of wind and rain hit her squarely in the face and she laughed. Frederick, astounded, kept his distance. Sheets of lightning exploded across the low sky. The corridors were bare, and the dim light gave the area an ethereal radiance. For a moment, Frederick thought he and Easter might be the only two passengers aboard, so empty and desolate was it in the fury of the storm. Then Easter turned, took his face in both her hands and kissed him hard on the lips. She led him back to the cabin, shed her clothes, and reclined on the bunk, uncovered. The cabin light swept across her in geometric patterns to reveal hollows and valleys he'd never seen. He looked away, embarrassed, and she reached across the small space to take his hand and pull him to her.

The storm died during the night and in the morning he found his bride fast asleep and only partially dressed. He reddened at the sight and recalled the feel of her, replaying the night's abandon. She was breathing evenly; there was color to her cheeks. He was sore, as if scorched with fine sandpaper in his most private places. There were three long scratches across his belly and, when he looked at the mirror, dark red round marks on his neck. His trousers, shirt and undergarments were in a pile on the floor.

His trousers showed a rip along the inseam. He carefully folded and hung the clothing in the diminutive closet. Then he sat on his bunk and tried to collect his thoughts. He felt a tinge of distaste. Civilized people did not rut like barnyard animals.

Frederick selected fresh clothes, dressed quietly and made his way to the dining room. The kitchen had weathered the storm and fired its ovens. On each table lay a basket of hot breads, and waiters served from covered trays. He ate lightly and shared boating experiences with an older gentleman who told him of a week spent aboard a ship in the Indian Ocean during the typhoon season. That, claimed the man, was a *serious* storm.

When Frederick returned to the cabin, Easter was awake but still in bed, her ill health restored to pre-storm days. Nothing in her face was out of the ordinary, but she was even paler than before. Neither mentioned the preceding night.

She slept most of the day, and in the late afternoon drank two cups of tea and ate a piece of toast. Ten minutes later it all came up. That night, Frederick woke from a confused dream with his hands curled protectively around his testicles and the sheets tangled about his feet. In his mind was a Mexican comic strip a friend had shown him, eight crude panels depicting an over-endowed postman and a willing housewife who resembled Easter a bit too much.

Sleep eluded him. He lay in his bunk thinking he did not know his new wife at all, and had never truly considered the changes this union would impose on his existence, and, for the first time, it frightened him.

Life in Chicago had been, if not boring, at least quotidian. He worked for his father's firm, where he was presented with problems whose solutions were rarely taxing and never irreversible. His secretary, Mary Meredith, never sick and familiar with all his foibles, arranged for his laundry to be picked up and delivered, brewed a perfect cup of coffee, screened the rare calls he received, and made sure his personal bills and rent were paid promptly. He took her to lunch twice a year and saw to it that her salary was above the norm of the company's other women employees.

Twice a week he played cards with male friends and once a month, with these same friends, he ate dinner at the same restaurant and visited a nightspot, usually one where there was music and dancing. He danced with the girls and on three different occasions, when they were willing, he'd bedded them quickly in hotels. He always left a small tip in an envelope as his friends had told him this was the proper thing to do after an encounter with a working girl. "They appreciate the hell out of it," one had said. "And if you ever want to have a second round, they're a lot more receptive."

Only one time had he seen the same girl twice and the second evening had ended early with a rapid and unhappy coupling at the apartment she shared with two others from the steno pool. Lying in her narrow bed was unsettling, and though he promised to be in touch the next day, he avoided for months returning to the club where they'd met.

One colleague, Jack Corrigan—the one with the dirty comic strip— was married and said it was the best of both worlds. "I get some at home—two, three times a night if I feel like it, any time of the week except Sunday—and I get some away from home whenever I want, and no one's the wiser." This seemed to be Corrigan's obsession and only topic of conversation. Truthfully, Frederick had never liked Corrigan at all, and found him a bore and a boor. In fact, he rarely enjoyed the twice-weekly gatherings. He went because young men of his age and social position did that. He had never bothered to ponder the lives of his companions, to inquire about their inner workings or their ideas, their families, their daily existences. He didn't know their middle names, where they lived, what they thought on most basic issues. The group seldom discussed anything more momentous than the latest baseball score or a recently opened show. When Frederick, on a few occasions, tried to turn the conversation to more consequential things, the group as one stared at him blankly, save for Corrigan who'd called him "our intellectual." They hadn't even given him a decent bachelor gift—instead anted up to purchase an illustrated marriage manual translated from the Japanese— and had roared at his discomfiture when he'd opened the package. He'd stashed the gift in a box full of old college clothes, and had not shown it to anyone.

Frederick wondered whether he might be a prude when it came to his wife. Were the marriage vows an entitlement for Easter to act as she did, so wantonly out of character? Perhaps this was where marital passion led, or perhaps there was something wrong with Easter. She might not be as well-balanced as it had appeared. Perhaps the recent loss of both her parents to influenza had deeply unsettled her.

Perhaps she was insane.

The idea hit him with such force that he sat up in his bunk. Much as he tried to dispel the notion, he began to categorize her actions, placing them in a harsh and demanding light. The thoughts cascaded; thoughts of her use of color and shapes in her paintings, colors that had nothing to do with reality—red skies, purple waters—of the elongated faces that looked like African masks. He thought of her manner of speech, how she addressed everyone in such a friendly way—was there more there than met the ear? What of how she dressed sometimes, with little care for current fashions? She showed a complete lack of interest in all things that should interest women: social events, gossip, magazine recipes. She had told him early on that she couldn't cook and would probably never learn. At the time, it had seemed a charming admission and he'd not given it a moment's reflection. Now that simple deficiency was foreboding. She kept a secret diary, claiming every woman was entitled to private convictions. The journal had irked him in the past but now took on darker significance. She refused to be called Catherine, but instead insisted on using her middle name, Easter, and again Frederick had thought this irresistible at first, another beguiling singularity. Was Easter really a name? That had been his mother's first question, for which he'd had no ready answer at the time. Why *would* a rational woman want to be called Easter?

What would she be like in Paris, where morals were worn like loose-fitting robes?

A few weeks before his marriage, Frederick had begun perusing the European edition of the *Chicago Tribune* with a mind to becoming familiar with events overseas and impressing his wife-to-be. He'd read about Paris, about the models who shed their clothes for a pittance and offered God knew what favors for a franc or two. There had been a breathless report by a special correspondent (the footnote identified the author as a well-known Christian painter from the Midwest; Frederick did not recognize the name) about an artists' benefit soirée—orgy might be a more appropriate word—held in Montparnasse. Young women (some no older than 16) had bared their breasts in a contest to see who would be crowned *la plus belle poitrine de Paris.* Hundreds of nymphs and nymphets had paraded semi-naked before a horde of drunken mustachioed men who clamored their assents or whistled their disapproval. He suddenly saw Easter's breasts in such a contest, smelled the unwashed artists' garlicky breath, and witnessed grubby hands reaching for her flesh.

He shook his head, rubbed his temples with two forefingers, rose from his bunk, threw a glance at his sleeping wife, and rearranged the covers where they had fallen from her feet.

The list of shortcomings grew.

He recalled Easter, bare-legged, insisting they have dinner together in an Irish bar where she was the only female, and telling a risqué story about a woman friend's involvement with a music hall performer. Indeed, her friends seemed inappropriate. One, Enid, had ground her hips suggestively against every man she'd danced with at the wedding party, then, deliriously drunk, had done an obscene shimmying gyration as Easter clapped delightedly.

Frederick checked his watch; it was 1:30 in the morning. He dressed quietly, made his way to the bar and ordered a straight gin and lime with ice. Three men sipped their drinks at a nearby table. Toward the rear of the small room, he spotted the French physician who raised his glass and beckoned. Frederick returned the toast, decided to join the man and perhaps, indirectly, lead the conversation to Easter's bizarre behavior.

In the end they spoke about the weather.

Chapter 5

In her dreams, Easter spoke French. She purchased quaint items in quaint shops, ordered exotic dishes at restaurants, conversed with people she met on the streets who assumed she was Parisian. In her dreams, her French was flawless. In her waking hours, she recited the phrases taught her by Mademoiselle Yvonne Février, the seamstress of her wedding dress. Mademoiselle, only in America two years, had an amusing accent, both guttural and sibilant, but was an excellent instructress.

Mademoiselle had lived in Paris prior to immigrating to Chicago, and, though only in her mid-20s, could lay claim to making acquaintances with Scandinavian novelists and poets, attending artists' *bals costumés,* and (this she only whispered) having an affair with a married man who arranged for her apprenticeship in a popular *maison de couture.* She mentioned artists who asked her to model, and why she had not done so—her hips and waist were not correctly proportioned, she said. Easter did not know if all these tales were true, but it didn't matter. Mademoiselle Février had supplied her young American friend with several names to look up once the couple got to Paris.

*****

Aboard La Savoie, Tuesday, April 8, 1919

Only six more days. The storm is past. I am still queasy and rarely venture from our cabin. Frederick says I should be feeling better. He has had the good grace to not refer to *that* night.

I have no explanation for it. Some unholy spirit took me, discarded my common sense and good upbringing, and substituted instead the soul of a harlot, for that is how I behaved with Frederick. I used words that never before crossed my tongue, employed my body in ways never even contemplated. Those realities make me blush.

I wonder what Frederick thinks? I don't know how deeply I shock him. I know he has had some experiences, but I am certain he never thought his wife capable of such ardor. We almost fell off the bunk twice!

*****

Easter tried to suppress a smile, then laughed. Her writing hand shook so that drops of ink spotted the page. She blotted them, continued.

*****

Should I be more ashamed of my behavior than I am? The truth is, I find a certain gratification in it. Though I cannot explain my actions (it's well known that some people react adversely to the full moon; perhaps my weakness is storms at sea), I did, for some moments, relish the power so inexplicably vested in me. When Frederick lay beneath, as I straddled him and made him do as I wished, I sensed something overwhelming occur. I frightened Frederick and enjoyed doing so. The look in his wide, pale eyes was one I had never witnessed before in another human. I kept moving even when he had stopped, even when I knew he had finished. I hadn't. I had several orgasms, I think, though of course I can't be sure since I've never, to my knowledge, had one before.

Will my new husband expect such a performance every time we lie together? If so, he will be sadly disappointed. I have felt neither need nor desire for his physical company in the days since the storm.

Frederick bears an expression of anticipation. I have caught him looking at me when he thought I was occupied, and the furrow in his brow is as readable as any book. He is unsure; he may even hope and secretly pray for inclement weather. I am unsure as well.

CHAPTER 6

"They look like everybody else," Easter said. "Except worse."

"And they don't even speak English," Frederick added with a smile. Easter looked up at him, saw he was gently reprimanding her.

"Well, I had expected they *would* look different somehow. They're *French.* It was understandable that everyone looks like us in England, but this is a different continent entirely."

Frederick couldn't tell if she was being serious. Her sense of humor routinely eluded him. Easter often said things he had difficulty interpreting.

La Savoie had berthed in its designated slip in the center of Le Havre's harbor. It was an overcast, chilly morning, and they stood with other passengers at the rail of the lowest deck watching the activity below them. It would be at least three hours before they could disembark, and stewards had set out tables of coffee, tea, cakes and wines on the deck. On the pier below, hundreds of workers manned cranes, unloaded the passengers' baggage from the holds and transported it by horse-drawn cart to a cavernous warehouse where customs officers waited.

On the next pier, workers blew whistles and shouted commands. Frederick saw that three cranes almost twice as high as the ones servicing *La Savoie* were working in concert to lift what looked like a railroad car. He nudged Easter, pointed. "Look at that!"

At first, only the roof of the wagon was visible. It looked to be some 80 feet long and shone whitely, and very slowly rose from the steamer's hold. Even the stewards stopped working to look. One, a young man with a pencil-thin mustache said, "That's Mr. West's car. You've seen him,

I'm sure. Very tall man, dressed like someone from the Buffalo Bill traveling show? He suffered an unfortunate accident during the storm."

Frederick remembered seeing a big man being pushed about the sundeck in a wheelchair, clad in an overlarge Stetson hat, chaps and boots with pointed toes. "One of the wealthiest men in the world," the steward continued. "He has his own ship, but I heard his cook vanished at the last minute and so he decided to travel with us."

The wagon, now free of the ship and held aloft by the three cranes, hung in the air. "Unbelievable," said Frederick. "That's a giant flag of Texas!"

And it was. Though the wagon's roof was white, its sides showed the star and colors of the 28th state. "That man must own a railroad," Frederick exclaimed. The steward corrected him. "No sir. Mr. West made his fortune prospecting gold."

The wagon was slowly lowered to the quay, and a hundred dockworkers pushed and pulled so that its 64 iron wheels fit perfectly on a spur line of rails that ran along the warehouses. They disengaged the cranes' iron cables and Frederick noticed men buffing the sides of the car with their shirt sleeves. With the wagon safely on the rails, the men stepped back and enjoyed the momentary silence that follows great labor.

"My God," said Easter. "We are an ostentatious lot, aren't we?"

The wagon they rode on the train from Le Havre to Paris was far less opulent. Frederick had reserved a private compartment for the four-hour ride and pursed his lips at the unkempt state of their cubicle and its odor: it was a mélange of stale tobacco, sweat and coal fumes. The floor was littered with cigarette butts. A used newspaper was haphazardly folded and wedged under their seat. He pulled it out gingerly. Easter took it from his hands, scanned the page. "This is almost a month old…"

A giant headline read *"Un Monstre Est Arrêté!"*

It says, 'A Monster Has Been Stopped.' Some sort of criminal, I presume." She read on, frowned. "Heavens! It's a man accused of murdering women and then burning them in his oven! My God! It says he lured them with advertisements in the newspapers, promised marriage, took their money and killed them!"

Frederick gave his bride a surprised look. "You can read all that?"

She nodded. "I've been studying French since we decided to come here. Oh, but this is horrid! They were mostly widows! How in the world could anyone be so depraved?"

Frederick was piqued. "You never told me you spoke the language."

Easter didn't look up. "'Speak' is hardly the word, dear. The seamstress taught me a few words during the fittings. I thought it would be appropriate. I didn't want us to be like those dreadful American couples who are incapable of uttering the simplest phrase in another language. What if I have to go to the bathroom? I'll have to ask someone. Look at him! Doesn't he look like the devil himself?"

The grainy photo showed a man of middling stature being escorted by two burly policemen. He was balding, wore a sharply barbered beard that grew to a point and a waxed mustache. He was glaring straight into the camera. "Look at those eyes," Easter said. "Murderous!"

Frederick frowned. He found the bathroom comment inappropriate. Easter continued to read aloud.

"His name is Henri Désiré Landru, and he is denying everything, but the police say they have proof. They found the remains of burned human bones in his villa! Those poor women! And it says he is married, with children!"

Frederick sighed. "I'm not sure this is the best way to begin our travels, talking about such things. Look at this scenery!" He tried to divert her attention.

She glanced out the window. "Farmland. Very exciting. It says here police found the names of 358 women with whom he corresponded. He apparently preyed on older ladies. They think he may have hypnotized them!"

She lowered the paper, folded it and reached for his hand. "Yes, we are in France and it's lovely. I'm sorry Frederick. You're absolutely right." She smiled, kissed him on the cheek. "There are certainly more edifying things to talk about than a deranged murderer." She shook her head, frowned. "But think of it, 358 women!"

The train was chugging through a wide field dotted here and there with leafless trees. In the distance, Frederick saw the steeple of a church, a barn, a farmhouse. The train flashed by a youth in knickers holding a stick and driving a trio of thin cows. The boy waved at the train.

"We're in France," Frederick said.

Easter lowered the paper and folded it. "Yes, we are." She smiled. "This is a wonderful trip! I'm sorry I was so ill on the ship, and I promise things will be better from this moment on."

An hour from Paris, the train ground to a halt. Frederick looked out the window and saw a military convoy passing by. "I think those are American boys!" They were. Throughout the train, compartment doors opened and men and women leaned out, cheered and applauded. Frederick struggled with the window but couldn't free it. Easter said, "I think they took the leather pull-straps to make belts for the soldiers…"

The line of men trudged past the train and disappeared around a curve in the road. Easter thought they looked very young, like the children she saw playing stickball in her Chicago neighborhood.

"Well," said Frederick. "It's nice to see the natives are friendly."

Easter didn't respond but pressed closer to him.

CHAPTER 7

James Johnson stared at the sketch; the sketch stared back. He stood, moved both the easel and canvas closer to a window.

The eyes were wrong. They failed to convey the young man's cavalier good looks, his daring and courage. Instead, the face showed a certain cruelty, a hint of rudeness in the lips and cast of the mouth. James tore a blank sheet of newsprint from a pad and, with a stick of charcoal, drew a new chin, softer lips, a thinner, more muscular throat.

From the apartment's open front door came a brief knock, a throat clearing. *"C'est votre frère? Your brother, yes?"*

Johnson turned, nodded and smiled.

Monsieur Hippolyte Lefebvre came twice daily, at 10 a.m. and 3 p.m., and though he rarely had correspondence of importance or interest, Johnson always welcomed the man's arrival.

The mailman was almost a foot shorter than Johnson but stood erect as a stake. For the first few months, M. Lefebvre had not been communicative, regarding the American artist more as a peculiarity of time and place than as a human. Johnson was a *Ricain,* a madman who had chosen wartime France over Philadelphia for unclear reasons that reflected what the mailman called *"la folie américaine."*

Over time the two had become friends, or, at least, close acquaintances. M. Lefebvre's, *"Bonjour, Monsieur Johnson!"* brightened the expatriate's day. The little *facteur* made the effort to pronounce Johnson's name as well as he could, though he failed to understand why there was an *h* between the *o* and the *n*. Plying him with an ocean of *café-crème*, Johnson had learned amazing things.

M. Lefebvre knew, for example, that the younger sister of Mademoiselle Gauthier, across the hall and down, was not a sister at all but a daughter, the issue of Mlle. Gauthier's brief encounter with an American Army captain in 1904. This, Johnson decided, accounted for Mlle. Gauthier's mother/sister aloofness when he accidentally met them in the hallway. The daughter/sister kept her eyes averted, but once flashed an irreverent grin when her mother/sister was not looking.

M. Lefebvre also knew that Monsieur Dupont, the dour baker at the nearby *boulangerie,* was conducting an affair of the heart with Madame Ribaud, owner of the flower shop across the street. Mme. Ribaud was far older than the 30-ish M. Dupont, a round, triple-chinned man, the product of his doughy environment. She, in turn, looked much like the pressed and faded flowers in her window display.

Then there was the Delâtre family, who had a boy, 6 years old now, with a head as large as a medicine ball, supported by complex braces attached to his waist and back. M. Lefebvre was friends with the Delâtre's maid, a country girl from Auvergne, who told him the boy was kept in a small room beneath the servants' stairway and fed only mashed potatoes and *boudin* sausage.

Of course, Mesdemoiselles Clothilde and Henriette, who lived in the apartment directly above Johnson's, were not sisters at all, but followers of Lesbos. With a disapproving look, Mr. Lefevbre told of the magazines the women received, publications singing the praises of same-sex love.

M. Lefevbre knew all this and more. The *facteur* had a Parisian way of erasing any doubt concerning his veracity: a raised eyebrow, a slightly curled upper lip, a deprecating hand gesture which might be effeminate anywhere else, but in Paris obviated the need for explanations.

The mailman was learning English from a thin, brown-cover book he kept in his satchel. He was proud of his growing vocabulary and had asked Johnson to write down one new word a day, which he repeated as he walked his mail route.

Yesterday the word was "chip." There had followed a bilingually complex conversation, and the mailman twice threw up his hands in despair and disgust as Johnson enunciated the differences between *chip, ship, cheap, sheep,* and *cheep.* To the postman's French ear, the five words sounded exactly the same. So did *bore, boor* and *boar. Big, bag, beg, bog* and *bug* tortured him. His lips generated grimaces that did nothing for his pronunciation. He found English grotesque yet fascinating.

Pepper, paper, peeper and piper. The more confusing the word, the longer M. Lefebvre lingered over his coffee. Johnson had thought to enter the dark domain of George Bernard Shaw's *ghoti,* where *gh* may be an *ef,* an *o* sounds like an *ee,* and *ti* becomes *sh,* so that *ghoti* is pronounced *fish,* but he decided the mailman might think this an American's revenge on the anarchistic French language, with its incomprehensible tenses, silent x's, silent h's, and barbarous use of vowels.

Hippolyte Lefebvre had the soul of an adventurer. He had read everything he could find in French written by Jack London, and though he did not approve of the author's scandalous divorce, he still wished he could emulate him. There were distant relatives in New York he had dreamed of joining after the war. He yearned to be a cowboy, or a taxi driver in Hollywood where customers paid in hundred-dollar bills and everyone owned a new Ford. M. Lefebvre, unmarried and occasionally despondent about his bachelor status, also thought of becoming a polygamist Mormon. Johnson thought it unwise to ask how the mailman planned to acquire several wives in Utah, when he had been so unsuccessful in getting a single one in postwar Paris, where the dearth of younger men made for astonishingly aggressive women.

Johnson did his best to keep the man's reveries within bounds by citing known American dangers: wild Indians with a penchant for scalps and influenza, murderous Mexicans, Irish and Italian thugs, and buffalo stampedes. Still, Johnson knew, Lefebvre would be an exemplary immigrant, and he sometimes felt a twinge of guilt over his own lack of patriotic encouragement.

From his ground-floor apartment next to the concierge, James Johnson could spy on the lives of his neighbors.

Not a day went by that he did not see a *grand mutilé,* one of the countless, brutally wounded war veterans—France's bitter war harvest. He shuddered every time, remembering the mud, the ambulance, the blood.

The disfigured were treated with great respect. Strangers opened doors, helped them cross the streets, viewed them with deference as the heroes they were. They received preferential treatment in shops, theaters and housing, and many still wore their medal-bedecked uniforms. Some were accompanied by attractive young women who, Johnson suspected, were not above calculating to the very last *centime* what the *assistance familiale* and *retraite militaire* might bring.

These maimed survivors were mostly farm boys from the Vosge, Bretagne, Camargue and Flandres.

Many were blind; those who still saw had weary, hooded eyes. They sat at the cafés, empty sleeves and pant legs neatly pinned, gazes fixed on something far distant. Many drank too much, and there were newspaper reports of their paltry crimes—petty thievery, nonpayment of bills after gargantuan meals in expensive restaurants. The authorities were lenient. Yesterday's *France-Soir* newspaper reported a fight among a group of *grands mutilés* during one of their battalion's monthly reunions held in Montmartre. It took almost 20 police officers to quell the riot. Mme. Bertrand, the concierge in Johnson's building, had told him in hushed tones that though she had the deepest respect for the *gueules cassées*— the broken mouths—she didn't want them in her building. They were known to complain incessantly.

After M. Lefebvre's morning visit, James Johnson planned to take his easel, palette, brushes and paints to the Opéra. He had found an interesting view of the grand old building, where shadows played across the statues of the Muses, bringing them to life. In the evening, there would be a meal and a walk to the Rotonde to watch the others discuss and argue their work. His French was improving, and once or twice he'd participated in discussions, but mostly he watched and he listened. The others called him *Le Grand Muet,* the tall silent one, and some, he knew, thought him a snob.

With luck, he'd see Kiki tonight. She often came to the Rotonde with a gaggle of loud girlfriends who dressed outrageously. Funny hats were the fashion; last week Kiki had worn an amazing *assemblage* of feathers, random pieces of silk and gossamer, all taped or pinned to a *cloche* perched precariously on her head.

M. Lefebvre did not like artists, or their entourage. He called them *sang-sus,* leeches, and opposed the government's modest sponsorship of the arts. He believed all painters, poets, playwrights, novelists, writers, sculptors, musicians, actors, dancers, and singers should be forced to bathe and get jobs, preferably menial ones. Johnson knew he was spared this contempt only because he was an American with means of his own. He was fortunate; Americans were popular. They had the reputation of being deferential and polite, were considered slow to anger and were expected to tip well. They had no need to explain their foibles to anyone, including M. Lefebvre.

The mailman, who had come an hour earlier for his English lesson, put down his coffee cup and smacked his lips. "*Excellent, Monsieur Johnson!* Like always, yes?"

Johnson corrected him, "*As* always, Monsieur Lefevbre. *As.*"

The mailman made a face, shouldered his big leather bag, "*As* always. *As* always."

He left with a smile and a wave, and Johnson glanced at the correspondence, which consisted of bills, a letter from his father in the States, and an envelope from *La Défense;* undoubtedly something about Daniel, his missing brother. He opened it. It had been several weeks since the last note from *La Défense* on its efforts to determine his brother's whereabouts, or those of his remains. Johnson knew that if the French government's attempts seemed halfhearted at best, there was at stake the reputation of the Lafayette Escadrille, with which Daniel had worked as a mechanic before he'd fancied himself a pilot and stolen a plane, presumably to prove that he could fly.

Their father, James Johnson Senior, could not accept that Daniel might be dead, and had for more than a year been engaged in a correspondence with Edgar Cayce, the spiritualist, who had persuaded him that Daniel had flown the airplane to Greece and was alive and well on one of the smaller islands—never mind that the Nieuport 11 could not carry enough fuel to attempt such a trip. Johnson Senior had asked his surviving son to contact the Greek Consul and secure that government's help.

Three of the Escadrille flyers with whom Johnson had corresponded believed Daniel had crashed his plane somewhere in the Massif Central. None of them seemed to bear him a grudge. Rather, they were bemused and somewhat impressed with his bravado. "It's not every day," said one flyer, "that a mechanic steals an airplane."

In the street, two children were kicking a red rubber ball. Johnson closed his eyes, recalled early memories—Daniel sitting on his chest, suffocating him with his weight, hitting him with a rock dead in the center of the forehead, where he still bore a faint scar, telling lies to their father, lies that were *always* believed. Plumbing the depths of his personal history, Johnson could not find a single example of Daniel's actions ever benefiting him.

I hope Daniel is alive, Johnson thought; I truly do, and I would be delighted to have him appear at my front door. I also hope I never see him again. I came to France partly to get away from my evil sibling.

God has a sense of humor.

CHAPTER 8

Henri Landru had lived in worse places—under bridges, in ditches, abandoned basements, unheated barracks, and village jails. The privations had forged him, had made him a giant of strength in a small vessel. Two weeks in the St. Lazare prison and they already respected him. He had a cell of his own—he was that important—and they fed him acceptable meals that filled his stomach and made him sleepy. He enjoyed sleeping, being in that daze just short of wakefulness when he could recall in details the women, the muscles in their legs, the colors of their nipples, the size of their breasts, how far the hair rose up their stomachs. He could bring back the smell of their fears, when their arm-pits exuded the warm and acrid aroma of barely baked bread. He never remembered voices, the colors of eyes, or their touch on him. He did not like being touched, but endured it and the actor in him could bench his dislike for contact because that was part of the work, part of what he did.

The Parisian prison was not a bad place. It was clean, and high above his head there was a *lucarne*, a tiny rectangular window. The sun shone almost directly into his cell 45 minutes every day. Because he called all the guards *Monsieur,* they gave him the mustache wax he preferred, and an occasional piece of hard candy. He knew the guards watched him covertly, wondered how this flea of a man had wielded such power over women.

He had a few minutes in the corridor every day and there he did knee bends, toe touches, pushups. He did them until he was breathless, then did some more. When the laundry cart came, he stripped his own bed, which he was not required to do, and that earned him the approval of the stout woman who manned the cart. He smiled at her and caught a softening on her lips. When he showered by himself in the cavernous washrooms, a guard he did not know brandished a long black club and watched him with disinterest. Once he unexpectedly got an erection and the guard laughed.

The days were monotonous. He could not trim his beard, and that irritated him. He had offered to pay for a barber but been told this was not possible. He did get three-day-old newspapers, and he read and memorized the stories about his exploits. He did not tear the articles out. As he steadfastly maintained his innocence, keeping souvenirs would certainly be misinterpreted.

He waited for Act 3 to begin.

CHAPTER 9

Kiki's real name was Alice Ernestine Prin. James Johnson found it rather prosaic for someone who caused such turbulence in others' lives. She was 18 years old, from a poor background in Burgundy. Her accent—guttural, clipped, and rural—gave her away and bespoke minimal schooling. She'd arrived in Paris at age 12, attended the *lycée* briefly, and like many girls of her age and lack of credentials, had started working a year after that, repairing soldiers' boots in a shoe factory. Then she worked in a *boulangerie,* but being covered with flour and tending ovens did not suit her disposition, so she ran away. Penniless, she modeled for a sculptor. That ended when her mother, who had apprenticed her at the bakery, forced her way into the artist's studio and threatened the man with a lawsuit for *assaut contre la moralité d'un mineur.* Johnson thought the immorality lay in a mother's willingness to sell her child's labor, an accepted principle of the French working class.

A week earlier, as Johnson sat at his usual table at the Rotonde, Kiki had arrived with several friends and, after minimal encouragement, had proceeded to act out scenes of her childhood, taking on by turn the role of her mother, the sculptor, and Kiki-the-child. The sculptor she portrayed as old, bent over and toothless, her mother as raging, herself as a winsome innocent. She was a good *comédienne,* and her audience had roared with laughter, then bought her several rounds of drinks and dinner, which she gulped down.

That same night, Johnson also got to witness Kiki furious. One of her inebriated friends, a tall gangly woman whom he'd never seen at the Rotonde before, shouted to the entourage: "I'll bet you didn't know that

Kiki's got no *poils sur son zizi.*" It took him a moment to translate what may have been one of Kiki's deepest secrets: she had no pubic hair.

A thunderous silence followed this announcement. Kiki rose from her chair, eyes flashing green fire. She slowly approached the drunken woman, looking very menacing indeed, and might have struck her had a young man not interceded. He grabbed Kiki by the elbow, whispered something in her ear which brought a smile, a laugh, and a passing of the storm.

The young man's name was Maurice Mendjizky. He was Polish, and a painter, and Kiki's lover. It galled Johnson that the man who took pleasure in her favors spoke a French even more abominable than his own.

The next evening, once again at the Rotonde, Johnson had ordered the *assiette de charcuterie,* a plate of cold meats with bread. Kiki had swept by his table, picked up the breadbasket without a word, and marched out the door with it. A few minutes later, she returned the empty basket, placed it before him with a charming smile, lifted his wineglass and took a healthy sip from it, patted him on the shoulder, kissed his cheek and said, "Merci."

Johnson immediately forgave her the Polish lover.

Chapter 10

The postman's latest tirade was against the Bretons.

James Johnson had been in France long enough to know that every decade or so, one or another region fomented a resurgence of local identity. This month, it was the Bretons, inhabitants of the French teapot's spout, a hardy lot of farmers and fishermen who acquitted themselves honorably during the war. They spoke several local patois and sought to preserve the cultures of their forefathers. The Parisians considered them country bumpkins.

A few days earlier, a delegation of Breton village heads had presented a list of demands to the Elysée and threatened general strikes if their wishes were not met. This infuriated Postman Lefebvre, a third-generation Parisian who, like many of the capital's natives, truthfully believed himself part of the French elite. Lefebvre's opinion was that no culture existed beyond the Paris city gates and he had no patience for illiterate peasants who should grow artichokes instead of making ultimatums.

Monsieur Lefebvre questioned Johnson at length on whether similar problems existed in the U.S. The American was often short of answers, responding that since his country was a nation of immigrants, Americans had learned to live with each other catch-as-catch-can. What, Lefebvre had demanded, of the Negroes? Wasn't that what the great civil insurrection was about, meeting their demands? The mailman was fascinated by American Negro musicians and assumed all Negroes could sing, dance, and play the banjo or trumpet. Johnson pointed out that most Negroes in America were poor, uneducated, and in menial jobs. Yes, they had on several occasions made demands to the U.S. government and continued to do so. M. Lefebvre nodded his head vigorously; they were like the Bretons.

Johnson knew many French citizens, M. Lefebvre included, who hovered between gratitude and mortification when it came to Americans. The Great War was an aching fresh wound. Calculations by both French and U.S. authorities put the number of American dead at more than 110,000. This was dwarfed by the number of French lives lost; almost a million-and-a-half at latest count, but already revisionists on both sides of the Atlantic were claiming the Allied powers could have won the war without U.S. involvement. M. Lefebvre knew better. He may have despised his country's leaders for being shamefully inadequate during the horrendous conflict, and he might deep in his heart, have resented the American rescue of France, but he would never forget the sacrifices made by young Americans to save his nation, and so it pleased him to hear his two countries had much in common, including Bretons here and Negroes there.

CHAPTER 11

Six days after landing in France, Easter retrieved her diary. She had spent almost all of her daylight hours on her feet, refusing to waste moments sitting. At night after dinner, if no specific activity was planned, she would force Frederick to hire a cab so they could be driven about Paris.

Her first purchase in Paris had been from a *papeterie* near their hotel. She bought a new blank book with 200 sheets of vellum paper nestled between thick suede covers. She also purchased a Lewis Waterman fountain pen with lever filler, and a bright green blotter.

One rainy evening, when Frederick pleaded exhaustion and fell into bed before nine, she took her purchases to the hotel's reading room, ordered tea with milk, and began writing.

*****

Paris, Monday, April 21, 1919

We are in Paris!! We are *really* in Paris!! It took no time at all for me to decide that I want to stay here awhile. I have not told Frederick this, but think I may be able to convince him that we should. Life here is relatively inexpensive for those with dollars in their pockets, and there is nothing pressing in Chicago. Frederick told me his father's firm can get along without him, though he remains on salary—a gift from Mr. C. Senior—for the duration of the trip, so we shall see.

The city has surpassed my every expectation. I have been in a state of constant delight ever since the train pulled into the Gare St. Lazare. The place *smells* alive. Emotions are palpable; relief at the war's end, sorrow that so many were lost, love for those who survived. You can feel the history, almost hear the hoof beats of Napoleon's cavalry returning from Egypt, almost see Marat, Charlotte Corday, and Robespierre on every street corner. I hardly slept the first night.

We are in an excellent-if-small suite at the Hotel Royal Deschamps. It is expensive; yet another reason for finding a more affordable residence. Since we have arrived here, there has been a tendency on Frederick's part to complain about the price of meals, transportation and other services. For example, I asked that the hotel send a seamstress to the room as my clothes hang on me after our sea voyage. Frederick frowned, asked how much this would cost. I didn't know, having not bothered to ask. Frederick frowned again, made a great show of producing his wallet and fanning through the roll of Franc notes. He looked unhappy at the prospect of parting with a single bill.

*****

Was that an indelicate thing to write? Frederick was not a tightwad, and only twice had he groused about the price of things, and yet it had surprised her; it was out of character. She thought for a moment, then continued.

*****

But Frederick has also been taken by the city. I have caught him staring at the latest men's fashions in store windows. He purchased a bottle of shaving cologne at a *parfumerie*, and tomorrow we shall look for a tailor who can make him some shirts.

I roam the streets like a common tourist. Frederick accompanied me the first day, but since then I've had mornings to myself. We meet for lunch, visit museums in the afternoon, and have attended two evening performances. The one last night was quite risqué. Frederick claims he was told by the hotel staff that it was a very entertaining spectacle, and so we attended. We sat in the dark for what seemed a long time. When the curtain finally rose, a line of dancers wearing brief costumes cavorted about the stage, sang songs, performed acrobatic feats of mild daring and told jokes that neither of us could understand. One skit about the murderer Landru, whom I have read about in newspapers, was obviously ill-rehearsed and disconcerting. An actor, wearing a pointed beard and a bowler hat, lures a young woman to his room. He persuades her to take off most of her clothes, which she does with a maximum of tasteless movements. The lights dim, and eerie strains rise from the musicians' pit. One hears the sounds of passion, and we are treated to a number of tableaux of Landru and his captive in compromising positions. The crowd applauds, shouts suggestions (I think) and generally carries on. Then a large black box—an oven—is produced. Landru wrestles the hapless woman into it while singing at the top of his lungs, then lights a match. Flames. Screams. Smoke. A crescendo of music. After a moment of anticipation, Landru wrests open the oven door and pulls out a skeleton with which he dances across the stage to an infernal rhythm. In the background, 10 thinly veiled women, whose breasts are barely hidden, sing a Greek chorus. Applause. The curtain drops, then rises. The actresses whip off their wigs and skirts, fling their fake bosoms to the ground and reveal themselves to be all men! Frederick, of course, knew. Why he chose this particular spectacle is beyond me. If he wanted to shock me, he succeeded.

*****

45

Easter poured more tea and signaled to a waiter for a fresh pot. It was hard to remember everything—so many discoveries, so little time, so much yet to see. How best to approach Frederick about staying longer than planned? He liked the city, or at least claimed to, but he missed American breakfasts, which no Parisian restaurant served. If he agreed to lengthen their stay, Easter decided she would cook Frederick eggs, bacon and pancakes every day, or at least once a week.

*****

Two days ago I sent a note to Mr. James Johnson, whom the seamstress of my wedding dress, Yvonne Février, suggested I contact. She told me he is a charming man who might be helpful in getting to know the city. Yesterday, having obtained a response from him welcoming me to France, I went to his residence.

I half-expected an artist's garret, the cold-water atelier of an impoverished painter, for Yvonne had told me that Mr. Johnson was struggling to establish himself. I had envisaged a handsome man besmeared with traces of ochre and magenta, and instead found a neat, ground-floor apartment and a young American with melancholy eyes. Yvonne had told me he'd driven an ambulance during the war.

Save for a foldable easel standing by a window, the tools of his trade were nowhere to be seen. I anticipated the smell of turpentine but was greeted by the aroma of cabbage and sausage wafting from the concierge's kitchen.

He was wearing a brown corduroy suit that had seen fresher days, and a gray foulard. His shoes, though scuffed, were clean and free of paint spots. I mention all this because I was taken aback. He apologized for the smell, asked for news of Yvonne and avoided my inquiries about his art.

The walls of his apartment were largely bare, save for some colorful posters and several portraits of a young woman. When I asked him, he admitted the paintings were his, and that the girl in question was a local model by the name of Kiki, but that he had painted them from memory. I sensed some embarrassment.

He mentioned in passing that he has a brother, Daniel, who is among the missing.

He offered me tea and cakes, and we then spoke for some time about the people whom I had read about in Chicago. *He knows Modigliani!!!*

I could not hide my exaltation, and he found this amusing.

"Tell me," he asked, "is Modi that well-known in the U.S.? I would have thought people there worshipped the *Fauves*, like Matisse or Dufy. Surely Americans are still enamored of wild colors and daring landscapes."

How embarrassing! I did not know who the *Fauves* or Dufy were. I've since found out. Dufy is a watercolorist. He illustrated some poetry books and became quite famous. The *Fauves*—it means "The Wild Animals"—are members of an artists' movement launched by Henri Matisse that is seeking to change the very concepts of what art is. At the time, however, I had to admit my ignorance.

Mr. Johnson—I shall call him James from now on, at his request—smiled at my lack of knowledge, and I might have been offended save that, for a moment, the sadness left his eyes. He is really quite handsome, but here is the exciting thing: he has promised to introduce me to Modigliani. He made the offer without prompting, as if he performed such services daily for American visitors, which, for all I know, he may.

Frederick did not accompany me on my visit. I hope James did not think it forward of me to come alone. The truth is that Frederick would have been bored and fidgety. Talk of culture fatigues him, and judging from his enjoyment of last night's performance, he is more at home in a popular music hall than in an artist's studio.

Tonight at dinner, I will broach the subject of lengthening our stay. James mentioned several inexpensive furnished apartments in his Montparnasse neighborhood, including two in his building. He also said he would gladly approach the concierge if I were interested in securing one. I told him I had not yet spoken to my husband and he winked at me, as if we shared a secret, which I suppose we do.

*****

Easter blotted the entry, drank the last of her now-tepid tea and left some change on the tray. She returned to her room and undressed quietly in the dark, slipped into her nightgown and got into bed. Frederick was sleeping on his back, mouth ajar, snoring very lightly. She thought for a moment of waking him, but then reconsidered. He might want to seduce her. Was that the right word? Seduce? Probably not. She kissed him on the cheek and he didn't stir. She turned on her side and in moments was asleep.

CHAPTER 12

And why, Frederick wondered, did the man at the hotel suggest that particular show? Granted, it had been great fun, a splendid tale to tell the boys back home, but not what he'd had in mind.

The subterfuge was obvious; those were men on the stage. It was evident to him and should have been to anyone, Easter included. She'd been shocked, or at least feigned her disapproval, and that had surprised him. Wasn't it obvious that the singers' falsettos were strained, that the legs were too stout, the hands too large? It seemed to him that everyone in the audience, save his bride, had recognized the buffoonery for what it was.

In fact, it was exactly the same sort of merriment he and his fraternity brothers had put on one year during the spring semester; excerpts from Romeo and Juliet with an all-male cast. The seniors cajoled him into playing Juliet; he hadn't wanted to, had done his best to overplay the female lead and to make her farcical, and been cheered for it. He had liked it. By the end of the skit, he understood how Juliet felt, had developed feelings for Romeo (played by a burly junior who forgot half the lines), and had relished the attention and ribald comments of the others who, after the performance, drunkenly pinched his rear and squeezed his padded breasts. He'd maintained the Juliet persona the entire evening, and the next day had felt a void as he put on his trousers, tie and blazer.

He dressed carefully for dinner. Tonight there would be an opera, something unobjectionable by Massenet; *Le Cid*, Easter had said. It would be in French, of course.

"Large costumed women bellowing their problems to a hushed crowd leave me cold," he told Easter. "I've never quite understood the attraction."

"It's an adventure story. You'll like it." She reached into her purse, brought out a small wrapped package. "Here, wear these. I purchased them today, and you'll look devastatingly handsome."

He stripped the paper wrapping and opened a small leather box. Four gold studs and a matching pair of cufflinks glinted within. He took them out and fitted them to his shirt.

"You shouldn't have, darling. They look expensive."

Easter shook her head. "They weren't. Don't be offended, but they're secondhand. I bought them in a shop that sells estate items and got quite a bargain. I think the shop owner had weak spot for American ladies." She adjusted his shirtfront, stepped back to inspect him. "Handsome and dashing. They fit you."

She went into the bathroom, fussed with her hair. "And anyway, I know how we can save a great deal of money. It's just an idea; we can talk about it over dinner. I've reserved a table at *La Tour d'Or*. It's reputed to be quite good." He had suggested she choose a place, still feeling some culpability for the preceding night's spectacle.

He nodded, took her in his arms. "And after dinner," he said, "we'll go somewhere special. La Rotonde. *Bechtel's Guide to Paris* says this is where all the artists meet."

She smiled, pondered the offer. "Then I shall have to wear a hat. I've heard it is gauche to enter La Rotonde bareheaded."

They took a taxi, a black Citroën driven by an older man who whipped the automobile around the Place de la Concorde and pounded his klaxon horn with abandon. A large tan and white dog was asleep on the seat beside him. The man drove with one hand, using the other to stroke the animal's flank. *"Mon meilleur ami.* A man's best friend, you say in England."

Frederick, not partial to dogs, nodded. "America, actually. And there, we seldom hire them as copilots." It seemed dangerous. "That's something I can't get used to in this country," he added to Easter. "You have to be exceedingly careful of where you step. Dogs everywhere."

Easter shrugged. "It doesn't bother me. In fact, I think it's rather sweet." She liked animals, had been raised with puppies and kittens. It surprised her—but not much—that Frederick didn't.

"Did you know," she continued, "that there were 29 million dogs and cats before the war, and now fewer than 2 million are left?"

The driver threw a glance over his shoulder. "People eated them. No food during the war. People eat dogs, cats, rats sometimes. People eat animals in zoo. Elephants and giraffes, monkeys, everything."

Frederick made a face. "That may explain some of the more esoteric items on the menus. I'm certain I saw one dish that said cheval, and that means horse. Horse steak."

Easter wasn't amused. "That's dreadful."

"It better than rat," the driver muttered.

Easter leaned forward, "You've eaten horsemeat?"

The driver nodded. "Oh yes. Not bad. A little hard, yes? My wife fixes. In soup."

The rest of the ride was silent. Easter made sure Frederick tipped generously.

Le Cid bored them both. Frederick dozed during the final act and Easter fidgeted. They were among the first spectators out of their seats.

"I think the term 'portentous' applies to this music; excuse me for taking the opportunity to catch up on my sleep," Frederick said. "Did I miss anything?"

Easter shook her head, arranged her hat properly. "No. But the program said someone called Gabrielle Chanel designed the costumes. Yvonne—the seamstress back home—mentioned that name. A milliner friend of hers, if memory serves. Makes *chapeaux.*" She pronounced the word emphatically.

They ate a leisurely dinner and arrived at the Rotonde shortly after 11 p.m. Though the night was chilly, most of the sidewalk tables were occupied. The maître d'hôtel, an immensely fat man with a friendly smile, led them to a table in the front room, but Easter shook her head. *"S'il vous plaît, l'autre salle."*

51

The man peered at her, said, "Very noisy there," in passable English, then shrugged and led them to the back room. Easter settled her hat, squared her shoulders and followed.

It was more than noisy. The room was teeming; smoke hung heavy and acrid; Frederick's eyes watered. Men in shirt sleeves shouted to overcome the din and added to it. Waiters in long white aprons ran obstacle courses past customers standing at the bar. The maître d'hôtel found a tiny table, asked, "Here?" Frederick was about to refuse but Easter smiled and quickly sat in the proffered chair.

"My God, Easter, this is intolerable!" Frederick made a show of wiping his brow with his handkerchief. "Please, let's leave. It must be a hundred degrees in here!"

Easter was already scanning the room. "Take off your jacket. Everyone else has."

It was true; all the men were in shirt sleeves rolled up to their elbows.

"I will not!" He stood. Easter remained seated. He sat back down, looked aggrieved. "Look at this rabble! If I take my jacket off, some thief will make off with it! Please, darling. Let's find someplace civilized."

She ignored him. A waiter slid a basket of bread on the table, looked at Frederick. "Monsieur?"

Easter answered, *"Deux anisettes, s'il vous plaît."*

Frederick's annoyance grew. "What did you get us?"

"Anisette. A licorice drink."

He made a face. She shot him a hard look, leaned close. "Frederick, I have wanted to come here for a decade. Don't spoil it."

Frederick opened his mouth to reply, thought better of it.

There were Arab men and black men, blond men smoking pipes, women with violently colored hair and make-up puffing on cigars. At the table next to theirs, an Oriental man in a tunic and bowl haircut played with the earring in his left lobe. The woman with him, a European with strangely slanted eyes, was arguing in a low voice. Frederick noticed the man had on leather sandals with straps wound about his bare lower legs.

The waiter brought their drinks. Easter sipped hers, then drank it down. Frederick put the glass tentatively to his lips. "This stuff is awful!" He wiped his mouth with the back of his hand. "Easter, I insist!"

The command didn't have the expected impact. "Order something else, Frederick. Or go back to the hotel if you prefer and I'll join you there later."

He tried looking petulant. "Oh, for heaven's sake!" Still, he remained seated.

The blanket of smoke made it hard to see. Easter stared, hoping to match faces to magazine photos she had seen. "The older man with the beard," she whispered, "the one with the shaven skull and bushy mustache, the fat fellow in the boater, they all look familiar. But then, so does the waiter." Her eyes swept the room, stopped, focused on a table close to the door. Frederick followed her gaze, saw nothing worth noting.

Easter squinted. "It's James Johnson," she said. The man she was looking at was in an animated discussion with a young woman. "That woman looks just like the one in the portraits hanging in his studio."

The woman was laughing loudly and Frederick glimpsed her white teeth, bright eyes. The man reached across the table, found the woman's hands, held them in both of his.

The woman glanced up and her eyes met Easter's. Easter turned away, unaccountably flustered.

Frederick asked, "This is the man you visited? The one you told me about?"

She nodded. He grimaced, added, "The place smells like a mine shaft, Easter. I know some of these people haven't bathed recently. I can smell it." He made a dismissive gesture with his wrist. "Phew! Really *very* unpleasant."

Easter was still watching Johnson's table. The woman with him was walking away, hips swaying beneath her tight skirt. She embraced a tall and thin auburn-haired man and wound an arm about his waist.

Johnson was watching the couple amble toward the back of the room.

"We should join him," said Easter. "I'll introduce you."

It took a minute, however, to hail their waiter and settle the bill and by the time they paid, Johnson was gone.

CHAPTER 13

The first woman was Jeanne-Marie Cuchet, a 39-year-old widow whose late husband had been killed in battle early in the war. She and her son, André, 17, died in Landru's rented villa in Vernouillet one night in May 1915.

The three had spent the night there, he and Jeanne-Marie in the upstairs bedroom, the son in the guest room on the second floor. She had been passionate, Landru less so. He did not really find the woman attractive—her nose was too large, her hips were rubbery, her pubic hair was beginning to gray—and he was annoyed by her voice, high-pitched and grating. Still, she had 17,000 francs in a savings account, and several pieces of acceptable furniture in her apartment. In bed that night they played a game where he bound a scarf over her mouth, supposedly to muffle her moans and protect her son's sensitivities. In fact, Landru had discovered, Jeanne-Marie liked to talk during the act, and he found this habit disagreeable and unnecessary.

The next morning he prepared a *petit déjeuner* of *café au lait et tartines.* He knew André and his mother each laced their coffee with 4 teaspoons of sugar—a habit that he, as a former soldier, found sinfully wasteful—and so to the sugar in the bowl he added a powdered cyanide-based rat poison bought at the local hardware store. The Cuchets, *mère et fils,* drank their coffee in one swallow. He turned his back to them and busied himself at the stove fixing more grilled bread. Within minutes, André dropped his bread and orange marmalade on the floor and convulsed. He fell off his chair, lay on his back and his breathing became labored. Jeanne-Marie screamed and Landru rushed to the boy's side just in time to see her fall as well. Landru rose, poured himself a cup of coffee, and watched as both died. By his watch, it took 12 minutes for André and nine for Jeanne-Marie. André had vomited, which Landru found reprehensible, and when he went to pick up Jeanne-Marie, he noticed her bowels had failed.

He grabbed the woman's body under the armpits and dragged her through the kitchen door to the walled backyard. He stripped off her clothes and, with a ladle, bath brush and a bucket of cold water, cleaned her. He repeated the process with her son. Then he knelt and carefully listened for heartbeats. There were none.

He checked his watch. The train for Paris would be leaving in an hour. Not enough time for dismemberment. He dragged the bodies to the garden shed, found a large, paint-splattered drop cloth, and wrapped it around the victims. He tucked the two bodies in a corner of the shed behind some gardening tools. Disposal would come later.

The day before, he had bought four train tickets to Vernouillet; three one-ways and one return. That had saved him seven francs. He found his ticket on the bedroom dresser, looked once around the house. He left the cups on the table, but made sure to put away the sugar bowl. He disliked ants. He left the house, carefully locked the front door, and walked to the train station.

He spent that night at home with his wife, Marie-Catherine, and three of his four children: Maurice, Suzanne and Charles. Marie, his oldest, was already married and living with her two children in Montpelier.

He entertained them by humming a recent Debussy composition, affecting different tonalities for the various instruments. Marie-Catherine laughed and clapped, but Maurice, his oldest son, was in a dark mood. Earlier, his father had said that in the morning Maurice was to help him transport the furniture of a Mme. Cuchet and her son to a holding garage. Five rooms would have to be moved, and the work would take all day.

Thérèse Laborde-Line died in June 1915. Born in Argentina and separated from a hotelier husband who abused her, she too had answered one of Landru's ads, had been wooed, taken to Vernouillet and poisoned. She was a medium-sized woman with large bones, small breasts and

56

strong hips, and most men would have called her plain. Full, pouty lips rescued her face from complete anonymity. She knew this and, free of her husband, had parlayed her marginal looks into three bad dalliances, one on the heels of the other. Landru—though she knew him as Marcel Veron—promised to change her life and carry her away.

Earlier that week, Landru had returned to Vernouillet and buried the remains of Jeanne-Marie and André Cuchet in a far corner of the local cemetery. The war produced graves daily; mounds of fresh earth in the graveyard were not suspect.

He had promised Thérèse Laborde-Line a lovers' weekend in his villa, but was silently repulsed by her lack of hygiene. She smelled poorly, and the skin on her neck was gray from lack of soap and water. He did not engage in sex with her, blaming an unexpected bout of colitis. Thérèse bore her disappointment well.

After feeding her a salad and some cold chicken, Landru this time chose strychnine, mixing a generous teaspoon of the chemical in Therese's evening cocoa. She made a slight face as she drank and complained briefly of the chocolate's bitterness, but he assured her it was a special mix from Abyssinia, and as she emptied the cup, Thérèse once again thanked the heavens for sending her such a devoted man. Imagine that! Chocolate from Abyssinia! For her!

He was amazed at the effect of the strychnine. Thérèse's neck seized, the cords and muscles etched in sharp relief to the gray skin. Her face froze into a toothy rictus, eyes wide open, frothed mouth in a distended O. Landru, watching, wondered if the odiferous woman knew what was happening to her. He doubted it.

Her arms flapped as if she were trying to fly, then her legs buckled. She jackknifed at the waist, repeatedly slamming the back of her head into the floor, moaning loudly, and Landru, concerned by the noise, squatted on her chest to hold her down. Her convulsions threw him off. She made a gurgling sound in her throat, arched her back until only her heels and head touched the bedroom rug. She collapsed and rose again once, twice. Her forehead running with sweat, she stared at her murderer with wondering eyes, seeing nothing. Her face turned a pale blue, and she bit her lower lip. The blood flowed down her chin and onto her blouse. In less than eight minutes, she was lifeless.

Landru sat in the leather easy chair that had belonged to Jeanne-Marie Cuchet, took out his pen, glanced at his watch and wrote the hour and minute carefully in the little notebook he always carried. The late Thérèse surprised him by farting once, very long and very loud like a balloon losing its air, and Landru waved the stink from his face. He frowned at the body, said, "*Vraiment, Thérèse, ce n'est pas très élégant, ça.*"

Later, he dismembered her with a butcher's saw. He wore a thick canvas apron that covered him from neck to ankle, and he worked methodically and without talent, cutting through muscle and bone and feeding the pieces of her into a large stove. He had overseen the stove's installation himself, ensuring a good strong draught in the flue, which rose straight through the roof and out the chimney.

Her remains were gone just before sunup, and by the time he cleaned his tools, scrubbed the floor, sink and apron with bleach and water, the morning was full on. He stirred the ashes with a long metal pole and was pleased to see nothing large remained unconsumed by the fire. He was exhausted and slept until late afternoon, then took a cab to the station and returned to Paris on the 7 o'clock train.

Chapter 14

Kiki arrived very early in the morning, banging on James Johnson's door, earning the ire of Mme. Bertrand, the concierge who moments earlier and with obvious misgivings had let her into the courtyard. When Johnson pulled the curtain aside to see who was making this racket, Kiki opened the rabbit-fur coat she was wearing to show that, save for her shoes, she was naked. Mme. Bertrand's eyes nearly popped out of her skull. Johnson saved the day by telling the outraged older lady that Kiki was his model, and that models often traveled in *deshabillé* to avoid getting tell-tale marks from their straps, elastic or garters.

Mme. Bertrand was doubtful. *"Vraiment, Monsieur Johnson?"*

Johnson nodded. *"Vraiment, Mme. Bertrand."*

Mme. Bertrand shook her head. *"La jeunesse... Très étrange."*

Johnson agreed. The youth today did behave in strange manners.

Mme. Bertrand spent a long time bitterly sweeping the courtyard, keeping a wary eye on Johnson's door. M. Lefebvre stopped by to speak to her, then shook his head in obvious consternation. Johnson knew his mores were under scrutiny and that the forgiveness of these two Catholic worthies would be hard to come by. A bottle of American whiskey might be in order.

Kiki thought the entire thing hilarious, mimed the concierge's dour expression, and put on her best American accent to mock Johnson's consternation. Then she took off her coat and, naked save for her red patent leather shoes, began wandering about the apartment.

Johnson suspected the model's visit was a follow-up, an outburst of her inquisitive nature, and, perhaps, a need for revenge.

The night before, he'd gone to the Rotonde hoping for a quick meal and an early night. He had been chilled and feverish, having had trouble falling asleep.

He'd ordered his dinner with a glass of *vin ordinaire* and had been reading the day's *Tribune* when Kiki pulled up a chair and helped herself to the breadbasket. He smiled, she smiled back. Spontaneity was not his strong suit and like M. Lefebvre, Johnson often found himself *bouche bée*—speechless—when faced with unfamiliar situations.

Kiki ate one piece of bread, then another. She asked the waiter to bring butter and mustard, and when he did, made a butter-and-mustard sandwich that emptied the basket.

She said, "I'm hungry." Then she said, "Also, I am very angry." (All this was in French, of course, since she spoke no English save for the unfortunate phrase, 'I like American *soldats*. Do you want to fock?')

Johnson bought Kiki dinner: deviled eggs, Parma ham, *pommes frites*. She ate with gusto and informed him that her fiancé, Maurice Mendjizky, had been unfaithful to her and had slept with one of his models. Then she asked, "You have a fiancée?"

Johnson shook his head. "No. I did once, but not anymore."

"You were in the war, yes?"

Johnson nodded, "Ambulances."

She looked up. "Verdun?"

He nodded.

She said, "*Pauvre chéri,*" dabbed at her lips with her napkin and reached for his hands across the table. She leaned forward and asked, "You had a bad time, yes? Like many… So, I know you paint. Everyone here paints. It is an affliction. What do you paint?"

Johnson told her he was working on watercolors, that he occasionally did portraits, and that, in fact, he had done hers from memory.

Kiki shrugged. "Everybody paints me. Sometimes they do my entire body. Maurice, my fiancé, did a portrait. Very ugly. I look like a school-teacher from Auvergne. Long nose, no chin. He did not like me very much that day, I think. What did you make me look like?"

Johnson smiled, felt sly. "Perhaps you should come and see. "

Kiki nodded, shifted her attention to the growing crowd in the room. Suddenly her mouth opened in a small, round 'o' which she covered with one hand. Johnson looked up and saw Maurice Mendjizky headed in their direction. Kiki stood, whispered, "Maybe tomorrow I'll come by," then ran off to embrace her lover. Mendjizky lanced Johnson with a dark look and took Kiki by the elbow. They walked away, their arms sliding about each other's waist. Johnson sat at his table, looked at the empty breadbasket and half-eaten eggs. He noted that he was both taller and broader than Mendjizky, who was thin, almost spindly, and did not look like much of a fighter.

Naked in the apartment, Kiki headed straight for the three portraits of herself, stood by them a moment and made a show of offering her profile. "Not bad. Much better than Maurice, *ce con.*" She wandered the room like an inquisitive cat, picking items up, inspecting them. "What is that?"

"A table lighter," Johnson explained. The lighter was in the shape of a small pistol, with the flame coming from the barrel. Kiki aimed it at Johnson, squeezed the trigger, went, "Pan!" She smiled. *"C'est mignon!* Can I have it?"

Johnson didn't smoke, but kept the lighter around for friends who did. He shrugged. Kiki went to her coat and put the lighter in a pocket.

Then she entered the bedroom and inspected items there. She dropped to the bed and said, "Come here. Sit by me."

Johnson did, feeling he was not really there but looking on, a third, voyeuristic party.

In the past few months, Kiki had invaded his fantasies and been the leading actress in his nighttime reveries. Now he looked at her dispassionately and noticed, as her girlfriend had revealed to La Rotonde's clients, that Kiki indeed had no pubic hair. He decided her breasts did deserve the title of *la plus belle poitrine de Paris.* She had rather small hands but largish feet. Her ankles were solid, made to anchor her to the earth, and her thighs were thick with muscle. She had a good waist and

61

a deep-set navel. He noted all this without a shiver of lust, as a painter might inspect a bowl of fruit.

She was in a hurry. She helped him undo his belt and pants, removed his shoes, slid the trousers off and let them drop in a heap on the floor. In time, she moaned, groaned, panted, bit her lip, rolled her eyes, and raised her hips to meet his thrusts. She mounted him, bucked and sweated mightily to a pretended orgasm and forced him to come without conviction. She was kind, swearing upon the graves of all her ancestors that she had been pleasured beyond her wildest dreams. She was lying; he knew it, she knew he knew it; it was acceptable to both. She went into the bathroom and, not bothering to close the door, sat on the toilet, then wiped her hairless self with his bath towel. When she saw him looking, she asked, "Do you know Fujita? The little Japanese with the earring and the sandals? When I pose for him, he gets down on all fours and inspects me like a doctor. 'Very funny. No hair!' Do you think it's funny, Mr. James Johnson?"

He said that, no, he didn't; he actually found her smoothness attractive.

She nodded. "Yes, a lot of men have told me that." She put on her coat, stroked his jaw with both her hands and gave him a lingering wet kiss. "Now we can be friends."

She left, waving gaily. Mme. Bertrand, still in the courtyard abusing her broom, turned her back and pretended not to see.

CHAPTER 15

Frederick slept, making strange bubbling noises in his throat. He was agitated; Easter jolted awake when he flung out his left arm and struck her shoulder.

It was still dark outside but light was beginning to creep above the horizon. They had a corner room with two windows, and the view displayed the changing face of the city. To the left were the Champs Elysées, glowing with a million incandescent lights. To the right was a much smaller street lit by gas lanterns.

Easter rose quietly, looked out to see a lamplighter extinguishing flames with a long bamboo pole ending in a candlesnuffer. What a strange existence, to be responsible for clarity and darkness, she thought. The worker was an older man wearing a slouch cap. He shuffled from lamp to lamp with a worn gait, and his dexterity was admirable. There was only a small aperture through which he could thrust the pole and, with a deft twist of his wrist, smother the flame. She remembered reading that workmen who paint long bridges never cease their labor, beginning one end of the structure as soon as they finish the other. This fellow's career, she thought, must be similar.

The morning before, she'd watched the *boulangerie's* cart delivering baskets of breads and croissants to the hotel's kitchen. Another truck brought flowers, still another, milk, eggs and butter.

A police vehicle sped by in silence, its distinctive siren hushed in deference to the hotel's slumbering guests.

She looked at the clock, opened her diary and began to write.

*****

Paris, Thursday, April 24, 1919

It is shortly after 5 a.m. I have had only a few hours' rest, but I love this city's early morning stillness. Paris gathers its strength, stretches in anticipation of the day.

Things are *right* here. Not that I pretend to be French; I don't. I am proud of my American-ness. Though many loathe admitting it, without the United States, there would be no France; or rather, there would be a France, but it would speak German—a repugnant thought.

I belong and have to let go certain of my ambitions already. For example, I realized yesterday, shortly after I saw James's portraits hanging on the walls of his apartment, that *I* did not come to paint. I would like to, and will, but right now, I simply want to witness.

Frederick is stirring. Whatever is he dreaming of to cause such agitation? What do men dream of? Women and sex? Politics, wealth and power? War and conquest, or more mundane things, cufflinks and shirt studs, razors that shave properly and shoes that fit?

*****

She paused, put down her pen. Frederick had thrown off the blanket; she carefully draped it back over his sleeping form.

*****

How little I know him. Is it a wife's duty to gentle a husband whose slumber is distraught? When he is first awake is when I like him best, without defenses and before he has marshalled

64

pretensions of manhood. Thank God Frederick is not a vain pop-injay, nor perpetually chasing skirts. Both Enid and Charlotte told me he does not fit the type, and he has never to my knowledge given even a passing glance to the pretty demoiselles strutting the boulevards. They look at him, though. Some ignore my presence and turn when he passes. Their admiring eyes are not lost on me. I am fortunate indeed to have found such a mate.

Why then do I harbor this lack of passion for him, this absence of desire? I *like* Frederick, and I am sure many lifelong relationships have begun and lasted on far less secure footing, but why don't I have the feeling Enid described after her affair with the dance band mandolin player?

The night aboard *La Savoie* had everything to do with me and nothing to do with Frederick, save that he was there, available and willing.

Perhaps something is seriously wrong with me; a flaw I did not know how to recognize until marriage.

Now, Frederick is talking in his sleep; it is unintelligible.

The Rotonde was a noisy disappointment. The food was indifferent, the smoke and unmistakable aroma of unwashed bodies quite revolting. Frederick noted this immediately, of course. James was there with his thick-ankled model. They were quite chummy, holding hands like sweethearts.

She was rather cheap, what Father used to call an 'overly made-up floozy.' I wonder if what I have read of the modeling profession is true. Are they really just a step above prostitutes, these women who disrobe at the whim of a man with a brush?

I have made too much of the encounter with James. He is a handsome man, but no more so than Frederick. His mannerisms imply a proper upbringing and his sad eyes yearn to tell stories. His missing brother must be a painful weight to bear.

Now it is past dawn. Frederick's eyes are open. I can feel them on my back. My "friend" has arrived. I am sure Frederick cannot be aware of this. Do men know of these things?

I shall take him to breakfast later and broach the idea of lengthening our stay.

Chapter 16

"Darling, it's out of the question. Our cabin is booked. My parents have already planned a dinner to celebrate our return. There are things we must do in Chicago: look for a home, purchase furnishings, and start a family, and frankly, I want our children to be American, not French."

Frederick buttered his croissant and carefully spread plum jam on it. Easter set her fork down, added a sugar cube to her tea and stirred. "Honestly, Easter," he went on, "the sooner we get home, the better. I don't know about you, but I haven't been sleeping well since we arrived." He chewed, swallowed, and smiled. "So, what do we have planned for today?"

"Not a single thing," Easter countered his smile with her best, "unless you start seriously considering what I just suggested. I'm quite insistent, Frederick. I want to spend more time here. The fortnight simply will not be enough. We can change the cabin reservations and send a telegram to your parents. As to starting a family, we have not discussed this yet and I'd like to voice my small opinion when we do." She flicked a crumb of bread from her sleeve and looked up. "I have my own views on that. I presume I will be involved?" She recognized the edge in her voice, lightened it with effort. "Or are you considering an Immaculate Conception?"

Frederick arranged the linen napkin on his lap, so its folds fell evenly on both sides of his legs. Weariness embraced him; he was suddenly exhausted, tired of this dirty city, the language he could not understand and the people who spoke it. He wished he were in Chicago having a drink and desultory conversation with his father. He longed for larger cups of coffee and softer breads, simpler meals of recognizable fares, bigger tables, wide wooden chairs with real seat cushions, and softer toilet paper. Even Easter fatigued him.

He wanted to walk back to the hotel, crawl into the too-small bed and draw the sheets over his head. He wanted to stay there until it was time to return to his country where things were done as they should be.

He took a silent, deep breath. "Easter, there are things one can do, and things one cannot. This," he made a sweeping gesture encompassing the city, the country, the continent, "this is not real life. It's a perfectly valid flight of fancy for a few weeks. You can see the sights, sit in the cafés and pretend you're an artist—"

The croissant and marmalade struck him in the middle of the chest, hung there a moment and slid down to his lap, leaving traces of orange on his white shirt. His mouth stayed opened as his wife carefully arranged the unused silverware by her plate, stood, and straightened her dress.

Her voice was barely a whisper. "Frederick, because I believe you're a gentleman, and a good man, I doubt you know how deeply you've just offended me. But at this very moment, I also believe you are a simpleton and a fool with whom I do not wish to spend the day." She pulled on her gloves, took her purse. Frederick found the croissant in his lap, returned it to his plate.

"Ask the waiter for some warm water so your shirt won't stain. Then please remain here and finish your meal. I am returning to the hotel to change."

She smoothed her skirt over her thighs. "I would prefer to do so in privacy. You may have the room for the rest of the day. I should be back early in the evening. I plan to go to dinner and to a show. I understand Charlie Chaplin's 'Little Tramp' is playing at the Théâtre Odéon. You can accompany me if you wish. Or not. Good day, Frederick." She dropped some coins on the table and swept out of the dining room, an empress.

Her fury carried her back to the hotel, past the concierge to whom she threw an over-the-shoulder, *"Bonjour, Monsieur,"* into the elevator where her stare burned through the back of the uniformed attendant. In the room, she threw off her dress and chemise, then doused cold water on her face and applied minimal makeup.

She selected a powder-blue two-piece suit matching the Parisian sky, a hip-length cream silk blouse and a large-crowned hat trimmed with silk threads and a silver buckle. Over this she threw a mid-calf cotton raincoat. She feared Frederick might return too early and try to stop her. If he did, she might very well succumb to the inevitable entreaties, so she buttoned the outfit hurriedly, sprayed a small cloud of perfume in the air—a new scent by Guerlain that she had paid a fortune for in the States—and walked through it.

In the hotel hallway, she stopped before a mirror, checked no other guests were present, and assumed several fashionable poses. A wisp of hair escaped and she tucked it back, then pulled it out again. When free, her auburn hair reached her shoulder blades. Stuffed in a bun under her hat, her coiffure was seriously out of fashion. In Chicago, she had resisted the boyish page-boy look both Enid and Charlotte wore and encouraged. In Paris, her longish hair was embarrassingly American.

The concierge was delighted to make an immediate reservation for her at a *salon de beauté* on Avenue Iena. On her way there, she passed the window display of a small *maison de couture*. She spotted a smashing black *crêpe de chine* evening outfit boasting a daringly low scooped neckline. She knew without asking that it would fit her perfectly. She purchased the accompanying shoes, belt, purse and, for good luck, a clever automatic umbrella that opened at the push of a button. The total, in Francs, came to just over $75. She kept the umbrella and had the ensemble delivered to the hotel.

Feeling immensely better, she walked to the Salon Dupêcher and was ushered into a private booth by the owner, a portly lady who cooed, undid her hair, and spoke a torrent of French to an assistant.

Mme. Dupêcher, Easter learned, had spent four years in England before the war, serving as the Duchess of York's private beautician, a lovely job though the Duchess was tightfisted. As the assistant chopped, snipped, and trimmed, she and Easter compared fashions in France with those in the U.S. Easter, knowing little on the subject, extemporized freely. They spoke of the War, English authors, the war again, husbands. Mme. Dupêcher lifted Easter's left hand. "You are recently married, yes? Of course. The ring has no scars..."

"Scars?"

"Scratches. I mean scratches."

Monsieur Dupêcher had been among the first to fall in battle at Charleroi.

"The fool volunteered," Mme. Dupêcher said with a sad smile. "The first day, pffft. Gone. What does a *coiffeur* know about war?"

Easter was talked into a facial, a *manucure et pédicure chinois,* and an *assainissement de la peau,* a deep skin cleansing that, according to Mme., was de rigueur for anyone spending time in Paris. "The air is filthy here; coal, kerosene, petrol. It destroys skin."

Easter left the salon three hours after she entered it, feeling rejuvenated if guilty. The afternoon had cost almost $100, more than half the funds she'd brought with her from the States. Frederick would be furious.

An hour later, without quite knowing how she'd gotten there, she knocked on James Johnson's door.

CHAPTER 17

When Frederick returned to the hotel, the concierge volunteered that Mme. had indeed left and was heading for the Salon Dupêcher a few blocks away. Frederick obtained directions from the man but got lost around the Etoile. After circling the Arc de Triomphe twice, he repaired to a café and had two small brandies against the early chill. The drinks left him angrier and somewhat tipsy. He paid, gathered his change and left, certain the waiter had shorted him.

Dark clouds drifted in and it began to rain. He found a taxi, but two pregnant women exercised their priority to public transportation and commandeered the vehicle. Neither thanked him. He returned to the café and had another brandy, counting his change with extreme care. The waiter watched him with open contempt, mustache quivering.

He ordered a *croque-monsieur,* a baked ham and cheese sandwich, but the cheese was too pungent for his taste so he ate one bite and left the rest on his plate. The waiter approached, muttered and pointed at the food. Frederick shook his head and waved the plate away. The waiter picked it up, brought it to his nose, sniffed, shrugged his shoulders, and returned it to the placemat. Frederick shook his head again, said, *"Pas bon,"* the two words he recalled from a phrase Easter had taught him. The waiter smiled, showing many uneven yellow teeth. *"Mais si, mais si. C'est très bon, croyez moi."*

Frederick remembered that *'Croyez moi'* meant believe me, and that was too much for the waiter to ask. Frederick assuredly did not believe him. The cheese was odiferous, nastily colored where it had melted on the bread. The ham was gamy.

Now, the waiter was piqued. *"Bon. Très bien."* He snapped his towel, whisked the plate away and walked off.

Some fruit, Frederick thought. Fruit would take the evil taste from his mouth. He waited for the waiter to return but the café's staff had vanished. People were looking at him, staring at the orange stains on his shirt. Could they divine what had happened, the croissant thrown by his insane wife? Certainly she was insane; why else would she throw food-stuff around in a restaurant?

He said it aloud but very softly, just to hear what it sounded like. "I fear my wife is insane."

He took a sip of brandy, then another. The waiter was slow in return-ing. In Chicago, Frederick might have spoken with the restaurant's man-ager but here in Paris he was at a loss.

He finished his brandy in one gulp, inspected the check, and left the exact amount of money on the table.

It had stopped raining and the cloud cover was breaking. He placed his wet trilby on his head at a jaunty angle and examined the day's possibilities.

It was still early. He could return to the hotel and wait for Easter like a chastened schoolboy. She might, of course, be there already. Had she gotten pangs of conscience, realized the depth of her abysmal behavior? Perhaps she'd gone to the beauty parlor to make herself especially attrac-tive and earn his forgiveness. Women were known to do just that, in which case he should not return immediately. Let her stew a bit, reflect upon her disgraceful actions, realize that he would not be one of those henpecked husbands who feared their spouses. What had his friend Corrigan said? "Show 'em who's in charge. Let 'em know right from the start that you won't stand for any of that female crap." Not a bad fellow, Corrigan. A little rough around the edges but his heart was in the right place. Certainly that was a good piece of advice.

He felt better. A passing woman gave him a radiant smile. He nodded his head, smiled back. She stopped, opened her handbag, dropped it, and made an alarmed sound as its contents spilled on the sidewalk. Frederick stooped, retrieved the bag and began gathering the items. Lipstick, loose change, a pack of Dots cigarettes and a small gold lighter.

The woman was quite attractive, almost as tall as he was with short auburn hair cut in a boyish fashion. Green eyes, he noticed, and very full lips. Nice white teeth. He took it all in at a glance.

She said, *"Ah, Monsieur! Comme vous êtes gentil!"*

He shook his head. *"Je ne parle pas…"*

Her smile widened; Frederick smiled as well.

"English? American?"

"American. Do you speak…"

"Ah! American! I love America…"

She'd been there, had traveled to New York, Boston and San Francisco with her husband, now deceased.

"The war?"

"La guerre. Yes. In the trenches."

They shared a necessary moment of respectful silence. Her eyes teared. She was standing very close to Frederick and he could smell her perfume, something autumny. He raised a hand, laid it on her wrist; it seemed the right thing to do. She took a deep breath, exhaled, did it again. "I try to think of this not often."

Frederick nodded, kept his hand where it was. They stood on the boulevard sidewalk, neither in a hurry to move.

"I am Micheline Barbot."

"Frederick Cowles."

There was an uneasy silence; then both spoke at the same time.

"I was going to…" They laughed.

"I was going," she tried again, "to have a cup of tea. You will accompany me?"

They sat in a booth with red leather banquettes and a white tablecloth. She had a pleasant voice. Frederick thought how enjoyable it was to be speaking English with someone other than Easter, someone who obviously enjoyed the language, laughed at his jokes, showed gratitude when he helped her find the right word and assisted her pronunciation.

She giggled a lot, twice reached across the table to give his hand a squeeze. When she asked if he might consider it uncivilized to have something stronger than tea this early in the day, he flamboyantly ordered a bottle of Veuve Clicquot. The waiter, a very nice chap, kissed his own fingertips in appreciation of Frederick's excellent choice and brought two fluted glasses. Micheline lit a Dots cigarette.

"American things," she said. "Very good. I like American things. Cigarettes, clothing; American everything at all."

They drank the Champagne and watched the traffic go by. Frederick rattled words off in English, Micheline provided the French equivalent. Then she attempted to explain the difference between the familiar *tu* and formal *vous* and Frederick had to admit that such nuances might indeed be helpful in everyday conversation.

He described his travels in America; she listened, mouth slightly open and eyes wide. They tried one of the slot machines at the rear of the brasserie. Frederick pulled the handle and a cascade of coins rewarded his effort. Micheline squealed with delight, stacked the winnings into neat little piles on their table. There was almost enough to pay for the tea and Champagne. She was really very nice, Frederick decided once again. It was turning into a wonderful day despite the dreadful scene with Easter.

By the time he realized Micheline's interest in him might be financial, he was following her up a set of dark stairs in a two-star hotel where she seemed to know the desk attendant.

CHAPTER 18

"What a pleasant surprise," said James Johnson.

Easter stood in the doorway, feeling exposed in her new short hair style and bright red fingernails. He was barefooted, wearing a tartan bathrobe over pale blue pajamas.

"I'm afraid I had a late night. Usually, I'm up and about by this time. If you'll give me a moment, I'll make myself presentable."

She waited, sitting on a worn green velvet couch. She could hear water running in the bathroom. She peered at the portraits on the wall, remembering the encounter at La Rotonde.

He was taking a long time to change, so she got up, headed for the front door, stopped, sat down again. The portraits demanded her attention.

Soon, James re-entered the room, buttoning the collar of a white shirt.

"You're looking at Kiki again. You haven't told me what you thought of them."

"Very…close resemblance."

He raised an eyebrow. "You know her?"

"I was at La Rotonde night before last with my husband. I believe you and the young lady were there as well. We were just leaving as you came in." Her words came in a rush and she hated herself for being so obvious in her lie.

"Well that's a shame." He bent to lace a shoe. "I could have introduced you. Kiki's delightful, and she always enjoys meeting new people. You'd like her."

"I'm sure." Easter let a silence pass. "She's very pretty."

James shook his head. "She's what's called wall-of-China beautiful. She looks better from a distance. I mean, she *is* attractive, but up close, her nose is a bit too large, and her eyes are close set. Also, she's rather short-necked."

He smiled awkwardly. "I'm speaking about proportions, of course. It doesn't seem to make her any less desirable. As a model, I mean."

There was a brief silence and Easter changed subjects.

"I should explain my unexpected visit," she said. "It's regarding the apartment. You mentioned you might be able to help; perhaps you could suggest a building? I haven't spoken to Mr. Cowles, Frederick, yet, but I plan to, and I thought if there were any possibilities, it might make my husband more receptive to the idea, because he... 'How embarrassing. She was babbling again.

If James noticed her discomfiture, he made no comment on it. "Ah. He doesn't share your enthusiasm. Well. We shall see what we can do to change that." He fiddled with his cravat, trying to center it. "As a matter of fact, your arrival is fortuitous." He glanced at his watch. "I'm meeting Modi for lunch. Would you like to join us? I'd be delighted, and I'm sure he would be as well."

"Modi? *Modigliani?*"

James smiled, then frowned like Janus. "Ah, but that the mention of *my* name could but only once arouse such emotions in a woman! Alas, it is probably not to be." He laughed, and his smile returned. "Yes, indeed, Modigliani, the one and only. He and I are friends. I don't spend that much time with other painters as a rule. They're overbearing, self-centered, egotistical and shallow. All of the above is true of Modi as well, but in lesser proportion. On occasion, he's been known to see beyond his brush, and I've had a couple of interesting conversations with him." He shrugged on his jacket, looked back at her expectantly.

"Actually," he went on, "you'd be doing me a favor. He's likely to be quite impressed if I show up with a beautiful companion. It's very Italian, you see. So, what do you say? A free meal, good company, and you'll be back at your hotel by three."

Easter hesitated the briefest moment, just to be proper. "If you're certain I won't be imposing."

James offered his arm. "Rest assured, but be warned as well. Modi thinks that to paint a woman is to possess her, so if he asks you to pose—which I suspect he might—well, you might want to give *that* offer second thought."

CHAPTER 19

The French woman was in a hurry. She'd hung her dress on a hook behind the door and carefully folded her underthings on the chair next to the bed. Conversation had ceased once they'd entered the room and he'd given her 20 francs in 5-franc bills. She was still smiling, but she wanted things to proceed.

Frederick felt no passion, no remorse or fear. He wondered how he'd come to be in a cheap and dimly lit room in Paris with a prostitute, and was trying to decide what he would do if Easter was waiting for him at home.

If his wife was not there, he would give his clothes to the laundry service and take a bath. Then he would get angry at her for leaving him stranded in a restaurant in a strange country, and, when she returned, he would make his exasperation plain to see. She was to blame for his present situation—one does not abandon one's husband where one's husband does not speak the language.

In the meantime, Micheline lay beneath him, urging his efforts with fluid movements of her hips and whispering, *"Dépêche-toi, chéri! Je n'ai pas toute la journée!* Hurry, hurry! There is not all the day!" She was due back at the office where she answered telephones part-time for an accountant and his partner and was paid, she said, very little.

Frederick was hurrying as best he could with the sad knowledge that—regardless of the pace of the action, be it slow, fast, or in between— the outcome of the event was no longer in question. He was erect but unexcited, and woozy as the brandy, tea and Champagne sloshed in his stomach with every stroke. What had started with so much promise, with Micheline's whisper of, *"Mon Dieu! Tu es énorme!"* as her round eyes gaped appreciatively at his midsection…all this was for naught.

If Micheline was irritated, she did not show it. After a while, she simply stopped moving and asked, "It does not work, yes?" She rolled from under to over, straddled him, pumped up and down a few times as if plunging a sink. This brought a sheen of perspiration to her forehead and some glow to her cheeks, but nothing else. She kissed him lightly on the lips. *"Mon bel Américain.* It does not matter. But I have now to go. The accountants are very strict."

She dressed quickly, checked that her money was in her purse and closed the door softly as she left. Frederick lay in the bed and stared upward. There were cobwebs in the corners and the painted paper was peeling. Beneath it, he could see traces of white and smears of dried paste. The bed was soft and he was tired. He allowed himself to drift off, thinking this too would make a good story for the boys back home if he changed the ending.

CHAPTER 20

To tell or not to tell?

Easter wrestled with the question. Surely even a married woman was allowed her secrets. Frederick would be livid if he knew that, first, she'd gone to James's apartment by herself again, and second, she'd had lunch with Johnson and another artist.

She thought about it a little more as she opened her diary, and decided that marriage did not mean subservience, or at least, that it shouldn't. Moistening her pen with the tip of her tongue, she began to write.

*****

Parris, Sunday, April 27, 1919

We met Modigliani at a restaurant that hardly merits the name, a one-room storefront on Avenue du Maine run by a former nurse, who opened it as an artists' canteen during the war. It is furnished with the odds and ends one might find abandoned on the street when people move from a large place to a smaller one: mismatched chairs and stools, a sagging, scruffy sofa, a dented two-burner stove. Yet, it is a treasure trove as well. James pointed out the works pinned to the wall: here a Picasso drawing, there a painting by Chagall. Several sketches by Modigliani himself. A sculpture by someone called Zadkine. The restaurant's owner, Marie Vassilieff, is herself a painter and has a studio on the second floor.

The place has a certain reputation. Two years ago, Modigliani showed up uninvited at a party here and was greeted by a gun-wielding guest who protested his presence. Later that evening, either from boredom or drunkenness, Picasso locked everyone in and ran away with the key!

Modigliani kept us waiting. When he did appear, I mistook him for a laborer. He grunted once to James, ordered and drank down a small carafe of wine and ate half a *baguette*—this before uttering a single word of greeting to me. Social niceties are not a major concern here. I shall have to get used to it.

Modi—that is what his friends call him—was unshaven, dressed in nondescript and baggy clothes, and looked very tired, pale save for dark circles about his eyes. Droplets of orange paint stained his hands, and his fingernails were ragged. He was handsome, though not exceedingly so—his teeth are in very poor condition and detract considerably from his appearance—and he smoked a pungent concoction which James told me later was tobacco and hashish!

He is of average height with thick lips. His hair curls and is parted on the left. There are tobacco stains between the fingers of his right hand. Did I say he was handsome? Let me amend that: he is unusual; his looks are distinctive.

The luncheon was held to discuss a business proposition. James has been asked by the owner of a New York gallery to arrange for the purchase of several of Modigliani's works. The discussion was put off until the cheese course (a rank smelling Camembert with an unsliced red apple) and I did not pay much attention.

The truth is, I had to force myself not to stare. I felt like a school-girl ogling a matinee idol. Modi swallowed his food (a smallish piece of rare meat and fried potatoes. I had a salad with Belgian endives) without chewing and, between mouthfuls, spoke incessantly of two women, Jeanne and Béatrice. James occasionally had to translate since Modigliani was wont to lapse into Italian, so my recollections may be a bit garbled. Béatrice—a British poet—apparently was (and perhaps still is) Modi's lover. James did not use the word, but implied it. Béatrice and Modigliani had a tempestuous relationship, and he is now enamored of another woman, Jeanne. Jeanne is only 19, an art student at the Académie Colarossi. She never smiles, he said, and this is a source of concern to Modi, who waxed eloquent over Béatrice's laugh and joyful demeanor. Jeanne adores him, and they now live together (without Béatrice, I surmise.)

Frankly, the discussion was too complex to follow. At one point, Modi complained that he suspected Jeanne of having an affair with a Japanese artist and I saw that James was surprised by this. Perhaps he knows the Oriental. Kiki's name also came up, and James blushed slightly, proving legitimate my suspicions. He did not translate whatever it was Modigliani said of that woman.

Modigliani is an entertaining person. By the time he left (without paying—James said this was in character as well) it was obvious that he was inebriated. He did not ask me to pose for him, and I don't know whether I am relieved or offended, probably a bit of both. James did inquire as to my interest in modeling for him (James) and I said I would think about it.

Another man dropped in toward the end of the meal. His name is Jean Cocteau. He is a successful writer, somewhat effeminate, quite courtly and polite. He has written a play and wants James to translate it into English. James agreed to do it, though he told me later he is not thrilled at the prospect.

We walked back to James's apartment, and he shook my hand in a most professional fashion, asking whether he might call on me in the near future. I suggested that I would visit him two days hence (I prefer not to involve Frederick and feel slightly abashed by this mild deception) so we might discuss my sitting for a portrait.

Frederick was sleeping when I returned. He did not stir, so I did not bother him. Later that evening, we had dinner and went to see the Charlie Chaplin movie. Frederick said he found my hair fetching and modern. I thanked him for the compliment but did not ask what he had done with his time. Neither did he inquire as to my whereabouts. I did not mention lengthening our stay.

*****

Easter closed the diary, went to the bathroom to run water over the pen's nib. She was vaguely curious about Frederick's day, but not enough to ask questions. She had sensed sadness in him, but that was gone by the time they returned from the motion picture. He had laughed until tears ran down his cheeks, and on the way back to the hotel and over a last brandy in their room, had told her how wonderful she looked and what a grand idea it had been to go see the Little Tramp.

She wondered whether he might feel amorous, but he didn't and she was relieved.

Easter remembered Modigliani's uneven teeth, the smell of his smoking mixture, James's smile, and she felt a warmth, a pulling, and what might have been an attraction.

CHAPTER 21

James Johnson returned to his apartment after the luncheon. How old, he wondered, is Modigliani now? Thirty-four? Thirty-five? The Italian's pale skin reminded him of the saintly translucence found in Renaissance paintings. Modi was smoking too much hashish and coughed constantly, a hacking, dry rattle. His hands trembled, and there was a facial tic Johnson had never noticed before; Modi's right eyelid jumped haphazardly as he drank wine to ease his cough.

Johnson had met Jeanne Hébuterne, Modi's latest obsession, and thought her an unusual and somewhat frightening creature with ethereal and vacant eyes. He feared she would never learn to take care of his Italian friend, to accept his genius, his passion, and fugues. Modi needed a nurse more than he needed a lover.

Modi and Johnson had struck a deal. In coming weeks, Modi would deliver Johnson fifteen assorted works, including some nudes and portraits. Johnson would ship these off to the United States, and Modi would earn the unbelievable sum of 12,000 francs. A New York gallery—the owner was a friend of Johnson, Sr.—had agreed to purchase the works outright, an unusual arrangement, enabling Modi to pay off some debts and, Johnson hoped, buy new clothes. Modi looked ragged and smelled unwashed.

The meal had killed two birds with one stone. First, by acting as an agent, Johnson was confident of buying some goodwill with the New York gallery, perhaps paving the way for an eventual show of his own. It had also allowed Johnson to introduce Modigliani to Easter Cowles who had shown up quite unexpectedly that very morning on his doorstep. This seemed to be something of a trend, women appearing at his home without notice. The young Mrs. Cowles had shown an eagerness to meet the Italian, and Johnson wondered if she'd been disappointed. Modi was not a polite man, and his table manners left much to be desired. He lapsed frequently into his native tongue, so much of the conversation had probably been lost on the American woman.

Mrs. Cowles was interesting. Johnson wondered what her husband must be like. She seldom mentioned him, was almost evasive on the subject, so he assumed Mr. Cowles was one of those well-off American businessmen who recently had begun arriving in droves to buy everything in sight—the worthless and the priceless, be it art, clothing, furniture, books, or antiques. A few weeks earlier, items from the Comtesse de Ségur's collection of miniature porcelain shoes had been sold to a Cincinnati entrepreneur for 50,000 Francs. Within a week, the buyer himself sold the collection to a San Francisco dowager for $50,000! The curio dealers, Johnson knew, were delighted, but personally he wondered whether this was to the good.

Jean Cocteau had made an appearance at the canteen shortly before the Italian's departure. Johnson did not know Cocteau well and had met him only twice, but knew of his achievements. The young man was a writer, composer, poet, musician (reputedly bad), playwright, and *cinéaste*. His English was quite good, and he was splendidly dressed, at least when compared to Modigliani. Johnson had observed that men who partnered with men often boasted excellent taste in clothing.

Cocteau had immediately charmed Easter. "I want your friend," he patted Johnson on the shoulder, "to translate one of my plays, *Le Boeuf sur le Toit*, The Ox on the Roof." He'd smiled, looking directly at her. "I know, a strange name, yes? Worthy of the Dadaists. And I am sure Mr. Johnson here will do a stellar job."

The indirect approach annoyed Johnson, who'd nevertheless agreed to do it because he could find no ready excuse to refuse. Cocteau was pleased, bussed Johnson on both cheeks as if they were fellow survivors of the trenches, ignored Modigliani, kissed Easter's hand, and sauntered off.

86

After lunch, Johnson had seen Easter off to her hotel in a cab and returned home to find M. Lefebvre finishing up his second round of mail delivery.

The *facteur*'s visit was punctuated by his ill-hidden curiosity—no doubt fostered by the concierge—regarding Kiki. He called her, "that woman whose picture appeared in *L'Echo de Paris*" which, two weeks earlier, had featured a photograph of Kiki showing her legs almost to the hips, above a caption naming her *"La Beautée de Montparnasse."*

In recent years, Montparnasse and Montmartre had almost come to be independent states within Paris. Bars and clubs were allowed to stay open all night, and prostitution was tolerated. Homosexuality and sexual deviance were overlooked. The neighborhoods had caught the fancy of readers everywhere, and reporters from twenty nations daily filed sensational reports depicting *la vie montparnassienne.* Most were rubbish that Johnson found distressing, even as the *quartier*'s reputation brought in money. The tourists' visits, however indirectly, did benefit the arts.

Johnson thought of what he'd come to call *his* artists as both odious and fascinating. It struck him that nowhere else in today's world would he encounter such a motley yet enchanting collection of personalities. Fujita alone, his hair cut like a monk's and garbed in toga and sandals, caused traffic jams.

The Japanese painter's name had come up today. Modi suspected him of having been Jeanne's first lover, and Johnson thought it indeed likely. Fujita entranced women by playing himself well. Japanese were a rarity in Paris, and ones dressed like Julius Caesar were even rarer.

Johnson's thoughts returned to M. Lefebvre, who had stared at Kiki's portraits with the practiced eye of one who knew many things but would not bring himself to ask whether Kiki and Johnson were romantically linked.

Were they?

Johnson often felt cursed with a sense of objectivity. Others, he knew, could fall in love on a daily basis. For them, the curve of a thigh, the rise of a cheekbone, were enough to inspire paintings, sonnets, compositions.

Not so for him. Feelings, he knew, were not facts, and it had taken him years to learn that emotions were best hidden, lest they cause harm. Marie, once almost his wife, often said she did not so much feel like his fiancée as she did a prize that, once won, was no longer of interest. He'd been barely twenty-two when he and Marie had announced their engagement, and twenty-four when he ran away to involve himself in a conflict that seemed both romantic and futile.

Kiki. Kiki *was* a prize, a gaudy bauble won by luck, not skill, and certainly won by many. She was sweet, amoral, untouched by guilt, happily impulsive and demanding of satisfaction. No doubt, she and her Polish painter would work out their differences, or, if they did not, Kiki would find another.

Johnson hoped he hadn't disappointed her. While they were in his bed, Kiki had briefly touched upon the sexual skills of nationalities she'd experienced. Poles? *Pfftt...* But then, she'd been having a tiff with her Polish painter and this tinged her judgment. Italians? Very showy. French? Quick. *Boum, boum, boum; comme des lapins et c'est fini.* Rabbits. Japanese? *Très ennuyeux.* Boring, "It is as if they have a book of instructions hidden under the pillow." Germans? She became angry. *"Jamais!* I'd never sleep with a *Boche!"* Americans? She smiled. *"Ah non, ça ne serait pas poli."* It wouldn't be polite to say.

He heated water for tea, glanced at the morning's l'*Echo.* There was a longish article on Landru. The accused murderer steadfastly maintained his innocence in the face of mounting evidence. Thanks to M. Lefebvre's inspector cousin, Johnson knew to within a button what the prisoner had been wearing, if his shoes were polished or his mustache waxed. M. Lefebvre had reenacted for him the last bout of questioning, playing both the accused and the accuser's parts. The mailman was an excellent actor.

CHAPTER 22

In his youth, when he was an altar boy, everyone had agreed that Henri Désiré Landru was a good child, smart, obedient, eager to please his parents and teachers. Physically, he did not stand out, being neither strong nor weak, handsome nor ugly. His father had clerked in a bookstore, his mother was a seamstress. There were three sisters and two brothers, and the family considered itself fortunate to be French, Catholic, and average.

While living in the Ile Saint-Louis, he quit school at fifteen and became an office boy in an architectural firm. His parents had hoped Henri's talent for free-hand drawing would serve him, and that he might become a draftsman, a well-paid and respected vocation.

At nineteen, Henri's interests veered from sketching buildings to sketching women. Shy and somewhat retiring, he met Marie-Catherine Rémy, a tall, svelte girl willing to share the bed of a diffident young man. She became pregnant just as he was called to do his military duty.

Upon discharge, Henri returned home and married her.

She soon mentioned to him that something had changed since he came back, now a sergeant with the 87th Infantry. The hesitant boy had become a taciturn man, unwilling to return to his former profession. Instead, with no license to practice, he advertised his services as an accountant and hired a delivery boy to fetch documents. He stole the young employee's bicycle and sold it. The boy, now without a means of transport, was regretfully fired by his boss. Landru perpetuated this pitiful scheme six times before being arrested and spending two years in the Lille prison. He and Marie-Catherine now had four children.

Landru's 24 months behind bars were not spent idly. He befriended other thieves and swindlers and learned lucrative ways to relieve the guileless of their valuables.

Back with his family, he set up a financial company promising large returns on investments of two to four thousand Francs. He kept his pyramid scheme alive for two years, robbing Pierre to pay Jean-Paul, but his hoax lacked true cunning. Found out, he evaded arrest for four more years but was taken in 1910. The magistrate recognized him as a habitual criminal and sentenced him to three years in prison.

Soon paroled for good behavior, Landru decided to change his ways. No more heavy-handed swindles for him—instead he embarked upon a career as a professional Lothario. Unfortunately, the first woman he met through a personal ad placed in a northern newspaper did not fall for his entreaties. She reported him to the police, which led to three more years in jail at Loos. Always a model prisoner, Landru shaved months from his sentence. He was released in late 1912 and immediately returned to his bad habits.

CHAPTER 23

Frederick and Easter agreed the two-bedroom apartment on Rue Vercingétorix in the city's 14th arrondissement was larger than it appeared. The living and dining rooms were separated by mirrored folding doors; windows gave out on the street in the front and on the courtyard in the rear. The kitchen was spacious, with a four-burner gas stove and two ovens, a pantry, china closet, and a small icebox attached to the window. The bathroom was tiny: a bathtub Frederick said midgets might have difficulty using, a sink, and a bidet. At the end of a long, dark hallway, the water closet's overhead tank whooshed and gurgled joyfully every time the chain was pulled.

The furniture was bourgeois utilitarian, large dark pieces from the preceding century set on a parquet floor covered with inexpensive Oriental rugs. On their first day there, Easter stripped the place of curtains and sent them all to the *blanchisserie* from which they returned a different, paler color. At night, they closed the exterior shutters, a task that fell to Frederick who disliked it but had longer arms.

"One day, Easter, you'll hear a scream and a thud. Don't be alarmed, it will only be your husband who has plummeted to the street below after having been told, once again, that the shutters are not closed properly."

The apartment belonged to an industrialist from Dijon who had purchased it for his only son, a student at the *École polytechnique*. The boy had died from a German bullet to the head in the first days of the war, and the shattered father hadn't had the heart to visit the place, much less empty it of his fallen son's belongings. The apartment had been vacant almost five years when James Johnson had found it through Mme. Bertrand's grapevine of concierges. The industrialist had been willing to

91

rent it to Easter and Frederick for a pittance, his only request that they carefully box the books, clothing and other personal effects still in the dead boy's rooms and send them to the father by post. Easter had done this, and Johnson had helped her draft a personal note of thanks and condolence. She and Frederick had a three-month lease with the option to renew.

It had all happened very quickly. Frederick's objections had never ceased while Easter remained adamant. On the verge of returning to the United States wifeless, Frederick received a cable from his father asking he finalize negotiations with a French tannery that wanted to purchase several thousand cowhides from Mr. Cowles Sr.'s company. Should the deal go through, others would be forthcoming and Frederick, in effect, would become the company's temporary agent in Europe. He'd admitted to Easter that it had a nice ring to it and a commensurate salary. That night, Easter, who did not believe in miracles, lit five candles at the local Catholic Church.

The cowhide negotiations showed that Frederick, to his own amazement, had a knack for such things. A week later, another deal surfaced and Frederick arranged for the purchase and delivery of 800 American fedora hats. Two more transactions (12,000 bottles of American hair lotion for men; 125,000 cakes of California-made avocado soap) established him as a bona fide entrepreneur.

The ventures allowed Frederick to mix with visiting American businessmen, and he fell to the task eagerly. He enjoyed their company far more than that of Easter's friends whom—with the exception of Jean Cocteau—he considered ill-mannered, unkempt, certainly prone to overindulging, and possibly drug addicted.

Frederick ran his office from the second bedroom and ordered personalized stationery and calling cards. His basic knowledge of Paris endeared him to travelers from the U.S., who counted upon him for the thickest steaks, the newest club featuring American singers, or the best café to meet unattached French women.

Easter discovered a vacant maid's garret on the top floor of the building, where the servants had their quarters. Though barely fifteen feet to the side, it had a huge, grimy skylight that, once cleaned by the grumbling son of the concierge, allowed light in for the better part of the day. She purchased a foldable oak easel, paints, assorted camel hair brushes, palettes, stretched canvases of varying sizes, and five smart white smocks.

The apartment became a home; she looked forward to every single day and prized how the neighborhood *commerçants* welcomed her daily visits.

James Johnson, whom she saw at least twice a week, told her, "There are 2,000 Americans living in Paris who claim to be artists. Most have far more money than their French counterparts. Of course, the *boulanger, boucher, pharmacien* and *épicier* are happy to see you. You have silver jingling in your pockets. I'm not trying to diminish your accomplishments," he continued. "I'm amazed at how quickly you've acclimated and how well you're learning the language. It's obvious everyone likes and respects you, but a lot of these people—the artists in particular, present company excepted—are like crows. Give them red wine—the cheaper the better—a half-chicken, and a *baguette,* and they'll be camping in your living room. You'll never get rid of them."

She was making money on her own; not much, but it was in U.S. dollars, the most desirable post-war currency. After closing out the savings account in Chicago and arranging for a transfer of funds to the Credit Lyonnais bank, she had, on a whim, written a humorous letter to her friend Charlotte describing the intricacies of the French currency exchange process. The writer Jean Cocteau had read the letter with amusement, asking here and there for clarification, and suggested she submit it to the European edition of the *Chicago Herald Tribune.* He knew the editor. To Easter's astonishment, the newspaper edited the piece and published it. Twelve dollars for not even an afternoon's work! With the aid of one of Modigliani's shadowy Italian acquaintances, the money had been converted on the black market and the $12 became almost $40. She did not tell Frederick about the transaction.

CHAPTER 24

The murders of Mesdames Cuchet and Laborde-Line, and the incidental murder of Mme. Cuchet's son, André, earned Landru 19,000 francs after expenses. The women's furniture was quickly sold to a large store just outside Paris where the buyer asked no questions. Before killing them, Landru had cajoled the women into revealing their bank account numbers, and he forged letters over their counterfeit signatures releasing all funds to him or his agent.

The moneys allowed him to pay his family's rent, back-owed for three months, and to give 1,000 francs to his wife Marie-Catherine for food, clothing, and other household needs. There was a debt of 200 francs which he paid to the doctor who, for almost a year had been treating his youngest son Charles for the croup. For himself, Henri Désiré bought two new suits, three shirts, a set of discrete navy blue suspenders, some cheery green socks and a pair of handsome English shoes.

Life, however, was unpleasant at home. The sudden influx of money seemed to weigh on Marie-Catherine who knew her husband was involved in shady affairs but never broached the subject. Five times in the past two years, the police had come to the door of the Landru apartment. They had questioned her, spoken roughly to the children, demanded to know where their father was. They mentioned names like Diard, Fremyet, Guillet and Raoul Dupont, claiming all those men were Henri Désiré's aliases. One detective, furious in the face of her denial, had kicked a chair and broken it, causing little Charles to burst into terrified tears. A uniformed policeman had threatened to arrest Maurice, their oldest son, for collusion. The young man had cursed and made a rude hand gesture that had enraged the *gendarme*, who struck him open-handed, bloodying his nose.

Marie Catherine loved her husband, though she knew with poignant certainty that he was not the faithful man she would have liked for a spouse. Sometimes she smelled perfume on him. Once, there was a pair of silver and gold earrings in a jacket pocket, and when she demanded to know their provenance, Landru had scolded her gently for ruining a birthday surprise. She had refused to wear the jewelry, knowing it had belonged to or been destined for another woman. She kept the earrings in the armoire drawer with her identity papers and the marriage certificate.

There were other problems too. Landru's father suffered from neurasthenia and, since the loss of his wife in 1891, he had dwindled in stature and wandered the apartment like a hunched and tearful ghost. His father's very presence so irritated Henri Désiré that he bubbled with anger and recrimination every time he saw the old man. M. Landru Sr. did nothing but complain about his son's criminal way of life, about his own miserable existence, about the shame brought on the family name by Landru's incarcerations. More than once, Landru had been tempted to jettison the old man out the window, or push him down the stairs, or perhaps even hire someone to kill him one night as he returned from the *café-tabac* with his Boyard cigarettes. Such were his fantasies, tempered only by the knowledge that a suspicious death in the family would immediately arouse the interest of the police. Had Landru believed in God, he might have thanked him some months later when the old man, in a fit of despair, embarrassment, and humiliation, hanged himself from a tree in the Bois de Boulogne.

Landru made the funeral arrangements using murder funds. He purchased a coffin of thick cardboard and arranged for his father's body to be interred in the paupers' section of the Cimetière de Bagneux. The undertaker was surprised that a well-dressed man would allot so little for a family burial and tried to talk Landru into a somewhat more elegant coffin—one made of stained pine, perhaps, with brass handles—but Henri was adamant and his demeanor turned icy. Cardboard was good enough for a man who had hanged himself.

CHAPTER 25

James Johnson and Frederick met for the first time some weeks after the Cowles had moved into their apartment on Rue Vercingétorix. Easter decided the place needed a proper housewarming, and she enlisted James's help in drafting a smart invitation list, ensuring the guests showed up for the celebration. James, in turn, conscripted Kiki to make the party a success, and so it was.

At 10:30 on a Friday night, a motley assortment of regulars from the Rotonde, the Dôme, the Café Versailles and a host of lesser restaurants and bistros, began arriving. Some Easter knew, others she did not, but all seemed to know each other. Victor Libion, the patriarchal owner of La Rotonde, surveyed the buffet table laden with wine, cold chicken, sausage, pâtés and other delicacies, nodded his head, twirled his gigantic mustache and told her she had done well. He suggested she count the rented silverware before allowing her guests to depart.

Kiki came bearing a single small bottle of Champagne. She was accompanied by several rowdy young men whom she did not introduce. These fell on the food like vultures, and Easter found it necessary to stop one from putting a full plate of *petits fours* in his pocket.

Someone brought Georges Hébert, the author of a scandalous new book on exercise, and his 19-year-old assistant Thérèse Maure, nicknamed Treize.

Pablo Picasso earned immediate *persona non grata* status by arriving drunk, pinching Easter's bottom, and emptying the bowl of his pipe into a wine goblet. Told that he'd offended the hostess, he shrugged, found a linen napkin, and with a borrowed fountain pen drew his and Easter's name entwined. "Here," he shoved the napkin at James. "Give her this, and tell her I'm sorry."

Modigliani and Jeanne Hébuterne clung to one another, and Easter noticed the Japanese painter Fujita took pains to avoid the couple.

More writers and poets came later in a cluster. They were less soiled, if more cliquish than the painters, but no less famished. Jean Cocteau offered Easter a housewarming present that delighted her—one of Guillaume Apollinaire's calligrams which, in English, read, "American woman learning painting, sculpture, etching, fashion, architecture, caricature, agriculture, literature, and making a thousand conjectures about nature."

A
mé ri caine apprenant
la
pein
tu
re
la sculp
ture la gra
vure la couture
l'architecture
la caricature
l'agriculture
la littérature
et faisant mille con
jectures sur la
na tu
re

The word drawing so pleased Easter that she ran into the bedroom, stripped a frame of its photograph of her as a child, and replaced it with the poet's work.

Johnson found Frederick in the bedroom office, morosely nursing a glass of whisky.

"We've never met," he said, by way of introduction, "but your wife speaks often of you."

Frederick rose, hand extended. "I'm told all this," he waved an arm to encompass the apartment in its entirety, "is thanks to you. I'm grateful." He pointed to a chair, and Johnson sat.

"This isn't to your enjoyment?"

Frederick looked up, rearranged some papers on his desk, set his glass down carefully, and shrugged: "My French is abysmal, which is no one's fault but my own. I haven't made much of an effort, and I've noticed that a lot of these people who do speak English make it a game to pretend they don't." He smiled without pleasure. "The truth is, this is Easter's world, not mine. I don't understand it. I haven't figured out what their motivations are. I don't really dislike her friends—or at least most of them. Some I find ridiculous; others are simply very difficult to approach."

"I suppose," he continued, "that I don't relate well. I don't see the attraction of daubing about with a paintbrush or scribbling one's most mundane thoughts, most of which aren't worth reading. I really don't see what these people contribute. Except," he forced a smile, "for you, of course. And for that man, Cocteau. A nice chap, very interested in American industry." He sipped at his drink, looked into his glass. "The ice is almost gone. It's damned hard to find ice in this country. A man delivered a hundred-pound block, and we put it in the bathtub, but I think it's just about all melted by now."

Johnson raised his own glass. "I've gotten used to everything at room temperature, but it takes a while."

Frederick stood, straightened his tie. "I'm being ungracious. I didn't even mention that I rather like the portrait you did of Easter. You caught her beautifully, save for her nose. I don't believe it's quite that pointed, and her nostrils most assuredly do not flare that way. And I kind of wish you hadn't made the cleavage so...pronounced..."

Johnson nodded, acknowledged the rebukes. "I'm sorry. I wasn't aware that it didn't please you. I must admit that I got much more out of it than Easter did."

Frederick paused. "Yes, you did, didn't you? It was odd, when Easter told me her likeness had been sold to someone who will probably gaze upon it every day, cleavage and all. It made me feel...inexplicably peculiar. As if a part of her had gone with it. Does that make sense?"

Johnson nodded, smiled faintly. "Yes. I felt the same way."

They both fell silent.

After a moment, Frederick rose. "I should rejoin my wife. I don't want to appear even more impolite than I am." He allowed Johnson to leave first, then made a point of locking the door behind them, muttering, "You never know, with some of these people..."

By three in the morning, the food was long gone and the alcohol diminishing. Victor Libion sent three guests to the Rotonde with instructions to bring back a case of assorted liquor and two cases of wine. Their return forty-five minutes later was met with enthusiastic cheers, and Johnson whispered to Easter, "Your *soirée* is a success."

She was lightly flushed, moderately drunk, and completely happy. She dragged him into the kitchen, threw her arms around his neck and kissed him roundly on the lips. "Thank you, thank you, thank you. This is the happiest, best, cheeriest night of my life, and I owe it all to you, James Johnson. Really, I do." Her speech was slurred. She hiccupped, whispered, "Picasso tried to pinch my rear but I slapped his hand. I think it surprised him. He's rather gross, isn't he?"

Johnson reached into his pocket. "Which reminds me. Here," he handed her the napkin on which the Picasso had entwined his and her name. "I'm sure he thought this could purchase at least a quick pinch."

Easter took the napkin, glanced at the work, threw the scribbles into the open pantry. "He probably does that for every woman he meets and offends, and no, it does not purchase *anything, m*uch less his hands on my *derrière."* She giggled, hiccupped again. "That's what Modi calls it. Now him, I like. Jeanne looks so frail, almost as if she isn't quite there. She doesn't say much, have you noticed?"

They spent another ten minutes in the kitchen, discussing the guests, the guests of the guests and the few unknowns who had gotten wind of the evening and appeared.

"Even Gertrude Stein came!" Easter was delighted. "I thought she never left the Rue de Fleury!" She lowered her voice to a stage whisper. "Really, she does look like a troll. She brought these small chocolate cakes Alice made, and people seemed to love them! They were all gone in minutes!"

"There was," Johnson told her, "a man from *l'Echo de Paris.* You'll be the talk of Paris by tomorrow evening, and all the people who didn't come tonight will claim to have been here." He took her hand, smiled, and Easter beamed back at him.

The crash of a body falling and the noise of shattering glass interrupted them.

"Oh my God!" Easter rushed out of the kitchen.

A large, red-faced man with a frightened mouth was shielding his belly with a porkpie hat. Threatening him with a carving fork was a smaller, darker man whose eyes brimmed with anger. Between them, hands over open mouth, stood a young woman Easter did not know. The rest of the guests surrounded the three at a respectable distance. The porkpie hat's crown and brim bore fork scars.

The smaller man circled his prey, holding the fork underhand and muttering in Spanish. The larger one, perhaps realizing his hat was a poor defense, grabbed a chair to hold his assailant at bay. Johnson stepped in, grabbed the cutlery wielder in a bear hug from the back and lifted him off the ground. The tableau collapsed. The man with the hat rushed to Frederick, whispered a few animated words, flung his porkpie into the middle of the room and made for the front door. His disarmed assailant fell into a *fauteuil* and gulped a glass of wine. The young woman vanished into the crowd. In less than a minute, life returned to normal.

Easter looked from Johnson to Frederick. "What in the world was that about?"

Johnson shook his head. "I didn't know they would both be here. I invited Pascin," he nodded towards the man in the chair, "and someone apparently invited John Quinn."

"I did," Frederick was pale with anger, his mouth petulant. "And he is at this very moment climbing into a taxi to escape from this dreadful evening. Really, Easter, your friends are savages. Quinn could have been very useful to the both of us."

Easter ignored her husband. "I know Pascin. He had a show in New York a few years ago. I read about him in one of the art magazines and ran into him at an opening recently. We exchanged some views on the city. I thought he was a very nice man. Who is Quinn?"

"An art collector!" Frederick had ice in his voice. "A very wealthy one whom I took great pains to coax to this party. He's in Paris for a month and I thought it might be good for you to meet him. I had no idea one of your friends would assault him with the silverware. Ruined his hat, for God's sake."

Johnson looked at Frederick, then at Easter. "I remember that Quinn bought a lot of Pascin's work—caricatures, drawings, sketches and whatnot. Then something happened, I'm not sure what." He paused, found a wine bottle and a glass, poured. "I think it had something to do with money, prices paid and such. But the point is, Pascin has been vilifying Quinn for weeks now."

Johnson watched the hired maid as she swept up the broken glass. He took a sip, added, "Pascin is rather high strung. He spent the war years in Cuba, and I think his contact with the Latins has made him more hot-blooded."

"Savages. Broke some of our better glasses," said Frederick. "Hooligans, every last one of them." As an afterthought, he added, "Except for you James. Or at least, I should hope." He stomped off to his office, slammed the door.

102

The party ended at four-thirty in the morning without further mishap, though both the next day's *L'Echo de Paris* and *Le Petit Parisien* described the Pascin/Quinn confrontation as a free-for-all witnessed by the *haut monde* of Montparnasse. Easter's first and last names were misspelled in the reports and *l'Echo* stated the police had been called, which they had not. The party made Easter a celebrity for a few days.

Frederick was not happy. "It's exactly as I told your friend James. These are not my people, and I should have known better than to involve myself. From now on, I'll keep to commerce, you keep to art. And please do try to control them when they're here. I find it distressing to have broken glass and bloodshed in my apartment, and I think the type of publicity you've garnered will certainly not serve my enterprises."

Later, Frederick would decide the party hadn't been all bad, though, for it was during that same evening that he and Jean Cocteau became better acquainted. Though he'd met the playwright once or twice before, he was charmed by the well-dressed young man who shared his disdain for the other guests' lifestyles.

Cocteau, bearing Apollinaire's calligram, had arrived at the party with the other writers, fresh from a set-to with his lover and having missed dinner.

When he spotted Frederick, he approached and said, "Ah! The man of the house." While spooning salmon mousse into his mouth, he waxed eloquent on all things American and mentioned looking for backers to produce a motion picture based on his ballet, *Parade*.

"Think of it, Frederick! I may call you Frederick, may I not? Diaghilev, Stravinski, Nijinski, my dear friend Pablo—whom I certainly hope you have invited tonight—and even that lovable, Satie...They all collaborated on the original presentation two years ago. I know they would help us again. What a show! We would stand the world on its ear!"

Frederick was not familiar with the names Cocteau mentioned, save for Picasso whom he knew Easter disliked. He was pretty certain that Cocteau's proposition would prove a failure and a poor investment, but he liked being seen as the man of the house, and he liked the cut of Cocteau's suit. They agreed to meet for lunch the following day.

Chapter 26

"It is opium, Frederick. A divine substance, with an exalted history! Half-naked yellow savages in Indochina and Asia pour their sweat and lives into fertile ground to grow the poppies. The British staked their legacy on it, and a million Orientals speak through it to their gods."

Cocteau, wearing a red velvet smoking jacket, reclined on the couch and waved his hands in the air. The apartment was smoky; a sickly sweet aroma attended the room. Frederick had never seen such an elaborately furnished place.

"Mon fumoir," Cocteau said. "My mother does not approve, the aroma bothers her, and since she and I share a home, I rent this place specifically to smoke. It is nice, no?"

The walls were a shade of warm burgundy, with black baseboards, wainscoting and crown molding. Oriental rugs were piled three deep on the floor. Cocteau's low-legged couch occupied a corner of the room with here and there a half-dozen North African ottomans.

"Frederick, please, your disapproving look saddens me. Even genius needs help. Come. Sit here and let me tempt you!"

This was not what Frederick had in mind when he'd accepted the luncheon invitation. He and Cocteau had eaten lean chopped steaks together—Cocteau had made a special trip to the butcher's to have the meat ground *à l'américaine*—and drunk Coca Cola and beer from Pennsylvania. They'd ended the meal with fudge and chocolate ice cream. Frederick had enjoyed the lunch more than any in the past several months, but now opium?

"Now is not the time to be provincial, Frederick. Look at me, do I appear an addict?" Cocteau jumped up, ran vigorously in place, touched his toes, and sparred with an invisible opponent. He grabbed a pair of drumsticks and beat a furious tattoo on a leather cushion while singing nonsense syllables. Then, slightly out of breath, he reclined again.

"You see? I play tennis, I dance, I ride my bicycle for miles, I am out every night until dawn. I play the drums. My life is full of people and events! I live by my wits! I create beauty! Could I be an addict and maintain such a *train de vie?* Come here, next to me," he pointed to an end of the couch. Frederick sat.

"And why, in any case, should I wish to harm you? I like you, Frederick. You are the future, you and your American colleagues. We need each other. Here, free yourself."

Frederick let his thoughts run at random. The risks, he decided, didn't faze him. Perhaps jaundiced Chinamen could get addicted to opium, but that wouldn't happen to him—he was an American and had more willpower than that. Jean, a constant user, seemed no worse for wear. More importantly, Frederick had heard that opium made people dream, and he desperately wanted dreams. He wanted dreams of home, of American friends and foods, of youth and college, and his parents' sitting room. He even missed his mother.

He took the long thin pipe, brought it to his lips. Cocteau flicked a gold lighter to life, applied the flame to the small brown pill-shaped ball. It sputtered and bubbled when the heat hit it.

Cocteau whispered, "Puff hard, Frederick, and inhale…"

Frederick did, then waited. Nothing. The strong cigars he smoked with his friends in Chicago had a greater kick.

Cocteau took the pipe from him.

"Harder, like this." He sucked until the end of the pipe glowed red. "Then like this." He inhaled deeply, shut his mouth, closed his eyes, and held his breath. After a few seconds, a wisp of smoke escaped his right nostril. "With opium, everyone is a virgin again. The heavens open, and deities share their secrets. We are smarter, stronger, and more vital in every way. Trust me, Frederick, there is nothing like it in the world, and it will seal our friendship." He smiled, eyes still closed, "I don't do this with everyone, you know."

Frederick took in a lungful. The colors in the room swam slightly. Cocteau smiled again. "You see? After you take a little more, that which now confounds you will do so no longer. Fears vanish, anxieties dissipate like morning fogs, and whatever weighed on you no longer matters. There is clarity; it is all around us in the air, but it is our task to seize it, master it. We can dominate reality, but we cannot do it alone. The old Chinese masters realized that. They knew you had to wrestle the dragon. This is where I get my scenery, my plot, my dialogue, the characters that people my stage. I invent worlds far more real than the streets outside." His voice dropped. "*Mon Dieu. Quel génie. Quelle métamorphose...*"

Frederick had ceased listening. Cocteau's voice was now just pleasing background noise with a French accent. There was a framed poster on the wall for a presentation of *Romeo et Juliette* by the *Théâtre du Bourg*. Frederick let his mind drift to the Juliet he had portrayed while in school. In his mind, he began reciting her plea to Romeo and he was delighted to discover he remembered every word. That had been fun; the crowd, the make-up, the camaraderie, in fact, had been the most fun he'd ever had in his life. Certainly, that had been better than now, stuck in this sad grey country where no one spoke proper English and even his own wife was mesmerized by things he couldn't understand.

He inhaled again, this time deeper and puffing harder. Cocteau seemed to be asleep, arms crossed over his chest, breathing deeply. Frederick found the lighter and relit the pipe. It was good to have a friend. In fact, he hadn't realized until quite recently how much he missed having friends. His "American colleagues" were all thousands of miles away, probably playing cards right now or entertaining each other in some normal, healthy fashion. They were certainly doing it in English, too.

Cocteau's eyes snapped open. He stood, took off his smoking jacket, slipped into a coat.

"Come Frederick. Come with me. Let's go for a walk. Your first time with the opium genies should not be spent indoors. Let's go have a drink at the Café Versailles and talk of interesting things."

Frederick did not move, so Cocteau prodded him with a toe. "Stand up, stand up! Show me some of that American vitality! We have time for a quick apéritif and then I must get home."

Frederick regretfully abandoned Juliet, school, his Chicago friends, and the card game. He struggled to his feet, swayed a bit. Cocteau took an elbow to steady him.

After a moment Frederick said, "It really is very pleasant, isn't it?" He smacked his lips. "I'm dying of thirst. Did you say we could go have a drink? That's a splendid idea. Perhaps a pastry as well?"

CHAPTER 27

Paris, Monday, July 15, 1919

It has been months since my last entry, but I forgive myself. So much has happened since then!

The apartment is a delight, so far removed from what I expected; a tiny upper floor was all I thought we could afford.

It was a sad place when we first entered it, and I had my doubts. Signs of the previous occupant were everywhere, and some brought tears to my eyes. The young man who had lived here went off to war thinking it a great adventure from which he'd soon return.

I often marvel at such innocence; did he really think he would come back in time to finish the open case of wine he left behind? I found a pile of forgotten dirty laundry in a closet, and a book of very lewd photos beneath the mattress of his bed. A cluster of petrified figs was in the icebox. In a drawer of his desk was a half-finished letter to a woman named Henriette, swearing eternal love and faithfulness and describing their last encounter in quite graphic and fleshy detail, which prompted me to immediately send the bed's linens, sheets, pillows and slipcover to my *blanchisseuse* a second time. Is this girl still waiting for him? Does she not know he's dead, shot in the head by a German, or has she moved on, like so many of the war's abandoned young lovers? Why did he never finish the letter? Was he afraid to send it?

I scrubbed, swept, waxed, painted, washed windows, and destroyed cobwebs. Frederick packed up the young man's belongings and made endless trips up and down the five flights of stairs, as the elevator has not worked since before the war. The concierge claims to have called a repairman who never showed up. We have opted to pay exorbitant fees in order to have gas and electricity; many homes still cannot afford it. Thank God for Frederick's work, which pays in dollars, and for the falling Franc, which enables us to splurge on what, back home, would be a meager income, and to host a most successful party.

I am now a painter with my own workplace. It is only a maid's room in the building's attic, and I've not yet had the time to actually paint there, but it is mine to do with as I wish. I have great plans and have already done rough sketches of several street scenes. Frederick, James, and I celebrated the opening of the *Atelier Pâques* (Pâques is French for Easter) on Beaujolais. We all got quite drunk and sang old show tunes together, which made me, for a moment only, nostalgic for home.

There is a somber side to all this happiness.

I had hoped to bridge the gap that has grown between Frederick and me, but as of yet I have not succeeded. It has been nine weeks since Frederick and I have been together intimately, and our last encounter was nothing if not desultory, more a result of his drinking than of any romantic or conjugal initiative. I didn't enjoy it, though my sense of duty is now somewhat assuaged. His erection lasted a few minutes at best, and he failed to enter me. I am just as glad. I don't miss the touch of his hands or the pressure of his body on mine, though there are times when I would like to be held.

In all other aspects of our relationship, Frederick and I appear to be a normal modern couple. We respond to invitations, entertain friends, and discuss the things that must be discussed (bills, rent, engagements). We gossip, we laugh. We make fun of the French, of the Italians, of the Poles and, occasionally, of the witless American tourists who have invaded Paris. In the company of others, we even flirt, but we hardly ever touch. His lips brush my cheek once a morning, once a night. Since that explosive conversation over breakfast, he has not broached the topic of our starting a family.

He now maintains his wardrobe in the closet of his office in the spare room. He enters our bedroom each evening in his pajamas and robe and leaves in the morning similarly attired. His modesty, if that is the name for it, must be contagious. I never show myself to him unclothed, always close the door when I bathe and lock it when I use the bidet; I no longer change in his presence.

Frederick does not appear to miss the physical release. Neither does he display the shy boyishness I once found endearing. Indeed, I'm astonished by the transformation he has undergone. The role of businessman suits him well. He has put on a few pounds, become more self-assured, more direct, less moody and temperamental, and he is good at what he does, or at least I think he is. We are not rich, but we never want, and he is a generous husband. Whatever needs he has seem to be met.

I wish I could say the same for myself.

While at the Cirque Medrano with Treize (of whom I shall write more at another time), I was positively overwhelmed by the sight

111

of the Kouski brothers, three aerialists from Krakow who, I later learned, have no lack of female admirers. One brother (if they really are brothers) was huge, a monster of a man more than six-and-a-half feet tall whose forte was catching his lighter siblings as they dove from a platform and flinging them back into the air. He was not, however, the focus of my attention; I have never liked large men. They frighten me. The brother who caused such an internal tumult was the smallest of the three, a sinewy youth with a dazzling smile, impossibly thin hips and broad shoulders. Perhaps it was his costume, or the sheen of perspiration that covered him, I don't know, but I felt myself melt and think I finally understand Enid's description of *loins on fire*. That is exactly the effect this acrobat occasioned. I squeezed my knees together and must have blushed, because Treize nudged me and asked if I was all right. When I told her I felt slightly faint, she laughed and said men in dancing tights have the same effect on her, and when we stopped for tea after the performance, she kept changing the conversation to matters of sex. She also said the Kouski brothers are well known in Paris for their escapades and that one of them is presently having an affair with the wife of a leading politician.

I'm glad such irresponsible emotions don't strike me too often. It would be embarrassing to go into a swoon each time I see an attractive man, or feel myself irresistibly drawn to every Tom, Dick and Harry (actually, *Jean, Pierre, et Jacques*).

I wonder what is going on with my husband.

I am not unattractive; I know this and have been approached a number of times by men interested in having what the French call the *cinq à sept*, surreptitious trysts from five to seven in the evening. Quite a few women entertain themselves thusly, or so says Treize, and they feel no guilt or compunction. I simply couldn't.

If anything, the scheduling of such encounters sounds ghastly, and though I'm no Mrs. Grundy, I find such frolics unseemly.

What does Frederick do, physically? The businessmen he meets seldom travel with their wives, so there is the possibility that in their company he frequents a *maison de passe*, one of those brothels that operate openly, but somehow I doubt this. My husband, for all the little I know him, simply is not the type to engage in such activities. He is too *fussy*. In our home, things must be just so, in their places, tidy, and ordered. He dresses with meticulous care, and I cannot picture him disrobing in a tawdry room. I may be wrong, but it seems to me that his sort of finicky mentality does not lend itself to languishing in brothels. On a more practical note, I have never once caught him coming home smelling of strange perfume or disheveled. There are no lipstick traces on his collar, no secret mementos in his pockets. Each day, he makes it a point to tell me where he is going, when, and with whom. True, he has taken to drinking a bit too much and has developed a taste for absinthe, but I can forgive that; everyone here drinks too much.

Obviously, I have never broached this subject with him. In my heart, I know Frederick is unwavering in his allegiance to me. In all ways but this, he has become a good and true mate.

Jean Cocteau appears to have taken a liking to him, but Jean harbors a fascination for all things American. They went out and purchased suits together, as well as horrid matching pale green shirts which Jean swears are the coming fashion. I could not wish a better, more amiable companion for my husband, but his friendship with Jean leaves me feeling odd... perhaps almost jealous. Of course, Jean is a true gentleman and talented beyond the imagination of most. He writes, draws, paints, and even plays the drums, although rather badly, I'm told. He is already producing plays, but dreams of making motion pictures.

Speaking of Jean, here is an amusing anecdote. Some months ago, he asked James to translate *Le Boeuf sur le Toit*, a play Jean is writing which will involve the Fratellini clown family. I don't think James was delighted by the idea, but he agreed to do the work for a pittance. It now turns out that Cocteau's play will be mimed, so that, in effect, Cocteau has hired James to translate nothing more than stage directions, which he, James, finds insulting. I must admit that when James told me of this *contretemps*, I laughed and probably hurt his feelings, but really, it is a little ridiculous.

Yesterday was July 14, Bastille Day, and the *Marseillaise* was played a thousand times. I was once again struck by how deeply war has maimed the nation. Paris was rife with gaiety, waiters' races, parties, the fluttering everywhere of the tricolor. The widows formed a sea of black dresses and veils. There are so many of them, and they are so young! Orphans took their places in the parades, proudly hoisting banners, thanking their American saviors in broken English. Thousands of veterans known as *gueules cassées*, or "smashed faces," horribly disfigured young men missing arms, legs, eyes, or jaws, marched or were wheeled through the streets. Still, France displayed its cannons and military vehicles, its battle flags and bemedaled officers. There is talk of forcing Germany to pay millions in reparations, but will this ease the widows' loneliness or replace the slain fathers? Frederick, who now reads newspapers and magazines voraciously and often discusses international issues with his colleagues, says the reparations will never be paid as Germany is bankrupt. He also thinks that if Europe is to grow into a strong economy, "squeezing the German turnip" will be counterproductive.

I know nothing of this. Certainly, Germans are not among my favorite people. I have met only a few, and these were dour, pinched, and unhappy. Almost two million of them perished during the conflict, and they too had families, lives, loves, and homes.

Well, it is late...I'm not sure what inspired all these depressing thoughts. The war is over and all hope, though few believe, that we have seen the last of such a massacre.

Tomorrow is likely to be sunny, and James has promised to take me to the Jardin du Luxembourg. He wants to start a new series of portraits, this time in an outdoor setting, and is looking for a suitable locale. He insists on paying me, and I plan to write a small piece for the *Tribune* on being a model.

Chapter 28

A few days earlier, Frederick had received a letter from his father:

My dear son:

I do not know whether being in Europe allows you to keep up with events in the States, but as you must be aware, the dour mood of prohibition is sweeping our nation. It is, indeed, sad when responsible citizens are prevented from their pursuit of happiness. I can write this to you, but would never dare voice such an opinion publicly; such is the vindictiveness of the bluenoses.

Your Mother has recently been elected Chief Officer of the Anti-Saloon Society's Chicago chapter. Almost nightly, she attends prohibitionist meetings and comes home chanting the League's rallying cry, "Temperate drinkers are the parents of all drunkards."

I am afraid that next week, we shall see laws passed, denying upstanding citizens like myself even a single drink!

In light of the above, I would very much like you to meet Mr. George Remus, who will be in Paris by the time you read this. He will call upon you, and I want you to listen to his proposal extremely carefully and with an open mind. It is important that you keep your meeting and conversation with him discreet. Mr. Remus is a cautious man whose plans may well benefit us. Please contact me by post after you have met and let me know how his proposal strikes you.

I trust all is well with you and your lovely wife. Your mother requested I ask whether we might soon be hearing news of a new family member.

Sincerely,

Your Father

Frederick searched his memory, but George Remus was not a familiar name. Frederick, of course, knew about the movement to ban alcohol in the States. Visiting Americans spoke of it often, and many purchased cases of fine cognac and other spirits before the last leg of their trip. Most *Amies* he spoke with thought the idea of prohibition ludicrous, but would only admit so much in private. In public, they agreed vigorously with the need to keep drunkards off the dole, and they applauded sacrificing alcohol "for the common good." Too many young men returning from the war turned first to the bottle, then to criminal activity. If the weak needed to be protected from themselves, so be it. A dry country, many believed, would surely be a strong country.

The French newspapers had a difficult time grasping the very concept of prohibition. In France, a meal without wine was unthinkable; the very foundations of civilization on the Continent leaned heavily on the production, consumption, and benefits of alcohol.

Europeans attributed America's temperance movement to the tantrums of an infant nation that had not yet realized the importance of good food, good company and, mostly, good drink.

A day after the letter's arrival, a portly gentleman with a firm handshake and a gap-toothed smile appeared at Frederick's door.

"George Remus, Mr. Cowles. I am a colleague of your father, who sends his best. I had the honor of speaking with him shortly before I embarked, and I can see at a glance that you are certainly his equal."

Remus was dressed expensively, but with little taste, in a cream-colored three-piece suit with wide lapels. He had small, porcine eyes set in a perfectly round face, and he badly needed a shave. Frederick took him for lunch at a local Italian brasserie where the man ate a remarkable amount of spaghetti and tortellini, polished off two bottles of Chianti, most of a loaf of bread and a plate of Sicilian country sausage. There was little conversation. Remus asked about the weather, the cost of living, and the availability of prostitutes. The questions weren't new to Frederick. Every American businessman, it seemed, had heard that French women were particularly talented in bed. Frederick answered that the weather was warm, the dollar highly valued, and suggested an expensive brothel that operated above a nightclub. Remus nodded, smiled, and spun pasta onto his fork.

When he was finished, he leaned back in his chair, unfastened the top button of his trousers and requested two slices of chocolate cake, a bottle of anisette, and a pot of strong coffee.

"Now," he said, "let us get down to business." He poured himself a small flute of anisette, inspected the clear liquid, and drained the glass.

"Did your father tell you what I do for a living?"

Frederick shook his head. "No."

Remus nodded. "Good. A wise man never puts anything in writing that may eventually be held against him. I am a pharmacist." He pronounced the last word with pride.

"I must tell you, Frederick," he continued, "that I love the trade. Had I been more fortunate as a youth, I would have become a doctor, but fate did not smile upon me. No sir. Fate made me poor, impoverished, actually, and quite unable to afford the cost of medical school, which, I might add, is a shame, as I would have been a most excellent physician. I seem to have a knack for diagnosis. I can look at a man's eyes and tell you what is troubling him. Yellowed iris? Liver, always. Bloodshot eyes? Perhaps gout, perhaps a hardening of the kidneys. A fluttery eye is a sign of a weak heart. A lid that droops is bile, my friend, an excess of bile. Protuberant eyeballs are often the sign of intestinal difficulties, while sunken ones bespeak melancholia."

He poured anisette, drank again, emptied and refilled his coffee cup.

"But this has little bearing on my presence here in this beautiful city. Tell me, Frederick, what do you think of the most recent amendment to our Constitution?"

Frederick shrugged. He didn't know the latest amendment, hazarded a guess. "The sixteenth?"

Remus' face showed minor annoyance. "No! No! The sixteenth has nothing to do with it, although it's almost as hateful. Established the income tax, is what the sixteenth did. I refer to the eighteenth, my boy, the eighteenth! Shall I quote it? 'The manufacture, sale, or transportation of intoxicating liquors within... something something something from the United States and all territory something something or other... is hereby prohibited.' I know it by heart but can't recall the exact wording at this moment. Does this ring a bell?"

Frederick nodded. "Prohibition?"

"Exactly," Remus was pleased. He sliced a small piece of chocolate cake with his fork, popped it into his mouth, and chewed thoughtfully. "Prohibition. No more wine, cognac, brandy, scotch, Armagnac, anisette, strong beer. No whisky, no gin or vodka. No rum, no ouzo, no liqueur. Say good-bye to rye and bourbon and malt and Canadian, say good-bye to... well, to everything." He forked more cake, sipped at the coffee. "Except," he paused, dramatically, "for medicinal alcohols." He looked up, stared into Frederick's eyes. "Do I make myself clear, dear boy?"

"And since you're a pharmacist..."

"Exactly. I am a pharmacist. It is my duty, my sacred trust, to ensure that my customers, my ailing clients, are able to purchase the medicaments necessary to cure their indispositions. And I do not take this duty lightly, I might tell you. It is the guiding principle of my life."

Frederick couldn't help it, smiled. "Mr. Remus, you're a smuggler!"

If Remus was insulted, he didn't show it.

"Call it what you will. The appellation has a long and respected history. More to the point, I own seventeen pharmacies in the great states of Illinois and Indiana, and I mean to see that all of them are properly supplied."

He looked around. By now, the room was almost empty; he pushed his chair back, stood.

"Shall we go for a walk? This is my first time in this glorious city." He took a large roll of banknotes from his pocket, dropped a twenty dollar bill on the table. "Will this do?"

Frederick finished his coffee, nodded. "More than adequately. You'll make friends for life with half that sum."

They walked along the Boulevard du Montparnasse towards the Place de Rennes. Remus stared openly at the women, stopped every few yards to inspect a shop front, a *boulangerie,* a *charcuterie.* "Wonderful town, simply wonderful."

Frederick tagged behind. "How do you know my father?"

Remus stopped, spotted a park bench and, sat. He pulled a large cigar from a jacket pocket, struck a match, and lit it. "A gentleman, your father, and an able businessman, I might add. Doesn't miss a trick. We met some months ago. Cowhides. Sharp as a tack, your dad. Drove a hard bargain."

"Cowhides?"

"One of my sidelines, young man; belts, suspenders, hat bands. I am looking into the production of wallets and briefcases for gentlemen. I've found it wise to diversify. Now," Remus expelled a cloud of blue smoke, watched it rise, "I'll need 4,000 cases a month, varied stock, delivered to Cherbourg. A little of everything, but no beer; beer I can get locally. But some wine, maybe two- or three-hundred cases. Hard stuff is what I'm really after, but no rotgut. And none of that fruity trash. Customers wouldn't like it. I have an elite clientele, and they deserve the best, you follow? Cheap stuff they can get anywhere. I specialize in the best, only the best."

Frederick was astounded; four thousand cases! That was forty-eight thousand bottles of liquor a year!

"I'll pay ten dollars a case, or fifteen if it's particularly fine Napoleon brandy, say, a very good year, but not a penny more. Whatever you pay for the goods is your business, and I don't want to know about it. First delivery in Cherbourg no later than mid November. Can you do it?"

Frederick pondered a moment. "Yes, of course. But…"

Remus frowned. "But what?"

"Fourteen a case, eighteen if it's premium."

After some negotiation, they settled on twelve and sixteen, then shook hands.

"Just like your dad," said Remus, "but I would have been disappointed if you weren't. Now," he stood, "you mentioned ladies. Are there any nearby?"

CHAPTER 29

Bastille Day had come and gone with all the necessary hoopla. James Johnson had spent the morning in his apartment, cleaning brushes and fighting off memories. He knew it was a losing battle.

*****

Dawn. They have not slept in 36 hours; their hands are covered with blood, and Johnson is no longer capable of thought. There are so many bodies in unnatural poses; a frozen arm sticking straight out of the soil, a head without a face, two boots—right and left—from which a pair of naked, white legs emerge. The corpses cling to the frozen soil. Johnson is walking among them, listening for a voice, a whimper, a plea. There! The slightest of movement, no more than a tremor! Johnson and Felker rush forward, fall to their knees. The boy is alive, though a great part of his chest is missing. His eyes are wide, he is panting. Johnson gingerly rolls him onto the stretcher, and he and Felker both run, stumble, jump over the bodies and step on some in their rush to get to the ambulance. Both know, deep inside, that the boy will die, but they run, they run. Breath coming harsh, steaming out of their mouths, they run desperately, and then Felker slows to a stop. Johnson, holding the rear arms of the stretcher wants to keep going, says "God damn it, Felker! Move! Move!" Felker doesn't move. He knows that they are now carrying a dead man. He drops the stretcher, sinks to his knees. This has happened to Felker before, and each time, within minutes, he has risen, shaken himself like a wet dog, and nodded to Johnson. They have always taken the body

123

not to the ambulance but to the field morgue, stacked it like a piece of wood upon other bodies, and returned to the carnage.

This time Felker does not rise.

Felker is a big, blond-haired boy from Southern Maryland. He is the oldest of five brothers, all crab fishermen. He was one of the first to join the ambulance corps, and he had done so because he wanted an adventure before getting married, settling down, and taking over the family crabbing business in Solomons Island. His girl, he'd confided to Johnson, hadn't wanted him to go, had cried, cajoled, withheld sex, but he'd gone anyway. Now he is on his knees in the mud, staring at the corpse of another boy who couldn't have been more than twenty.

Johnson tugs at him, says, pleading, "Come one Felker, we've got to get him over there. Get up, man, get up!" Felker does, but as he rises he unleashes a haymaker that catches Johnson just above the jaw and drops him. Now Johnson is on his knees in the mud, and Felker is running around in small circles, screaming, stomping, kicking at the dirt. Then he stops, mutters something, and turns to Johnson.

"Whaddya doing down there, Jimmy? Come on, get up! We gotta get this poor son of a bitch to the infirmary..."

*****

Johnson tried to avoid the Bastille Day celebrations, but could not. Treize had spread kohl around Johnson's eyes, draped a sheet about his shoulders, toga-like, and dragged him to the festivities. In Montparnasse, they'd helped drink a river of wine and attended a costume *bal* to watch the mighty behave like morons. Johnson, slightly drunk and more than slightly embarrassed, had no idea who he was supposed to be, and only stayed an hour or so. He noted that Brancusi took the necessary photos of the revelers garbed as gypsies, Saracens, Hercules, muses, Neptunes, naiads, Roman warriors, Hellenic seers, and other heroic figures. Treize went dressed as a shrimp. Her costume had taken weeks to make and so severely hampered movement that some mistook her for a sculpture. Easter was supposed to come with her husband, but at the last minute, Frederick claimed a stomach illness, so Easter went alone, dressed as Cary Nations with a hatchet. Cocteau came as himself, resplendent as usual, and said he had seen Gertrude Stein and Alice Toklas dressed as nasty old biddies. Then he added that he was mistaken—those were not costumes.

The celebration could not wash all the city's gloom away. There remained fifty empty-eyed widows and a hundred orphans for every Bacchanalian. The trumpets' flourishes had an empty ring, and the gold epaulets on the generals' uniforms reflected a tarnished light. Johnson knew that as the crowds drank and roared, there were growing numbers of people without homes, families driven into the streets by the cost of caring for their young invalids.

The day before, a very young woman pushing a handcart of pitiable belongings somehow managed to creep past Mme. Bertrand's vigilance. The waif, unwashed and in rags, stood mute in the courtyard of Johnson's apartment building with a sign about her neck that read "*Je suis pauvre.*" He'd purchased some needless items from her—a set of mismatched cutlery, a pair of rusty scissors—and had paid her five times what she was asking. She'd taken his money with a nod and shambled away. There were two babies in the cart, and Johnson had the horrendous suspicion that for a price she would have sold them as well.

The world powers had finally signed the treaty in Versailles, and now the populace was force-fed a feast of parades, speeches, horsemen, and Republican guards in full regalia. Pundits waxed eloquent on the triumph of good over evil, but not so much as a stray morsel from this self-serving banquet found its way to the woman pushing her handcart and so many like her.

*****

Three weeks later Felker is dead. A stray bullet catches him square in the back of the head. Johnson is with him. When Felker drops the stretcher, Johnson thinks another of Felker's fits might be coming, but Felker has never lain motionless and face down in the mud before. He's never been this quiet. The man they've been carrying curses. He is an older poilu *with a relatively minor wound to the groin, and he tells Johnson,* "Ton copain, il est mort." *Then Johnson too falls to the mud, arms hugging his knees. The* poilu *reaches a hand over and using Johnson's shoulder pushes himself upright, grunting in pain. He says,* "You need to help me, or else we'll both die here." *Johnson, unthinking, gets to his feet and they both walk and stumble the quarter mile to the infirmary. Johnson will learn that the* poilu *died of septicemia ten days later, but by that time Johnson has been restationed to another front.*

*****

Johnson inventoried his paints, saw he needed a new brush and a fresh supply of cadmium yellow. Monsieur Lefebvre had stayed a few minutes after delivering the mail to show off a new English book he'd bought in his quest for fluency. According to the instructions in the first chapter, M. Lefebvre must recite aloud all the tenses of a particular verb just before going to bed, and then place the book under his pillow. The author proposed that the mailman's brain would work feverishly during the night to memorize the words. By this method, M. Lefebvre would become an adept English speaker in no time at all.

Johnson and the *facteur* briefly explored the mysteries of the silent *w* versus the exhaled *h*. M. Lefebvre struggled with *horde, hoard, whored,* with *whirred, word, heard, herd* and *world, whirled,* and *hurled.* He left complaining that his head was so swollen his service cap no longer fit.

CHAPTER 30

Easter took her diary from the drawer where it lay wrapped in a silk square. She leafed through it and was amazed to see how few pages she had filled.

*****

Paris, Sunday, July 20, 1919

My suspicions, sadly, turn out to be correct.

Treize came by early this morning looking distraught, at a rare loss for words. She hemmed and hawed as I offered her coffee, which she accepted and gulped in one swallow. She even ate a croissant, a singular event since she eschews butter and white flour. She apologized three or four times for being the bearer of bad tidings, and after much prompting finally told me that yesterday she saw Jean Cocteau and Frederick nuzzling like newlyweds over supper at *Le Monocle*, an establishment frequented by homosexuals and lesbians. I did not ask Treize why *she* was there, and she did not offer an explanation.

I cried a little when she told me, and she took me in her arms. She patted my back, my hair, my cheek, murmuring, "*Je sais, je sais, mon poussin. C'est très triste, très très triste.*"

Well, it *is* very sad, but not in the manner Treize suspects. It is sad because I fear Frederick has chosen a path from which he might never be able to deviate, and I cannot help but think that, in the long run, it will not be a happy one for him.

However, Treize's revelation was not unexpected. I came to the conclusion some time back that Jean and Frederick were involved, but a part of me still hoped the relationship might be a banal one based on Cocteau's love for all things American. I can't help but wonder if I am the one responsible for Frederick's change of attitude. No, it's more than that; my husband is now sexually involved with a *man*.

Our brief time together was not blessed with peace and quietude. I am afraid I imposed my will on my poor husband, and that he has resented me ever since that day when I told him I wanted to stay in Paris. I was not the nicest of wives. I hope God will forgive me and give me an opportunity to make up for this somehow.

I cried some more that night over lost expectations and hopes not attained. Then I cried for the deaths of Mother and Father, for my fears, for Frederick's survival in a strange new world, for obstacles to overcome. By next morning I had no more tears.

CHAPTER 31

Perhaps the Jardin du Luxembourg had not been such a good idea. A week earlier, James Johnson had been forced to cancel the outing with Easter because of rain, but today's weather was no cheerier. The clouds were low on the horizon, and an air of desolation clung to the place. The ponds remained empty of duck and fish caught and eaten by starving Parisians. A gamekeeper interviewed in *Le Matin* had said he was certain the waterfowls would come back in a year or two. In the meantime, good French citizens had been emptying their aquariums into the Jardin's basins so that eventually the giant, graceful carps would once again allow children to hand-feed them pieces of bread and cake.

Easter and Johnson paid to sit by one of the fountains and watch the nannies of the rich wheel baby carriages to and fro. There were a lot of babies. Easter suspected the sexual energy of the French reappeared as the war neared its end. There would be many children whose fathers were old enough to have been grandfathers. With so many young soldiers killed, the young would-be brides turned to the aging men left behind.

They sat in silence, and Easter asked Johnson whether he'd ever wanted a family, a wife and children. He said that yes, there had been a time when it had seemed important to him to further the lineage, and he told her about his once-upon-a-time love for Marie who, for all he knew, was probably now a happy bride and mother somewhere in America.

"Do you miss her?"

He thought for a moment before responding. "No. Sometimes I think I do, but it's not Marie that I miss as much as the *idea* of Marie; the concept of being settled. I miss the fantasy of quiet, orderly life, but

Marie? No. I'm a fairly happy man, though I can have my bad moments like everyone else. All in all, life is good."

Easter laughed. "'We are in the best of places, in the best of times with the best of people.' I overheard Gertrude Stein say that at the party."

Then she surprised him by lighting a cigarette. Johnson raised an eyebrow, asked when she'd started smoking.

"Just now." She coughed, dabbed at her lips with a handkerchief. "I read that it has both a calming effect and can relieve tiredness, and occasionally I feel both weary and nervous, if the two can coexist. I love this place, James, but it sometimes fatigues me."

He said he thought she was a very busy woman.

"I don't think it's that. I've always been active. Perhaps I'm simply afraid of turning into one of *them*." Easter shot a pointed look in the direction of a group of women, all clad in black. *"Les corbeaux.* The crows. That's what people call the widows now. The French are losing their patience for sorrow." She dropped the cigarette, ground it under foot, fidgeted a moment, then looked up.

"I'm glad we came out here, James. There's something I've wanted to speak to you about."

He fell silent, expected the worst. She had taken the initiative away from him. He had planned to hint at his feelings for her, to try to determine if there was any hope of a future together. It had been his idea to meet with her, and his intention to speak out. Now she would tell him she wanted to curtail their relationship, or, worse, return to the States.

She said, "Frederick is a homosexual."

Her statement, so flat and unadorned in its finality, caught him up short; *bouche bée,* once again. No words came, so he put an arm around her shoulder and drew her close. She did not resist, instead lowered her head and began crying softly.

She allowed him to hold her for a few minutes, then straightened, retrieved her handkerchief, wiped at her eyes, and blew her nose. She said, "Treize told me," then began talking very quickly, as if ridding herself of a burden.

"May I be frank, James? You are the best friend I have here, and I trust you implicitly. You have always had my best interest at heart."

James opened his mouth to reply, but Easter held up a warning hand.

"Please, James. This is very difficult. Please don't interrupt me." She lit another cigarette, coughed. "Frederick and I have not been…together," she hesitated on the word, "as man and wife for months. *Months.* I realize it's unseemly to even bring such an issue up, and it honestly would not concern me were I not aware that he is involved with someone else; not just someone else, but a man."

"Ah. Cocteau?"

She looked up at him, wide-eyed.

"My God! Is it already common knowledge?"

He reluctantly informed her that Cocteau was loose-lipped and had boasted of going to *Le Monocle* with a young American businessman.

"Treize," said Easter, "told me she saw them there."

Johnson nodded. "*Le Monocle* has a special night for men, the third Friday of every month, or so I've heard. Cocteau has been telling people he had a most wonderful time and that his companion did not speak French, which has led to a great deal of gossip about your… about Frederick, I'm afraid."

Easter took all this in perfect silence, then nodded. "How amazing."

She looked at the widows again. "*Les corbeaux.* That's one uncertainty they don't have to face." She laughed dryly. "What a horribly unkind thing I've said. Those poor women. Look at them; some are younger than me."

"Well." She sat up, squared her shoulders. "In a way it's a relief. I was certain something was wrong with *me;* that I was a poor excuse for a wife, somehow, not holding up my end. There are times Frederick makes me feel undesirable. It's odd, living with a man who never touches you."

Johnson turned his head so they were face to face.

"Easter, you are one of the most desirable women I've ever met. If Frederick is too great a fool to realize that, then it is his loss, not yours."

He blurted all that out, surprising himself, but, to his embarrassment, Easter only laughed. "Dear James! I do hope you haven't chosen this moment to make a pass. That would be terribly ungentlemanly."

He was about to protest his innocence when she patted his knee. "That was humor, James. I find it lessens tension even better than cigarettes do. Rest assured, I know you would never take advantage of me."

Was there a note of warning or wanting in her voice? He barely had time to hope before Easter began speaking again.

"Did I tell you that both my parents died during the influenza epidemic? That was just a bit more than two years ago. They were among the very first, before it was even properly diagnosed. I remember the doctor telling me it was a touch of ague. I didn't even ask what ague was. I thought perhaps it was like a stomach ache, some minor indisposition. It was only when others started to die that the physician realized what he was dealing with. It was so fast; one day my father took ill and stayed home from work. He complained a bit, a sore throat, a cough. A week later he was gone. Four days after his funeral, my mother developed the same symptoms, the sore throat, the cough, and then she became very ill. It was horrible to watch her pain. She was a strong woman, always had been. She lasted 72 hours. I have no idea why it is that I wasn't struck down. By all accounts, I should have been. I suppose I was lucky. There was a bit of money, enough to tide me over for six months while I trained to become a secretary. A few weeks after their deaths, I met Frederick at an interview. There was an opening in his father's company. Frederick was charming, but he never once attempted any familiarity. I'd only been out with one other boy before that, and *whatever* we did, *wherever* we went, I spent the better part of the evening fending that boy off, removing his hands from me. I thought it was normal."

She smiled sadly and continued. "I have two friends, Charlotte and Enid, who took me under their wings when Mother and Father passed away, and they both told me this was how men behave, that they're only interested in one thing. You can imagine how being with Frederick was a relief." She fell silent for a moment.

"It took him three months to kiss me, and when he did, it was almost as a brother. We were engaged that same week. Only once after that did he ever touch me, and I think it was almost experimental. I didn't respond; we both pretended it had been an accident. It didn't even occur to me to refuse his marriage proposal. If you had asked me then what a homosexual was, I couldn't have told you, and you know the most amazing thing, James? I don't think Frederick knew either. All this happened because I brought him here, because I insisted we stay in Paris."

She began crying, soft sobs that gently shook her. Then, once again, she regained her composure, stared at the women dressed in black.

Johnson was quiet. It had always been his contention that people were what they were and, by and large, remained that way. Few people, despite good intentions, underwent drastic changes save perhaps those like himself who had faced war or other cataclysmic events they could not begin to understand. He told Easter that, from what she had recounted, it appeared Frederick had always been what he was now but merely undiscovered. She seemed to take some solace in that.

"Do you really think so, James? Because I've had the same thought from time to time. You aren't only saying those things to assuage my guilt, are you? You mustn't, you know."

He assured her that guilt was inappropriate. "We're in an age where things once forbidden are now commonplace," he said. "We're establishing new norms, redefining the nature of 'acceptable.' Look at Gertrude and Alice, living together quite openly, making no secret of their relationship. Homosexuality is not prohibited here, and the fact is, Montparnasse is a haven for those whose behavior might be banned elsewhere. I don't know if this is good or not, Easter; I'm no seer. I am, however, totally certain you're not at fault. Frederick is a grown man. He chose his own path."

She nodded, perhaps persuaded, perhaps not. "There are times when I see him as totally childlike; no doubt I've babied him, have even looked down on him. That may also have had something to do with it. I don't know, James. I'm horribly confused and at my wits' end. If things like this happened in the United States, I certainly never heard of them. Being wronged by one's husband with another woman is one thing, but with another man?" She barely paused, and then asked, "Are you sleeping with Kiki?"

Johnson was astonished. "Excuse me?"

Easter spared him further discomfiture by averting her eyes. "James, I'm not a fool. It's an indiscreet question, but we're having an indiscreet conversation. I've told you the worst secret of my life—that my husband prefers sharing his bed with a man than with me. Now I want something in return for this degrading admission. It'll make me feel better, as if we're on somewhat even grounds." She paused, looked back at Johnson. "So, are you?"

He stammered, "No. It... that is... it happened only once."

Easter considered this.

"A shame, that. You deserve someone nice, James. Still, perhaps she's not for you. She seems a bit promiscuous, in my opinion. You should find yourself a pleasant woman—French or American, that's immaterial—someone who will care for you. Do you know that the first time I saw you and her together, I was jealous?" She smiled, waved at a little girl who was staring at them. The child waved back, ran away laughing. "Oh my, I really am baring my soul. Let's talk of something else."

From the moment Easter had mentioned her husband's dereliction, Johnson had been wrestling with his conscience. Surely this was more than enough ill news for one day, and she did not need the further burden of his suspicions. He decided not to mention Frederick's opium use.

Then she said, "And Frederick's using drugs. Opium. Cocteau again, I suspect."

James sighed. "Easter, you're reading my mind..."

She ignored him.

"The apartment reeks of it. He thinks I don't notice, but the smell reaches the hallway. He sleeps a lot lately, and his appetite is off. He hides it in his office desk, in a tin of cocaine pills for headaches. He must really think me stupid. I was looking for something to take for a migraine when I remembered seeing the tin. The pills are gone, replaced by these things that look like rabbit droppings. Don't look at me that way, James; I *have* spent some time on a farm. My grandparents raised rabbits."

The little girl was back, gazing at them with bright blue eyes. Easter made a face, and the little girl giggled. This went on for some time—Easter making increasingly deformed grimaces and the child returning them tit for tat. Then the nanny called, and the child scampered off.

"There was an article," Easter continued, "on how inveterate users of opium lose interest in everything—food, money, people, even sex."

Johnson had read the very same periodical. "Is Frederick that numb?"

She shook her head. "No. If anything, his business is thriving. There seems to be a bottomless hunger for American products right now, and Frederick has a knack for identifying a need and filling it. His father is delighted. I assume the profits are handsome on both sides of the Atlantic. At least I have no fear of being destitute. If anything, Frederick has become ridiculously generous. Guilt, I suppose. He actually encourages my spending, and he's thinking of purchasing an automobile, a Citroën. I've seen the advertisements."

It was getting warm. Johnson took off his jacket, wrestled a sense of discouraging helplessness mixed with desire and admiration. He told Easter he would this very day call Cocteau to inform him he would not participate in the production of his play.

"Why in the world would you do that, James? I don't blame Jean. He did not subvert Frederick. Don't be foolish, please. I'm grateful for the gesture, truly I am, but it would do little to solve my predicament."

She stood, balled her handkerchief into the pocket of her coat.

"Could we leave now? I'm hungry. All these confessions… Let's go eat."

On the way to the restaurant, they passed a neighborhood merry-go-round, and Easter spotted the little girl again. The child was sitting on a wooden elephant that rode up and down as the calliope blared. When the ride stopped, Easter bought two tickets from the attendant and mounted a giraffe—directly behind the child. The nanny looked momentarily concerned, but softened when Easter gave her the brightest of smiles.

Johnson watched as the two—a little girl and a grown woman—rode the carousel. He tried to find meaning therein and failed.

CHAPTER 32

Easter walked Johnson to his apartment, then continued home alone, prey to a strange sense of fragility and lightness. Her feet scarcely touched the *trottoir's* cobblestones, and she hardly cared where she was going. She ended up at Mme. Desroches's salon where, a lifetime ago, she'd spent a pleasant morning being manicured, pedicured, and given a *coupe moderne*. Mme. Desroches recognized her, and the two spent an hour together as the salon staff washed her hair, massaged her scalp and tried to talk her into changing her hair color to one that was all the rage. Easter demurred and gave the salon proprietor a hug and kisses on both cheeks before leaving.

When she got home, the apartment was empty. She brewed some tea and found her diary.

*****

Paris, Monday, July 21, 1919

Frederick and I will never have children. A little girl at the Jardin du Luxembourg let me know this. She was pretty, as children usually are, wearing a sailor costume. I took a turn on a merry-go-round with her and wondered whether I'd ever do this with a daughter of my own. I suppose motherhood is something I shall have to hold in abeyance. I hadn't given it much thought until now. Frederick mentioned becoming parents only once, months ago, when I attacked him with the croissant and marmalade.

Tempus fugit. Time must be malleable. Nothing else explains how my former life in Chicago could seem so ephemeral and distant when compared to these few months in Paris. Recently, I went to the cinema with Treize and something happened—the employee manning the projector must have tripped the wrong switch because suddenly the images on the screen sped by so that Douglas Fairbanks looked like a woodpecker kissing Mary Pickford. That is the image I have of my life right now—everything speeds forward. Days and weeks are flashes in a shadow-box. In a matter of months, I marry, I leave my home, we move to Paris to find a new one far more to my liking; I make friends, discover my husband is a homosexual and perhaps a drug addict. I am subject to strange and strong urges at the sight of men I do not know. I find myself occasionally thinking in French.

And, of course, I meet James, whose friendship I take advantage of by burdening it with all my doubts and fears. I wish he would do the same. He speaks only in passing of his Service with the Ambulance Corps, but his eyes are haunted. Poor James. I know he finds me attractive, but, surely, I am a trying companion. I enjoy teasing him; I welcome his befuddlement when I cause it; today I surprised him with a blunt question about Kiki. He is such a good, strong man that I'm amazed no woman has set her sights on him. He claims to enjoy being a bachelor at 32, but I frankly don't believe it. I sense loneliness in him, a patch of shadows behind his smiles, and I am relieved to learn he is not Kiki's lover (how easily that once-forbidden word comes now. Scant months ago, it was too suggestive, even lurid.) Part of me makes it a game to guess what he might be like in bed. He *is* handsome, and his height and coloring make him unusual in France. He has talent, far more so than he willingly admits. His portraits of me, and yes, of Kiki as well, are bold and striking. We never did get around to discussing another series of paintings.

The door opened and Frederick walked in, dressed in a dark blue suit, a pink shirt, and two-tone shoes. He brushed Easter's cheek with his lips, smiled, waved at her and without a word went into his office and closed the door. A minute later, she heard him walk to the bathroom.

*****

There is news from home. Enid wrote that a professor from Massachusetts, a Dr. Goddard, has seriously proposed that a trip to the moon is possible. I suspect poor Dr. Goddard has spent too much time in the company of Jules Verne novels. Charlie Chaplin, D.W. Griffiths, and other Hollywood figures have created a new film company. Enid, who would spend her life in movie theaters if she could, is all atwitter. War heroes were given a downtown parade attended by thousands, and Charlotte has met a soldier. Enid says he is not that handsome, but I can tell she is envious. She now dreams of meeting Jack Dempsey, a boxer who earlier this month won some sort of title. Of a more worrisome nature are reports of Negroes attacking whites in Washington and Norfolk. Several men, women, and children have been injured within sight of the White House by roving bands of these thugs. The European papers have carried very little of this news. I hope such riots will not spread to Chicago. I don't think they will. The Negroes there are more settled than the ones in our Southern states. There is also much debate about the Bolsheviks, who parade openly beneath the Red flag.

I must give some serious thought to my situation with Frederick who, at this very moment, is smoking opium in the bathroom and thinking I don't know it. Perhaps the drug has made him stupid.

It is possible, I suppose, that his new sexual orientation is a passing fancy, and that he will revert, in time, to become again the man I married. This particular eventuality leaves me cold. The sad truth is whatever love I may have had for Frederick has greatly diminished. Certainly, his presence eased the shock of Mother and Father's death, and for this I will always be grateful. I would not be in France now were it not for him. Forgive this cruelty, but was he ever anything more than a vehicle I employed to get from there to here? Had he said, "We'll spend a few weeks in the Dakotas after the wedding," I might have given his offer less positive consideration.

I have just caught a glimpse of him, eyes swollen and low-lidded. I am sure he has left the bathroom window open to vent the *toilettes*. His pretense at temperance *is* rather ludicrous, and I suppose I am ludicrous as well, feigning ignorance as I do, but I am not in the mood for a fight.

Frederick has provided for us well since our arrival here. He is inordinately proud of the fact that his father's company—very largely thanks to his initiatives in Paris—has made more money in the last three months than it did in all of 1918. Mr. Cowles Sr. has announced that next quarter, Frederick will become a Vice President in Charge of European Affairs. Notice the Capital Letters; this is the way Frederick pronounces his future title. He has already ordered new cards and stationery, and plans to have two telephone lines installed, to be answered by a British secretary. He has also told me that he will soon be doing some extended traveling throughout the country; I don't know why.

Louis Pascin and his wife Hermine came by earlier today and gave me a delightful caricature of me that he has drawn. It is framed and under glass. Their visit and their gift were totally unexpected, but Hermine (whom I barely know) said she had been after her husband to apologize for his dreadful behavior the night he assaulted poor Mr. Quinn during my party. I had almost forgotten about it. She asked for Mr. Quinn's address in New York so she might a send him a new hat.

In no time at all, I shall best Gertrude Stein at collecting artists' works. I now have Apollinaire's calligram, Picasso's napkin, Pascin's drawing, and James's second portrait (a copy of the one he sold). Lest I forget, Modigliani sent me by post a tiny watercolor of Jeanne's face, and Kiki designed a flowery hat for me that I shall never wear.

Frederick objects to having these items displayed in the apartment, except of course for the portrait, which he claims does not do me justice. I have therefore created my own small museum in the *Atelier Pâques*. I have even kept poor Mr. Quinn's fork-punctured boater. Perhaps one day I'll use it as part of a costume.

Per and Lucy Krohg, who live on the rue Joseph Bara, have invited a number of Montparnassiens to come to their vacation home later this summer. I know both Per and Lucy only slightly. James has also been asked to come. I mention this invitation because a few days ago I ran into Lucy at the *pâtisserie* (she is very fond of the profiteroles they make there), and she showed me some photographs of the villa they have rented. It is a splendid place on the coast near Biarritz, with full amenities and a swimming pool. I was a bit taken aback when she proudly displayed pictures of her and Per enjoying the waters completely naked. I suspect a stay with them may call for nudity while bathing, and while I am not a prude, neither am I used to ablutions in the altogether. On the other hand, I am very curious to see how the males in such company behave. What happens if they get excited by the sight of all that female flesh? Are we supposed to pretend we don't notice? What is the etiquette for entertaining *au naturel*?

Ah, and I'll note just one last, rather odd event.

For weeks now, I have been shopping in the same neighborhood and seeing the same residents and *commerçants*. In fact, it is sometimes hard to believe I'm in a city, rather than a village. As I walk from the apartment to the stores I patronize, I will encounter a dozen or more familiar faces. Some I greet with a "Bonjour, Madame" or "Bonjour, Monsieur," as appropriate, while with others I may share a smile and a nod. Two or three extend their hands for a firm handshake, which still surprises me. Women seldom shake hands in the United States and doing so here is one of those small habits I still do not take for granted.

There are three beggars in my neighborhood. The French call them *clochards*. I have not been able to find the origins of the word—whether it has anything to do with bells, *cloches*, or not. At any rate, the first is an elderly Negro man who is quite demented. He mutters to himself as he reads a book and seems prey to many demons. He is meticulously dressed and only close inspection will reveal that his pants are frayed and his jacket tattered. I routinely give him some change, and he does not acknowledge my donation, which is just fine.

The second is an ageless, run-of-the-mill alcoholic with a mouthful of brown teeth. Most of the time, he is slumped over and surrounded by empty bottles of cheap wine. He wears the clothing of a laborer—soiled black pants and a dark blue shirt that may never have been laundered. I do not give him money as I have no desire to foster his vice.

The third is a younger man, with a copious beard and a mane of reddish hair. He has on an old French army uniform that is too small for him. The pant legs rise above his ankles, and the jacket will not close. He is blind, I think, and wears dark tinted glasses that do not sit correctly on his nose, giving him a truly cockeyed look. I don't know whether his blindness is the result of the war, or perhaps he was born that way. He taps a white cane on the sidewalk. I always give him whatever change I might have left after my purchases. About a week ago, I dropped coins into his tin cup and he said, "Thank you."

I did not imagine this. It took a moment for it to register, and I had walked three steps before I stopped, turned and said, "Excuse me?"

He tapped his cane on the pavement.

I repeated, "Excuse me?" and he said, "Madame?"

In English, I said, "Are you American?" He ignored me. I repeated the question in French. He shook his head, muttered, "Non, Madame. Belge." Then he put his tin cup in the pocket of his jacket and walked away. I was tempted to follow him but didn't.

Here is what I am sure of: He is not Belgian.

This small mystery was with me all day, and I mentioned it to Frederick over dinner.

"Not bloody likely," he said. (Frederick has taken to using British expressions lately and his speech is laced with 'bloody' and 'blasted' and 'this chap' and 'that chap.' It's a strange and irking affectation. I have taken great pains not to chide him.)

"No American chaps begging in the streets of Paris, that's for sure. Embassy wouldn't stand for it. Make us look bloody poorly."

Frederick has made some friends at the American Embassy. He won a small contract to supply the Ambassador's residence with some household item or other and now claims familiarity with the Embassy's staff.

"Any American in France can get a ticket home by asking for one at the Embassy or Consulates. Law was passed by Congress a few days after the treaties were signed. We want our boys to come home, not wander around Europe like lost souls." He chewed on the bone of his lamb chop, "So it wouldn't make much sense for one of ours to be here begging in the streets of Paris, now would it?"

I let the subject lapse and made a mental note to talk to James about it.

The next day, the blind man was gone from his usual spot. I spotted him some blocks away. I began to cross the street to get closer to him but was stopped in mid-traffic by a surge of cars and trucks. When I reached the other side, he was gone. That was a week ago and I have not seen the man since.

CHAPTER 33

Henri Désiré Landru killed Mme. Ernestine Guillin by striking the back of her head with an Italian grape hoe. It made a strange noise. Landru was reminded of being with his mother at a street market decades earlier, when she had thumped melons with her closed fist before buying them. It was the same sound, but louder.

The hoe had not been his first choice. Landru, a smallish man aware of his physical limitations, was not sure, at first, that the blow had killed her. Then Mme. Guillin crumpled like shed clothing, and Landru knelt and saw a trickle of blood draining from the nape of her neck. The blow had indeed been fatal, which both pleased and surprised him.

He wrestled her into a burlap potato sack, which was dusty and left a smear of soil on her face, offending his sense of neatness. He wiped Mme. Guillin's cheeks with a linen handkerchief, then dumped that, too, into the sack.

He had abandoned the villa at Vernouillet and rented another one near Gambais. This was a dark, multi-roomed home slightly off the main road and far enough away from neighbors that his comings and goings would go unnoticed. Tall trees bordered three sides of the lot. He had professionals move and install the large stove, and he furnished the house sparsely with items from his warehouse: a hodge-podge of good and bad sofas, side tables, and unmatched dining room chairs. He chose a small bed, barely large enough for two, and a poorly made Oriental rug frayed at the edges.

His first victim was Mme. Heon, a large, meek widow. He slept with her twice, leaving her breathless, shaken, and melting with gratitude. Shortly thereafter, she accepted his proposal of marriage and was thrilled to learn that they would soon be posted to Indochina, where she would be the wife of a vice-consul. Landru extracted from her a promise not to tell anyone of their future plans, as issues of *sécurité nationale* were involved.

Mme. Heon was killed December 26, 1916, shortly after a meal of Christmas goose and *foie gras* at the villa. Her death was noisome and flatulent, very similar to that of Mme. Laborde-Line. As he dismembered her with his butcher saw, Landru decided never to use strychnine again.

CHAPTER 34

James Johnson's *facteur* had something to say. M. Lefebvre shuffled his feet, smiled, and a little sweat seeped from his hairline. Johnson had to coax and cajole quite a bit before M. Lefebvre admitted he'd met a woman.

The mailman had mentioned once in passing that he and the *inspecteur* cousin investigating the charges against Landru had enjoyed their usual *pot au feux* in their usual restaurant. Johnson had not paid much attention until Lefebvre said, "She seems very pleasant…" Johnson looked up, stopped his pottering with the tomato juicer. *"She?"*

The *facteur* tried to make light of it with the familiar Gallic shrug but Johnson could see this momentous event was to be the focus of the morning's conversation.

"She is not very pretty," M. Lefebvre said. "Not like her," and here he pointed to one of Easter's portraits. "Maybe a little bit fat," he added, making a largish figure eight in the air with his hands. "But the world is not perfect, *n'est-ce pas?*"

Normally by the time M. Lefebvre reached Johnson's apartment building on his first tour, his five-o'clock shadow was pronounced. This morning he was shaven to the quick and, Johnson suspected, talcumed as well. His shoes were buffed to a high gleam, and he'd taken pains to press his uniform and polish the silver postal service insignia on his cap. His medal, awarded for fifteen years with *la poste,* was carefully pinned to his chest. He looked well put together, and Johnson told him so.

After one *café-crème* and a bit of patience on Johnson's part, the postman grew voluble. The lady's name was Marcelle Colombini, and she was a childless widow in her early forties. She cleaned offices at the Sécurité where M. Lefebvre's cousin pursued the *interrogatoire définitif* of Henri Desiré Landru. She was also attempting to learn English, hoping this might lead to a better future. When the mailman's cousin saw her repeating, "How. Are. You. Today. I. Am. Fine. Thank you," as she dusted, he mentioned M. Lefebvre's Anglophonic efforts, and *voilà*.

The situation, however, was problematic for the mailman. Mme. Colombini's mastery of the language was greater than his, a vexing situation. If the relationship was to develop, the mailman explained, it would not do to start off on uneven linguistic footing. "She already knows the *pepper* and *paper* words. Her accent is very good. *British,*" he added with a dark look implying that Johnson's New England intonations were sorely lacking. "Also," he continued, "she can read and translate the American newspapers without effort. Her instruction book is better than mine."

So, thought Johnson, no more etymological jokes at M. Lefebvre's expense. This was serious business. The mailman's future might well depend on Johnson's teaching skills.

They agreed to meet weekly as soon as Johnson returned from vacation, and that Johnson would draw up a full course of instructions, complete with assignments and dictations.

Once this issue was settled, M. Lefebvre hesitantly sought advice on a much more delicate problem. Mme. Colombini apparently already had a suitor, a swarthy Corsican coworker whom she had hinted was pursuing her affections with great determination. How, M. Lefebvre asked, would Johnson handle the situation? "You are American," he said, "and so far this year, more than 3,000 French women have married American men. Your concierge told me how popular you are with ladies. They come to your apartment all hours of day and night." M. Lefebvre said this in such a certain, admiring way that Johnson felt unable to demur.

Johnson had from the first recognized his *facteur* as an intelligent man who read copiously. At the moment in France and throughout Europe, every novelty was American. An American restaurant and bar had opened near the Parc Monceau a fortnight earlier, touting a menu of ribs, burgers, and *chiens chauds* (hot dogs). There had been a recipe for meatloaf in *La Belle Parisienne*, a women's magazine. American music was all the rage, and certainly American dollars were welcomed in anyone's pocket. American movie stars were the latest heartthrobs, and the European fantasy of the American West still held substantial sway.

So, M. Lefebvre's conclusion that Johnson—as an American—must have hidden romantic talents and valuable advice for the lovelorn subsequently made perfect sense. To Lefebvre, Johnson's people were the wealthy victors, the unabashed heroes, the ones with answers.

Johnson told him he would give the matter of Mme. Colombini's suitor some thought, as this was not something to be handled carelessly. He meant it, as M. Lefebvre had become a friend. Johnson recognized that his own history of relationships with the opposite sex was tatty at best, and he dared not speak his views on marriage in the modern world, lest he appall M. Lefebvre.

As they talked, the mailman outlined his plans for the next decade: once Anglophone, he and Mme. Colombini—or rather, the future Mme. Lefebvre—would both learn to speak and write English. They would take a Dutch ship from Rotterdam to New York (the fares were cheaper than those of the French Line) and, once there, find high-paying jobs. He would drive a taxi, and she would be hired by a rich American family in need of a French *nounou*. After ten years, not a day more, saving as many dollars as possible, they would return to France and open a brasserie.

Johnson heartily wished M. Lefebvre all success. His own immediate prospects were far less grandiose.

Per and Lucy Krohg, back from Norway where Per was hailed a genius, had asked him to spend three weeks in their villa near Biarritz, and he'd accepted their invitation. A few weeks by the sea would do him good. Per had mentioned that Easter and Frederick had been invited as well, but that Frederick would not be coming. Johnson tried to appear uninterested by this news and was delighted when Easter suggested they travel to Biarritz together by train.

The invitation, of course, had strings attached. He (and Easter, more than likely) would be expected to speak English during all the meals so the largely Scandinavian assembly could practice the language. In exchange for English lessons, the Krohgs had promised to teach everyone to dance.

In Montparnasse, Per and Lucy were the Golden Couple, famous both as dancers and highly successful artists. They'd danced professionally in Scandinavia for almost eight years and knew all the steps to the crayfish, the bear, the tango, the *rouli rouli,* and of course the *matchiche brésili-enne.* The money they earned dancing during the summers provided for winters undisturbed in Paris practicing their crafts: he painted, she made dolls.

Easter was thrilled at the idea of learning the wild "Apache" dance on the ballroom floor and had already tagged Johnson as her partner in crime.

Later while shopping, Johnson ruminated on the perfect symmetry of events. In Paris, M. Lefebvre had found a paramour; in Biarritz, the Swedes were throwing him and Easter together.

When Johnson returned to his apartment, he found that a member of the Lafayette Escadrille had left his card with Mme. Bertrand, who had been impressed by the flyer's uniform. The man's name was William Thaw, and Johnson suspected that, like most members of that celebrated squad, the flyer was writing his memoirs and needed whatever information Johnson might be able to supply on Daniel, Johnson's brother, the airplane thief. Thaw's note asked if he could call on Johnson next month, as he was going to the country but would very much like to speak with him upon his return.

The visit gave Johnson pause. The public had already forgotten how few of these daring flyers there had been, never more than twenty, and their number was never commensurate with their fame. Johnson supposed his brother Daniel had earned some notoriety of his own; certainly, all of the Escadrille fighters were likely to know his name. Daniel's primary talent had always been his knack for getting attention, and he was forgiven and occasionally singled out and respected for behavior that was often boorish, at best foolish, and at worst suicidal.

CHAPTER 35

"In August," Frederick wrote in a letter to his father, "Paris is deserted, save for the tourists. Shops and restaurants close for the entire month. The trains to the Atlantic and Mediterranean coasts overflow with families bearing beach umbrellas, massive picnic hampers, folding lounge chairs, sacks of reeking food, and *pétanque* sets weighting dozens of pounds. Passengers who are not able to afford railway seats stand in the wagons' aisles and smoke all night, play cards, and compare the attractions of beach towns and villages. Many, sad to say, are unwashed and smell strongly in such small confines."

He did not tell his father that the last few weeks had not been pleasant. Easter had confronted him with the two secrets he least wanted to discuss: his use of opium and his relationship with Jean Cocteau.

Frederick, outraged, denied the accusations in their totality, putting on an agitated performance of livid rage and disbelief. "Cocteau is my *friend!* How could you have the gall to imply anything else?"

When he saw his words were not swaying Easter's opinion, he shouted: "I would think you should be pleased that Jean and I have become close. Aren't you the one who wanted me to be friends with your damned artists?"

This, of course, was a lie.

Easter's claims that he smoked opium were harder to deny. She had found his cache of the drug and waved it in his face as she spoke. The off-and-on argument, punctuated with tears and accusations, counter-accusations and threats had lasted four days. Frederick had taken refuge in his bedroom office and eaten all his meals at cafés and restaurants, and he smoked his opium at the Cimetière du Montparnasse near the train station.

He liked it there and had found a park bench beneath a large oak shadowing a crypt where no one had been entombed for half a decade. There, he could walk in peace among the vaults and abandoned sepulchers. The carved stone angels, virgins, Christs on crosses, and weeping cherubs never disputed his thoughts or castigated his actions.

He often fell asleep beneath the oak tree, and once he awoke at dusk and only barely escaped being locked in the cemetery for the night. Another time, he arranged to meet Cocteau there, but the latter did not like it at all.

"I detest death," Cocteau had said. "It is a negative thing, and I am a positive person. Doesn't it repel you to know you are treading on the bones of others?" The playwright shuddered dramatically. "I walk in cemeteries, and souls scream at me. The dust of the past flies in my eyes."

When Easter left for her holiday at the Krohgs, Frederick treated himself to an expensive meal at the Restaurant Sainte-Cécile, followed by several drinks at the Café Voltaire on Place de l'Odéon. Soon he would be touring France in a grand automobile, purchasing alcohol for a thirsty America. Feeling a celebration was in order, he went to Cocteau's tailor and ordered two suits—one charcoal gray, one navy blue—as well as several shirts and trousers.

Then, even though he could have smoked in peace at home, he went to the cemetery.

It was a bright, cloudless day. Easter was on her way to Biarritz, and Frederick did not miss her. Her stridency annoyed him; it was a poor recompense for the lifestyle he'd given her.

Of course, James Johnson was also going to Biarritz. Would they sleep together? Frederick didn't think so; Easter took her vows seriously, and Johnson did not look like a philanderer. Still, it was not a matter of *if,* Frederick corrected himself, it was a matter of *when,* and he didn't care, which amazed him.

Under the oak tree, with the bluish gray smoke wafting away, Frederick took as deep a look inside himself as the drug would allow and once again came to the same conclusion. He felt no jealousy, regret, or even resentment at the idea of Easter's infidelity; frankly, he welcomed it. The marriage had been a blunder, the biggest mistake committed in his adult life.

It amused him how Easter prattled on about being a changed woman, a person reborn. She was so consumed with herself, her life, her interests, her circle of friends, that she never noticed how *he* had changed. His metamorphosis had been just as intense as hers, if not as visible.

Just five brief months had altered him. Though he'd never dream of admitting it to Easter, Paris was a pleasant city for a man of his discernment. One did not need to speak the language—it had taken him some time to figure this out—or have native friends, or eat the food, or subject one's self to the indignities the natives heaped upon tourists. There was an American world in Paris, and he was well on his way to becoming one of its regents.

He was well-off, and quickly becoming rich from the French obsession with American products. The old men could smoke their corn-paper Boyards and stinking pipes, but the younger generation wanted blonde Virginia tobacco, safety razors and blades from King Camp Gillette, and Colgate tooth powder, Fords and Chevrolets. The chic American fashions were all the rage, and every French worker dreamed of sturdy American cowhide boots. How many French students—adults and children—studied English? American movies drew overflow audiences; American inventions were revolutionizing the world.

True, the cost of almost everything was rising in America. A rare letter from Frederick's mother was a litany of complaints:

"Every time I go shopping I am appalled at the amounts one must spend for the most elementary items. The market charges usurious prices for the beefsteaks your father consumes daily. I sought to buy a new dining room table, an inelegant thing of mahogany to replace

the one we have, and was aghast when the cabinet-maker wanted more than one hundred dollars! And I have ceased going to the dressmaker, who must think me a fool, charging as she does eight dollars for a simple skirt."

Frederick paid little attention. Life might be getting harder in the States, but in Europe, he knew, America represented everything bright and shiny, from newly invented household products to moral and ethical values. There would come a time, he was certain, when English would become the *lingua franca*—a small joke there—and when everything that was shopworn, faded, and jaded would give way to the innovations from those brash upstarts across the Atlantic.

So what if many Europeans didn't like it? During his first weeks in Paris, Frederick had been put off by the high-handedness of some Parisians. Waiters were rude, store clerks acted as if foreign customers were a hindrance, editorials in many French newspapers (or so he'd been told) hinted darkly at the end of civilized French society. Now he saw it all for what it really was: fear. This small country, hardly the size of Texas, incapable of fighting and winning its own war, was terrified. Change was sweeping the nation, and Frederick was part of it. Soon, with the help of Pharmacist Remus, he would be rich beyond his dreams.

He looked around. The cemetery was old and unkempt. Weeds sprouted between the cobblestones and here and there small trees overtook the plots, their roots tilting the headstones. Wind, weather, and lack of care eroded the names of the dead. Leaning statues honored long-passed citizens whose accomplishments were forgotten generations ago. In one caved-in pit, he'd actually spotted moss-covered bones.

Few French understood where the world was going. Cocteau and a select clique of his *avant-garde* friends had caught glimpses, but they were chroniclers, not *doers*. They might start trends, influence and amuse the public; they might even write the histories, but it was up to people like Frederick to launch the changes, increase the momentum, mold, sculpt, and forge the future.

Then, of course, there was this sexual…discovery. "Discovery" was the word Frederick had settled on.

Their first encounter had been in the *fumoir* Cocteau rented so as not to disturb his mother. It had been unhurried, almost placid. One moment they were fully dressed enjoying the effects of the opium ("from Formosa, dear Frederick. For you, only the best.") and the next they were stark naked, trying on the playwright's collection of North African *djellabahs.* Cocteau and Frederick were about the same size, and the loose-fitting caftans, though itchy, were a welcome relief from tight shirt collars, cuffs and and waistbands.

Cocteau spoke at length about "men like ourselves."

"Two, three, maybe four out of a hundred. That's us. We are the superior males, the creative ones. The rest, they merely breed. Are you a student of history, Frederick? No? Ah. That is because you come from such a young country; you have no history yet, not really, and you don't yet feel the burden of time. The past shows us that some of the most powerful men were like us; males who knew that true love is that of one man for another man. Alexander, Suleiman, the Greeks, and the Romans; of course, God is a male. Angels are always male. Oscar Wilde, Shakespeare, I'm almost certain, were like us. Your own Abraham Lincoln and Walt Whitman…"

Frederick had stopped listening. The opium had made him sleepy and vivid dreams full of shapes and color were within grasp.

Cocteau sat up. "Do you like women?"

The query seemed to come from far away and gave Frederick pause. After a moment, he mumbled, "I don't know." Then, quite without realizing it, he found himself in an embrace, imagining himself Juliet to Cocteau's Romeo.

They had spent the better part of the afternoon in bed. Cocteau's first reaction upon seeing Frederick erect was a quiet, *"Mon Dieu…"* In his few prior experiences with women, Frederick had always been embarrassed by his partners' first look, but with Cocteau it was different. Frederick enjoyed it, reveled in having something the writer admired.

Cocteau's awe was unabashed. *"Quel spécimen magnifique, Frederick. I never would have suspected it, though of course, we all know Americans are large and magnificent in every manner."*

Frederick had woken later to find Cocteau gone. There was a note on the table next to the sofa asking him to lock up, and a key to the *fumoir*. He felt extraordinarily good, as if a great, basic question he'd never thought of asking had been answered.

Frederick was amazed and relieved by his lack of remorse or jealousy. As he doffed the caftan and buttoned his shirt, he realized he was suffused with satisfaction and totally devoid of the usual attendant perplexities. Cocteau had other men, whom Frederick knew tested the limitations of the writer's patience, enjoying Cocteau's displays of possessiveness. Frederick felt no such need. He liked Cocteau but knew the physical delight he had achieved could just as easily be attained with another man. The realization filled him with power. He was not dependent. For the first time in his life, Frederick felt whole, unencumbered, and entirely himself.

Sitting on the bench beneath the oak tree in the cemetery, Frederick sensed that almost everything in his life had changed profoundly. He could master a destiny of his making, could amass wealth and power, dismissing anyone useless to him.

He took a silver cigar case from his pocket, assembled the ivory stem and ceramic bowl of his pipe. He rolled a small ball of opium between his thumb and forefinger, placed it carefully in the bowl on the tip of the pipe. He lit the opium, inhaled deeply, and closed his eyes. The smoke added to the totality of his serenity.

He organized his mind and made a checklist of chores to be completed that day; he must finalize the plans for his trip. First, though, he would purchase more opium.

Chapter 36

Easter sat in a folding chair beneath a grape arbor, ignoring the insects whirring about her head. Her stay at Lucy and Per's summer villa had been both uneventful and delightful. The days, spectacular and windless, reminded her of cloudless times when she was little and had spent weeks at her grandparents' Illinois farm. Now, she was in *France!* It still amazed her.

She balanced the diary on her knee with the inkwell on the ground next to her feet.

*****

Berck-sur-Mer, Friday, August 8, 1919

Well, I did it. I went swimming in the sea totally naked, nude, unclothed, without a stitch, for all eyes to see. Of course, there were only women there (save for Lucy's baby, Guy, who grabs at everything and doesn't yet appear to care about anatomical differences between men and women) but still, I consider it a major breakthrough. Delightful too, I might add. This was my first time in the sea (I bathed in the lake in Chicago, but of course I wore a full suit), and it was so cold my teeth chattered. The wind threatened to take my breath away and I slipped on some rocks and almost fell, but all in all, I never could have imagined the sense of freedom one might attain by being unfettered in water. I splashed like a child, screamed when waves broke over my head, had a water fight with Lucy, and felt light as a feather caught in a spring breeze. Treize showed me how to float motionless on my back with only my breasts breaking the surface of the water and bobbing there like two small buoys. There were no others at the beach save myself, Kiki, Treize, Lucy, and Jeanne—Modi's ethereal lover—who refused to go in and so served as our lookout.

Lucy had found the isolated beach some time ago. It is away from the main bathing areas, barely twenty yards long, and ensconced between two rocky promontories that jut into the ocean. She drove us there in Per's Taylor automobile; she drives very poorly and claims the car has a will of its own. We took blankets, towels, a large picnic lunch, and several bottles of wine that we drank promptly to warm ourselves. We all chattered and gossiped, save for Jeanne.

Truly, Modi's friend is a strange person. Her eyes are fascinating, and this is not the first time I've noticed them. They stare, as if in a trance, all seeing and yet unseeing. She is amazingly beautiful in a fragile-as-porcelain way. Her features are so delicate that an errant draft might damage them. Her conversation is monosyllabic and she refuses to be drawn into the gaiety. I told her that I found Modi a most fascinating man, thinking a confidence or two might breach her reserve, but she merely smiled, nodded, said, "I do as well." Having now met Fujita a time or two, I am dying to know whether she did, indeed, have an affair with the Oriental, but of course, I wouldn't dream of asking outright.

The other women—Kiki in particular—dislike her. Treize, a kind person by nature and self-described observer of psychology, opined that Jeanne had a *bouleversement*—a shattering experience—as a child and that this explains her remoteness. Kiki— who I think speaks from jealousy—believes no such thing. "*Elle est folle, complétement cinglée. Un vrai vol-au-vent!*" A real fruit-cake is, I think, the translation. Insanity, Kiki believes, runs in the Hébuterne family, though how she would know this is beyond me. At any rate, Jeanne seemed content to gather flowers and grasses, arranging them in a pretty bouquet she presented to Lucy.

Kiki, of course, had to be more outrageous than anyone else. She posed on the beach in a most risqué fashion and I noticed something very odd about her; she has no pubic hair. At first, I thought she might shave her private parts, like North African women are said to do, but this is not the case. There are traces of shadow, but this is because she applies *charcoal* down there!

I've come to like Kiki, but she does thrive on the indiscreet. We were hardly out of the car when she asked me, "*Et James? Tu l'as baisé?*" Of course I misunderstood her question. In French, a baiser is a kiss. I thought she had asked whether I'd ever kissed James, and I admitted that I had, but only once at my party after drinking too much champagne. Treize, who was listening to the conversation, nudged me with her elbow and whispered in English. "I think she mean, you have fuck him?"

I'm sure I turned crimson from head to toe, but I also learned a valuable lesson in French grammar. *Un baiser*—the noun—means a kiss. *Baiser*—the verb—means, well, *fucking*... I wanted to set the record straight, to correct the impression Kiki must have had of me, but by the time Treize had explained the nuances, Kiki was in the ocean pretending to be a whale and spouting a thin stream of water from a gap between her teeth.

Treize gave us quite a scare. One forgets that her slim figure is that of a dedicated athlete and that she is a professional physical educator. At one point, she took to the water and began swimming away from the beach. We paid little attention, until Jeanne uncharacteristically spoke up.

Lucy was about to drive to the village to seek the local police—there is a dangerous undertow, and drownings are not all that uncommon—when we spotted someone floating motionless in the water. My heart stopped—I was certain tragedy had struck. Then the figure moved and began stroking in the Australian crawl fashion. Soon, Treize stepped from the water, shaking moisture from her hair and vastly amused at our consternation. She has been swimming since she was five, she explained, and is training to cross the British Channel unaided.

During the late afternoon it began to rain; a *crachin*, more mist than drops. We repaired to the house for a game of royal auction bridge. I am still learning the rules. The men played chess and checkers, and, liberally fueled with Pernod, accused each other good-naturedly of cheating and lying.

I am relieved that Frederick chose not to come. His presence would have darkened my mood. He claimed to need time to prepare for his business trip but I suspect the only business at hand is opium, upon which he is becoming increasingly dependent. Strangely, it does not seem to affect him when he is pursuing professional interests. I have listened to him expound quite intelligently on coming trends, and there is no doubt he has a touch for commerce. In the brief months we have been here, he has maximized profit upon profit, seemingly with no reversals. There is a constant exchange of cables between him and his father, and from other marketers in England, Canada, Holland, and Germany. Our bank accounts are healthy, so much so that he has opened another two, one in Switzerland, the other in London.

Even so, the opium is always there. We had a serious set-to a few days before my departure when I walked into the apartment one afternoon to find him asleep on the floor next to a spilled cup of tea.

The place gave off the sweet stench I've come to recognize and so dislike, and he had dropped his pipe and burned a jagged hole in the carpet. I shook him awake, and when he did not respond quickly enough, I poured the tea on his face. He bounded to his feet, furious and dripping, but I don't know which of us was the angriest. He stupidly denied using the drug when the evidence was obvious. I found his cache of opium (or at least one of them; he probably has several) and flushed it down the toilet. He turned white and for a moment I thought he might strike me. I could see him struggling to regain his composure and, to his credit, he did.

Then he lectured me on the benefits of opium, and that made me even more irascible. Hearing Frederick speak of the greats with whom he shares his addiction was too much, and mentioning Jean Cocteau as the apotheosis of wisdom was the last straw. I said something to the effect that his idol probably buggered small children, and would he (Frederick) follow that example as well?

He stormed out of the apartment without his raincoat, although it was pouring, and did not return until very late that night, quite drunk. He slept in his office and was gone when I rose the next morning.

I don't know what I shall do. Obviously, our union is a failure. I suppose getting a divorce is not out of the question, but initiating such proceedings so soon after our vows would be inappropriate.

Frederick and Cocteau appear to be estranged as well. Cocteau is presently in Tangiers, according to Kiki, who knows him well. "Probably," and here she made an obscene gesture with the index of one hand and a closed fist, "with little Arab boys."

Frederick has not mentioned him as often as he used to, though he did receive an unsigned postcard from Morocco bearing the picture of a handsome young Tuareg.

Frederick has not suggested divorce, and neither will I. James offered to make funds available to me, if it came to a separation. I thanked him for his kindness but told him I had no interest in becoming a kept woman. The comment, though made in jest, flustered him, which was not my intention.

Money is not an issue; I am not afraid of becoming poor. I have sold a few more stories to the *Tribune*, and I have standing invitations to model. There are opportunities for American women in Paris and these increase as my French improves, so I am not morose. Today I am surrounded by friendship and the beauty of the coast, and it is difficult to feel sad when I witness Per Krohg, dancer, artist, wit, and supreme accordionist, belting out the seafaring chanteys of his alleged Viking forebears.

We have done some touristy things. One day, Per led us to a small one-room church tucked in a hollow. He made a great show of telling us we would be amazed at what the church would reveal, but I think "disgusted" is a better word. When we arrived there, Per enlisted James's aid in moving the pews to expose a trap door set in the dusty floor. There was a large iron ring attached, and after a mighty heave, the door swung open amid a cloud of dust. Per shone a battery-powered light into the hole and to our horror we saw the mummified remains of a small man in armor, who Per claims was a crusader. I could tell that James was taken aback, and I suspect more than one of us thought Per's amusement sacrilegious. I think he would have jumped into the grave had James not held him back. According to village legend, the crusader arises from his entombment twice a year and visits the chateau, where he once lived, to make sure all is in order. Per said the chateau's owner claims to have seen the crusader wandering the dark halls at midnight. Some locals use the ghost as a threat when their children do not behave.

James has done some colorful landscapes, but he ran out of both yellow and green paint, so his skies look somewhat grayish. Per, who apparently moved his entire atelier with him from Paris, is at work on something mysterious. He rises before dawn, paints until sunrise, then covers his creation with a large piece of burlap. I gather he sleeps only a few hours, believing life is too short for any part of it to be spent comatose. He promises to reveal all before we leave.

Treize led us twice in physical exercise. We bounced up and down like so many marionettes, touched our toes, breathed deeply through our noses and exhaled through our mouths to get the maximum benefit of the country air. We engaged in a tug of war (the men won, of course), hopped about the courtyard on one foot, and did jumping jacks, which require some coordination. Then we ran around the house four times and sat down to an enormous breakfast of cheese, salted herring, ham and eggs that, Treize said, negated all our efforts. I have noticed that she eats quite sparsely; mostly vegetables, which she claims are all man was ever meant to consume. Modi disagrees, and once said that if God had not wanted man to eat animals, he would not have made them out of meat—a difficult argument to refute.

Picasso arrived unannounced in a Mercer automobile driven by Francis Picabia. The latter I do not know at all, save that he claims to be an anarchist. James told me Picabia funds a magazine called *Littérature* published by a number of poets, including Aragon, whom I sort of like. (I once heard him read some of his poems from what he calls 'a future collection' to be entitled *Feu de Joie*.) They were driving a circuitous route from Paris to Nice and heard Per and Lucy were in the area.

I'm afraid it turned into a poor afternoon for Picasso. He arrived precisely as Per and some of his Norse friends were choosing sides for a *grande bataille* where Per said he would demonstrate Viking martial arts. They were one man short for the shirted army (it was shirts versus bare chests), and Picasso volunteered, squaring his shoulders and jutting out his chin. Each man was armed with a stick (a sword) and the idea was that they would duel until one or the other side gave up. Per began and promptly defeated four foes (he was very graceful and enjoyed using his dancing skills to avoid the thrusts.) Picasso sought to employ trickery, and rushed Per when the latter was not looking. Per, sensing movement, swung his 'sword' in a great arc that caught Picasso just above the left ear. The Spaniard dropped to the ground like a bag of potatoes and left less than an hour later in a great huff, with a large welt on his head. Per claims the blow was an accident, but I detected a small smile on his face.

The childishness of these men astounds me. James insisted on taking part in the battle and did so with infantile glee, waving his weapon in the air and grunting like an orangutan. He acquitted himself proudly, but later confessed he had been number two on the fencing team at his college.

The mealtime English lessons are proceeding well. James and I have created a curriculum for lunch and dinner. At midday, we speak of the news and encourage our Nordic hosts to discuss the events of the week. At night, the conversation turns to the arts and is always more lively. Then out comes the accordion and later the dance lessons.

James is not particularly agile, but we have been complimented for our rendition of the Argentinian Tango.

Per is always encouraging my dance partner to be less stiff and formal with me.

"You are making luff," Per says, "yah? Standing up, you make luff to each other, you use the music for rhythm, for movement, like this! Like Norsemen and Valkyries!" And he grabs his willing Lucy, and sweeps her off her feet, slings her this way and that while she laughs wildly. James has tried mightily to replicate the moves but succeeds only in making me feel like a rag doll. Still, he has already mastered several dances in that inimitably serious American way. He frowns, he concentrates, his steps are precisely what they should be, and yet they lack grace. His wooden movements make the others laugh, and he takes it in good spirit.

I really do like him.

Chapter 37

Frederick knew he was not the only man scouring the French country-side on behalf of American "pharmacists." On the eve of the Volstead Act that would officially prohibit drinking alcohol in the United States, U.S. businessmen or their representatives sought to purchase massive quantities of liquor from any source on the Continent.

Frederick did his research well and realized quickly that the U.S. had inadvertently created a seller's market in Europe, with inflated prices and diminishing supplies. Greek villages saw a run on ouzo. A traveling silk trader by the name of Spyros Metaxas proudly told Frederick about cornering the market for a Greek liqueur, and offered a good deal on a thousand cases. Frederick agreed and they sealed the contract with a handshake and a glass of the trader's product. Frederick gagged, coughed, and his eyes watered. The dealer laughed and poured another glass.

Travelers returning from Spain and Portugal told of shortages of brandy and Port wine. In Scotland and Ireland, local producers sold out their stock, much to the displeasure of local consumers who, on several occasions, burned down pubs in protest. In Italy, the harsh *grappa* ran out. In northern France, Cognac, Armagnac, Cointreau, Cinzano, Byrrh, Benedictine, calvados, and every other sort of liqueur vanished. In the south, supplies of Pernod, Ricard and anisette ran dangerously low or disappeared.

Not wanting to travel alone, Frederick lured a young American studying French literature at the Sorbonne away from his classes with promises of extraordinarily high pay.

Alan Stabler spoke French fluently, was acquainted with the country's geography, and knew how to drive and repair a car. Even more important, he was a self-described oenophile and cognac expert with excellent references—a letter from La Rotonde's owner, Victor Libion, stating in the most flowery of language that Monsieur Stabler had an uncanny knowledge of wine and liqueurs for one so young, particularly for an American.

Storehouses in Paris were already depleted, so Frederick and Alan rented an extravagant Panhard 10 horsepower Coupe de Ville automobile and began visiting local producers and suppliers.

For the right price, anything was available. The sellers almost always smiled, offered a glass of the local product, then shook their heads when Prohibition was mentioned. "*C'est de la folie...*Why not ask people to stop breathing?" Deals were finalized with a handshake and a down payment. In a week, Frederick had lined up a three-month supply—12,000 cases—of varied products. He had paid outrageous prices by European standards, but still stood to make an immense profit once he resold the stock to George Remus, the Michigan pharmacist.

As they drove through the countryside from vineyard to vineyard, Alan, a collector of French trivia, sought to educate Frederick.

"There are some 150,000 cafés in France. I find that amazing—that's one for every twenty-five inhabitants. The average Frenchman consumes almost six gallons of hard liquor a year, and almost sixty gallons of wine."

The statistic did not surprise Frederick, who thought most Frenchmen were born drunks.

On occasion, Frederick found Stabler's encyclopedic knowledge tedious. "The Beaujolais is only seven miles long and thirty-five miles wide. The four thousand vineyards produce 100 million bottles of wine annually. Can you believe that? And some of the growers believe in a few years, they'll be able to double production."

If Frederick was bored by the recitations, Stabler failed to notice. "There are nine *crus* in the Beaujolais region," he listed them, pronouncing the names with care. "Brouilly and Côte de Brouilly—you have to be careful and not confuse the two—Chenas, Moulin-à-Vent—that means windmill—Chiroubles and Juliénas, which was named after Julius Caesar."

"That's only six." Frederick was driving the Panhard at a steady sixty kilometers per hour. The car was noisy, uncomfortable, and emitted a foul exhaust that soiled his clothing. Still, he liked its looks. It had a certain panache.

"I didn't think you were paying attention. There's also Fleury, Morgon, and Saint-Amour."

"Which is the best?"

Stabler thought for a moment. "That's hard to say. Last year it was the Chiroubles. I only had a bottle or two but it was very good. This year it seems to be a toss-up between the Fleury and the Moulin-à-Vent."

"Well then," Frederick guided the car through a series of potholes, held the vehicle steady as a large truck passed them, "let's go get some."

They bought two thousand cases of each Beaujolais from the owner of a minor chateau in need of repairs. The man was curious. "I thought Americans drank beer, not wine."

Frederick answered through Alan. "Tell him that Americans will drink almost anything and are willing to pay a high price for it."

They stayed at inelegant hotels and ate inelegant foods. Frederick learned to order an omelet at nearly every meal but Alan made it a point to sample the local cuisine. He ate veal head, tripe, blood sausage, kidneys, cow brains, and sheep stomachs with relish. His favorite dish was a ghastly mess of offal and onions bathed in a brown, swampy sauce. More than once, Frederick came close to gagging.

"I don't see how you can tolerate this stuff. It's vile, truly beyond repulsive."

Stabler ignored Frederick and devoured whatever was placed before him. "I'm from Colorado. I was raised on Rocky Mountain oysters. Had 'em every Sunday after church. Do you know what Rocky Mountain oysters are?"

Frederick shook his head.

"Bull balls."

In Macon, they found the young widow of a grower killed during the war who had cached several hundred bottles of absinthe in her barn and cellar. They bought her entire stock, and when they left the overjoyed woman, both men had traces of lipstick on their cheeks.

As they rejoined the main highway, Stabler pointed to the road's shoulder. "Artemisia absinthium."

Frederick looked, saw nothing unusual.

"Wormwood. That's what it's called in the U.S." He pointed again. "Those small yellow flowers over there. That's what the absinthe is made from, along with anise seed. It's illegal, you know."

Frederick didn't. "But everybody drinks it. It's everywhere…"

"Drink it or not, it's been illegal since 1915 here in France. 1908 in Switzerland. There was a massacre in the countryside in Savoie. A peasant killed his entire family with an ax. Chopped them to pieces. Five children and his wife. He claimed it was because he'd been drinking absinthe."

"That's like saying they should ban cars because there have been accidents."

Stabler shrugged. "All sorts of experts claimed absinthe can cause delusions, insanity, sterility, and moral debilitation. So they made its manufacture illegal. But, obviously, people still produce it. The thing is, if it's not distilled properly, it can kill people, particularly the elderly, folks with weak hearts…"

"Absinthe makes the heart grow fonder," Frederick said.

Stabler smiled, nodded. "That's not original… In any case, you're going to have to find an alternate way of shipping it out. You certainly won't be able to go through French customs with it."

While having lunch at a café overlooking the Saône, Stabler had a discreet conversation with the establishment's owner, and Frederick saw a bundle of franc notes change hands. After their meal, the owner led them to a farmhouse and introduced them to a swarthy man who could expertly counterfeit labels on a small printing press he kept in his cellar. More money was exchanged and the man suggested the bottles be labeled as Pernod. He would forge labels, complete with a seal from the mayor of Taragonia, where Pernod Fils manufactured absinthe-free liquor that tasted like the real thing but was distilled without wormwood.

They shook hands all around, were offered and accepted *un coup de blanc pour la route.*

Later, as they stopped for dinner, Stabler said, "Did you ever hear of a painter called Picasso? He did a work called 'A Glass of Absinthe.' I saw it at a gallery. Very striking."

Frederick couldn't resist. "My wife knows him. He came to our apartment a few months ago."

Stabler was stunned. "You *know* Picasso?"

Frederick nodded. "He has a very large nose."

Throughout the week-long trip, Frederick smoked his opium. Though he tried to hide his use from the younger man, Stabler recognized the odor.

"I've tried it, you know. Several times. It's very popular among the American students here. I don't particularly like it. Makes me feel sleepy and gives me awful dreams. I don't understand the attraction at all." Which gladdened Frederick's heart, as he had no intention of sharing his diminishing supply with anyone.

The first shipment of alcohol would leave Le Havre less than ten days after Frederick purchased it. It would cross the Atlantic in a little more than a week, then be quickly off-loaded in Boston. The precious cases of bottles would then be trucked to Michigan where Mr. Remus' agents would distribute them to eager clients.

In time, eight cases of absinthe would be delivered to Charlie DiMarco, owner of several speakeasies in Indiana and Illinois.

Chapter 38

The men agreed: Something about sea air brought adolescence to the forefront. During the past days, they had behaved like children without parental supervision—staying up late, eating and drinking too much, lazing in the sun, shouting, cursing, and speaking ill of both the living and the dead. James Johnson found it delightful.

The area had not suffered much from the war. Fruit, fish, cheeses and vegetables were abundant and cheaper than in the North. The guests stuffed themselves with a cornucopia of fares, including local sausages, patés, and the Swedish *rollmops* Per and Lucy had brought with them in an ice chest, along with several bottles of aquavit.

Everyone knew Easter's marriage was floundering, although they took care never to speak of it when she was in the room. Frederick, of course, had opted not to come; he'd made no effort to hide his dislike for Easter's friends, and they couldn't imagine him thrashing about with a wooden saber or frolicking in the sea.

The water was frigid, the sun warm, and the weather exceptional. There was always something to do, and Per and Lucy were wonderful hosts. Johnson had learned a few dance steps he would never dream of attempting in public, and the Krohgs' command of English was improving. It amazed him when he realized, a week into his vacation, he hadn't once thought of the war.

A few days into his stay, he received three letters forwarded from Paris by Mme. Bertrand. The concierge had also attached a note from William Thaw, the Escadrille pilot, who proposed he and Johnson meet at Johnson's apartment the day after his return.

Johnson had recognized the handwriting of the first dispatch immediately yet it took him several minutes to open the envelope. This was only the second missive he'd received from Marie since the canceled nuptials. It was a long letter, with news from many fronts.

Her father had died. Marie, an only child, was now an immensely wealthy young woman.

She had married. The man's name was Robert Shelley Lightfoot, a stockbroker with an important firm in New York, and they'd met during last year's Harvest Ball. The best man at the wedding was a Republican Congressman by the name of La Guardia. Robert Shelley Lightfoot was eighteen years her senior. The courtship was rapid and Marie was expecting their first child in October. They lived in a brownstone row house on Washington Square and she was a member of several charity boards.

Mr. Lightfoot belonged to the American Defense Society and Marie was a leading light of its ladies' auxiliary.

"Like all good citizens of this most favored nation, she wrote, *we are anxious, even alarmed, by the Bolshevik threat. We fear the very heart and soul of America are at risk, and so we have stopped going to the cinema. The film industry is a hotbed of communism, as everyone knows. The Red Menace threatens us all, and since Robert is in a position of authority, we are eternally vigilant."*

Johnson had shaken his head and smiled. Poor Marie. What would she think of this assembly of radicals, ne'er do wells, malcontents, complainers—artists all? It amused him that this woman who, when he knew her, could not name the current American president, should so suddenly be well-versed in the evils of Communism.

She bore him no ill will, she wrote, and now realized that his flight was perhaps the sanest of moves.

"Indeed, dear James, you have done me a great favor. Had we wed, I fear my life might have been spent in the shadow of your accomplishments. You are an artist, a decorated war hero, and I have little to show for my years. Thankfully, Robert is supportive of all my endeavors and allows me great leeway. I am forging a life of my own, a life of which I am quite proud, and I am confident that, all in all, everything turned out for the best."

So, she forgave him and, she added, hoped to see him next summer when she and Mr. Lightfoot toured Europe.

The second letter was from the *Societé Générale pour l'Identification des Soldats Inconnus*. Johnson had written to them some months ago asking, without much optimism, for their help in finding his brother Daniel. The *Societé's* charter was to help families identify and recover the remains of soldiers whose bodies were still missing. The very name of the *Societé* implied that it did not hold out much hope that missing fighters might still be alive, and, of course, it was concerned primarily with *French* soldiers. Johnson knew that four hundred thousand soldiers were missing at the end of the war; a staggering number.

The letter requested he visit their office in person upon his return to Paris. They had questions about Daniel. Johnson had already told what he knew of his brother's last days to at least a dozen *fonctionnaires;* he had no objection to doing it once more. It couldn't hurt.

The last missive was from M. Lefebvre, the mailman. It was in English, and in spite of a few grammatical errors, remarkably well drafted. Formal, an exact translation of the French and precisely in the style of the textbooks Mr. Lefebvre had no doubt studied as a youth, the note informed Johnson that the mailman's pursuit of Mme. Colombini was going well; that he had so far managed to repel his Corsican adversary's attempts to reap Mme. Colombini's favors, and that Mme. Colombini had met his parents, who accepted her after making sure she was not—as her name might imply—Italian.

The mailman also hinted that they had consummated their relationship, though this tidbit was in such flowery language that Johnson thought he might be mistaken. The letter's last line noted that the concierge, Mme. Bertrand, had fallen and twisted her ankle while cleaning the windows of a *rez-de-chaussée* apartment, or so she claimed. M. Lefebvre thought she was actually standing on a rickety chair, peeping into the apartment of a new tenant when the chair collapsed.

Only Modi's worsening health cast a shadow over Johnson's holiday. The Italian had lost a great deal of weight and ate little. The sun brought no color to his face, and he drank without respite. He confided to Johnson that almost all the money from the sale of his paintings to the New York gallery was gone, though when pressed he could not recount how he had spent it, or where. He and Jeanne still lived in the fourth-floor garret on Rue de la Grande Chaumière, a sad and decrepit place. Easter spent some time talking with Modi, and came away obviously depressed. The Italian often lapsed into reveries in the midst of conversation and referred to "taking a boat to a miraculous country." Once Johnson found him some distance from the house eating green grapes from a vine and talking in Italian to a flock of ducks.

Jeanne was of little assistance. She had given up everything for him and been disowned for it by her bourgeois parents. She believed Modi was a god, had often spoken of him as a being whom life would not violate, but she was wrong. Life was indeed taking its toll, though what it was that so tormented his Italian friend, Johnson simply did not know.

Johnson feared for Modi and worried over Jeanne. If something were to happen to Modi, he reflected, God only knew what Jeanne might do.

Chapter 39

Berck-sur-Mer, Tuesday, August 12, 1919

The appropriate words—even written—fail me, so I'll be blunt: James is not as large as Frederick. His *thing* is far shorter than my husband's and has a noticeable bend to the right. And his pubic area is not as hairy as I would have thought.

Putting James and Frederick in the same sentence, considering the context, seems wanton, yet I do not feel wanton at all. In fact, bearing in mind that it was I who initiated the event (though in my defense, I can attest that I did not plan it), I feel strangely fulfilled and at peace.

I suppose I knew all along this would happen. Surely Fate orchestrated this encounter. I know I shall not be punished for violating the trust of my marriage, since, indeed, very little of that "trust" even remains. Frederick betrayed me first—and with a man! This may or may not be a valid defense of my actions, but, as said Monsieur Prudhomme, "It is my opinion, and I share it."

This is what happened. Yesterday morning, Per announced that he knew of another site where the remains of several Crusaders could be viewed. Brancusi, Satie, and Modi—all morbid male voyeurs—decided this was indeed worth a trip. Kiki, Treize, and some of the other women were at the market buying food for the coming few days, and James had left earlier in the morning to sketch a meadow that had caught his fancy. I declined to join the men's grotesque journey. When they left, I found myself alone with Modi's Jeanne.

For a time, we sat in the sunshine. Jeanne is not a talker, and though I tried to initiate conversation, she was at best monosyllabic. She said she missed her little daughter who was spending a month with some country cousins, and then the exchange limped to a halt. After some minutes, I became nervous in her presence. She is such a strange woman, so wraith-like and removed from reality; an otherworldly aura emanates from her. We shared an uneasy silence until she rose and shimmered off. Jeanne gathers flowers every day; this is her main activity. I assumed she was once again doing just that, and thought no more of it.

I dozed for a while and awoke sometime after noon, then decided to gather a picnic for two, thinking to surprise James who had now been gone several hours. I took a tablecloth, a bottle of wine, half a baguette, a bottle of mustard from Quiquempoix, a small round Camembert cheese, and some very good local ham. I knew the whereabouts of his meadow, and so, basket under one arm, I wended my way down the path and through the woods. It was a gorgeous day and amazingly quiet, as if Nature had decided the buzzing of crickets and the song of birds were the only accompaniment She desired. The colors were brighter than usual; a thousand shades of green against a cerulean sky with here and there a patch of Queen Anne's lace. The forest smelled of honeysuckle.

I saw James before he saw me.

He had removed his shirt and was sitting on the trunk of a long-fallen tree, his sketchpad on one knee. His shoulders were reddened from the sun. I could see his drawing hand moving in quick slashes, working the charcoal stick with authority. I was no more than fifteen yards from him when he moved suddenly, cursed and slapped his shoulder with his free hand. An eternity passed. Then James scratched his shoulder with the charcoal stick, leaving traces of black on his skin. I was strangely enthralled, feeling we could stay this way forever, a *tableau vivant* frozen in time, when something in me blossomed—a thought, an emotion, a desire.

I crept away silently, leaving the basket behind and retracing my steps. When I was forty meters away, I began circling to his left and soon I had made a half-circle; in front of him but still out of sight.

How can I account for what I did next? I cannot, save to say that it felt natural, in the spirit of the moment.

I removed all my clothes but my stockings and shoes, leaving my skirt, blouse, petticoat and undergarments in a pile on the ground. I stepped onto the path, but James did not move or look up, still focusing his gaze on his drawing. I picked up a small stick that lay at my feet and threw it in his direction. It landed close enough that his concentration wavered. He looked up, saw me.

He dropped the sketchbook and charcoal, his mouth a wide O of surprise. I may have smiled. He stood, approached, and stopped just out of arm's reach, swallowed, and blinked. I said, "I brought lunch..."

He nodded, as if this were the most natural thing in the world, but maintained his distance. We stood across from each other for a moment, awkward, tense. I felt powerful under James's gaze, desirable, desirous.

"James," I said.

He enveloped me in his arms, his hands stroking my back and buttocks. We would have lain down amidst the twigs, flowers and grass, but I bade him wait. I gently disentangled himself from his embrace, retrieved the picnic basket, spread the tablecloth on the earth. Then I unfastened his belt and drew him to me.

We lay together for a while, side by side, our naked selves sharing a heat warmer than the sun, lips exploring shoulders and necks, and then he rolled on top of me. It was the gentlest of penetrations. I closed my eyes and lost myself in his motion. His breathing came hard in my ear and his perspiration ran between my breasts. I thought I heard a sound not ours and opened an eye; I caught a flash of scarlet, a wash of white. Though I did not mean to, I screamed.

Jeanne Hébuterne, her wide empty eyes smiling, stood over us, a bouquet of assorted wildflowers cradled in her arms. James's thrusts intensified. I felt him lunge, stiffen, pulse. Jeanne's expression did not change. I turned my head to speak and in that barest instant, Jeanne was gone.

James must have thought me addled. I ran back into the forest, losing a shoe. I gathered my clothes, slipped into them haphazardly, fastening every other button on my blouse. When I returned, he was sitting on the tablecloth clad only in his underwear. I would have been willing to believe in apparitions, phantasms, specters or whatever spirits had it not been for the bouquet of wildflowers Jeanne had left behind.

James claims he never saw her. When I pointed to the dropped spray of blossoms, he said, "Maybe she left them behind on purpose. As a gift." He may be right.

I think he was ready to perform the act again but I was not.

When we returned to the house, everyone was engaged in a madcap game of croquet save for Modi, who sat on a lawn chair with Jeanne nestled on his lap. She glanced in our direction but her gaze swept unhindered past us to a swarm of swallows circling a nearby apple tree.

James took my hand in his and squeezed it, whispered, "Everything Jeanne sees and knows, she keeps inside. She will never speak of us, even to Modi."

Later that night, James told me he loved me and he hugged me hard enough to crush my ribs. We sat outside together watching the stars and listening to the hum of a million insects. He was very quiet, and when I asked him if something was the matter, he shrugged, sighed, said, "I'm a bit scared. The last time, it ended badly."

I promised him this time it wouldn't, and meant it.

CHAPTER 40

In two days, the holiday would be over, and they would return to Paris. Johnson thought this good—he was both anxious and eager to spend some private hours with Easter.

He asked her to move into his apartment upon their return to Paris, and though she assured him she was touched by his offer, she refused. Easter admitted she and Frederick shared nothing but their lodging, but said she nevertheless felt she had to give her marriage one last chance. She announced she would tell Frederick he must give up the opium, and if he refused, she would leave him.

"God forgive me," said Johnson, "but I pray his addiction will be stronger than his sentiments."

He had found their stay idyllic, with Per, Lucy, Modi and his mate, the entire motley crew of Swedes, Danes, and other Norsemen, Kiki and her cohorts. Their thirst for life and enthusiasm was immature, insatiable, and precious. Not a day went by without some reason for celebration, some spontaneous special event. The day before their departures, Treize had organized a field day, with awards given for both best and worst feats. In the evening, Kiki and Lucy, accompanied by Per on the accordion and Satie on the violin, minced through renditions of the latest popular songs. Many had found Satie's music disconcerting, Johnson among them, but after a few minutes he began hearing subtleties, undercurrents, and charming innuendos. Soon he found himself laughing, thoughtful, sad; Satie's composition rang in him a host of emotions, and one brief off-the-cuff composition Satie titled *Les Hasards de la Vie* left Johnson pondering exactly that—the vagaries of life.

183

As he listened, he'd watched Modi and his Jeanne, sitting together on a low-slung divan. They, certainly, lived in a world of their own, and right now it didn't look like a happy one. Kiki, he knew, was orphaned in her heart, and when caught in a bad moment the deepest sorrows of childhood were written on her face. Three of the Danes bore wounds from the war. Like Johnson, Per had spent freezing nights when he served in the Vosges with a volunteer ambulance corps. All had lost close friends in battle. Easter's mother and father had both succumbed to influenza in a month. Even in the midst of all this joy and vigor for life, there were lingering sorrows.

Shortly before the group's last meal in the villa, Kiki had told Johnson in confidence that she'd run into Frederick just before taking the train to the beach, and that Easter's husband looked prosperous, though unfocused. *"Un regard de drogué"* were her words, and if anyone was familiar with the wasted visage of drug users, it was her.

They would be back in Paris on Saturday morning. He missed the city, missed Mme. Bertrand, his busybody concierge. He missed M. Lefebvre's adventures and was eager to know how the mailman fared with Mme. Colombini. Most of all, he was eager to return to the city with Easter, to begin sharing with her some of the day-to-day humdrum of existence.

Johnson was also curious about meeting Mr. Thaw of the Lafayette Escadrille, who would probably quiz him about his brother. He wondered if he should tell Mr. Thaw the truth and say that Daniel was a fearsome bully who had tormented Johnson with unabashed glee all his life. Perhaps not.

While at the beach he'd dreamed of Daniel, big as life, wearing goggles and the leather coveralls favored by pilots. His enormous, mean laugh filled all the space in Johnson's mind, drowning out his surroundings.

CHAPTER 41

There was a cockroach in the cell, and Landru fed it crumbs of bread moistened with his own saliva. He decided early on that the insect was not trainable—it never ate from his hand—but he liked the company of a creature so inferior. His attorney, Monsieur de Moro-Giafferi, visited him daily, and never with good news. Each day, there was more evidence against him, each day more of the populace hated him. Landru's imprisonment was the talk of Paris and indeed, of all villages and cities in France. The prosecutor would, naturally, want Landru's head. Landru thought him an inferior creature too.

So Landru read, thought, watched, memorized small events such as the exact time of the guard change, the size of the laundry cart, the width and length of the bed sheets he was issued. He smiled at the girl with the laundry cart, and she responded shyly with a smile of her own. He befriended guards, some of whom, he knew from overheard conversations, were misogynists to the bone and who secretly admired him. One young *gendarme* fresh from the country sought Landru's advice: What did Monsieur Landru think of the young man bringing his fiancée to Paris? Would she be safe here? Would she find work? She was just a farm girl of little experience. Landru pondered the questions a full day before responding and, in the end, suggested that no, she should not come here. The young man should amass some savings and return to the land. Paris was a sewer, a cesspool of crime and danger, a pit that devoured young farm girls. The *gendarme* was grateful and shook Landru's hand.

Landru watched everything.

He saw that there were seldom very many dirty sheets in the cart, and that a small man, huddled, might fit beneath these sheets and not be noticed. At night, when the guards were dozing, he quietly practiced making a life-size dummy of sheets and blankets. He reread the hundreds of letters and postcards sent to him, some with death threats, others with marriage proposals. Three letters in particular he kept in the middle of the pile. They were from a woman who had loved him, one he had spared because she had nothing worth dying for, and he had particularly liked the way her legs became dainty ankles. She had smelled wonderfully good when they were together, and when he was on her and in her, the seriousness in her face was fetching. Their union had occurred at her home and not at his villa, and he did not consider himself a cruel man, so she had lived. Her name was Brigitte Bonjean, she was a part-time comedienne who sang in cafés or worked as a chorus girl in out-of-the-way musical comedies. In his own way, Landru had come to love her.

Chapter 42

Frederick's reactions to traveling through France surprised him. He didn't like the French and sensed they did not care for him either, yet he was developing a grudging admiration for the country itself. He enjoyed the villages, even as he could not fathom how people could live there. The grayness of the lesser cities pleased him, risen as they were, fully formed from the granite quarries dotting the landscape. Over a period of days and with Alan Stabler's constant running commentary, Frederick began to better understand what brought workers to the fields, vineyards, and wineries.

He preferred to let Stabler initiate the bargaining, but before the deal was done, he often found himself haggling in halting French with the small-town *commerçants*. He seldom won, but began to develop a certain pride in being able to hold his own with the locals. His proudest moment during the trip was when he persuaded a bar owner to sweeten their deal by throwing in two cases of local Armagnac. He repeated and rehashed the details of the transaction with such enthusiasm that even the patient Stabler begged for silence.

After almost a full ten days on the road, Frederick decided it was time to return to Paris. There would be endless paperwork and forms to fill out in order to get the shipment of alcohols and wines ready for George Remus. The French authorities, Frederick had discovered, had no issue with sending drink to a place where it was illegal, but they did want the travel of every bottle exhaustively documented.

On the last day of the trip, as they reached the outskirts of the capital, Stabler said, "I'll never leave here. I'll never go back. I'm going to apply for French citizenship."

The conviction in the younger man's voice surprised Frederick. "Whatever for? A boy like yourself? You're in the best of both worlds. You're in Europe, but should anything happen, the U.S. will be there to take care of you."

Stabler shook his head. "I don't want it to take care of me." He paused. "I love Paris! Do you know that the city is built on six million graves? *Six million!*"

Frederick rolled his eyes; another lecture on Paris. Stabler continued, undaunted. "In 1786, the authorities started transferring the bones they found whenever a new building was excavated, and they're still doing it. All the skeletons go to a quarry that's under the Place Denfert-Rochereau. I went there once; it wasn't frightening at all. A field of bones—tibias, skulls, ribs…Do you know that only one Parisian in five is actually born there? One in ten has a Parisian parent, and only one in twenty-five has two native Parisian parents. The real Parisians are like a very small tribe."

"What does that have to do with giving up your American citizenship?" Frederick asked.

Stabler smiled. "I don't have a clue."

They stopped in Saint-Maur-des-Fossés, just outside Paris, because, "Rabelais lived there," Stabler said, "And I've always wanted to see his house. You've heard of Rabelais, haven't you?"

Frederick had not.

"My god, Frederick. *Rabelais!* Gargantua! Pantagruel! Tasteless gross excess! Doesn't that ring a bell? Even in Chicago, higher education must teach you something to earn its name."

"In Chicago, they taught us useful things," Frederick answered. "Like business, profit, enterprise; the American trio." He stopped the Panhard Coupe de Ville in front of a bistro. "There's a restaurant. Let's stop and eat."

The food was simple country fare. They ate and drank in silence until Stabler whispered, "You have an admirer."

Frederick looked up from his dessert.

Seated two tables away, a handsome youth stared at him with unabashed boldness. He was slim, dark-haired, cradling an open book of loose-leaf pages. In his right hand was a fountain pen. There were ink stains on his thumb and index finger. Frederick returned the stare for a moment with feigned disinterest. The young man rose, approached, stuck out his hand.

"Radiguet," he said, "Raymond. You are Americans?" His accent was thick, provincial, and inescapably French. He pulled out a chair and sat down. "I speak English. I write French." He pointed to his notebook. "Poetry."

A waiter appeared with a glass, looked questioningly at Frederick who nodded. The waiter placed the glass before the young man and poured wine from the carafe.

"Poetry," the young man said again, and drained the glass.

Frederick peered more closely as Stabler broke into rapid French. The boy had a helmet of black hair that rose in spikes from his head, a prominent nose, and a Spanish mouth. His eyes were dull green, his skin pale and unblemished.

"I go to Paris," he said. "I go with you?"

The boy was looking at Frederick as if reading his every thought.

Frederick shivered imperceptibly. "Yes. Of course."

The ride to Paris was punctuated with Radiguet reading from his notebook as Stabler heaped praise. Once or twice, Frederick said, "*Très bien! Bravo!*" without knowing exactly what he was bravo-ing.

That same evening, back in the capital, Frederick had Stabler drop Radiguet off at a small hotel near the Bois de Vincennes. He paid for a week's rent for the boy, and gave him enough money for a meal and a haircut. Later that night he returned to the hotel, but the boy was out, so Frederick left a note suggesting they meet for lunch the next day.

CHAPTER 43

Easter and James shared a cab from the Gare St. Lazare. The return trip from the beach had afforded them a few hours together in a private compartment, and Easter had embarrassed him by suggesting they "do it" next time they traveled in such style. She'd been joking, and had to remind herself once again that his sense of risqué humor was marginal.

She unpacked quickly and found her diary.

*****

Paris, Monday, September 1, 1919

It was, at best, a strange homecoming. Frederick is traveling. I entered the apartment to find a woman of indeterminate age on her hands and knees in the kitchen, scrubbing the floor. She barely looked up at me as I stood over her, merely moved her bucket of soapy water from one spot to another. Her name, I learned, is Mathilde, and she is a Bretonne. When out in public, she wears the *coiffe* of her village and dresses all in black, although she is, I understand, not a widow. Frederick hired her as a housekeeper while I was gone.

I shouldn't be surprised. Frederick, in spite of his fussiness, is not the type to clean house. Still, Mathilde's appearance in our home surprised me, as Frederick and I had agreed that a live-in housekeeper was not a necessity. Yes, she is live-in, though her room is one of those top-floor twelve-by-twelve cubes, similar to the one where I set up *l'Atelier Paques*. How a grown person can live in such a cramped space I do not know, but Mathilde is grateful almost to the point of tears at being given work and a place to live. A brief conversation with her revealed that she feared being a burden to her family, and that she feels finding work here was miraculous.

She is a taciturn woman. Her husband and son, fishermen in Quimper, lost their boat during the war; she saves her money and can account for every *centime* she earns and spends. Every fourth weekend, she will take the Friday evening train from the Gare Montparnasse to St. Malo, then another train from St. Malo to Quimper, and return on Monday morning.

It's odd having someone usurp some of my duties. I am happy to give up washing windows and fighting the cobwebs, doing the dishes and making the bed, but I insist on purchasing the day's food and flowers, and on pursuing the small errands I've grown fond of.

James pressures me to file for divorce. "Everyone who knows Frederick is aware of his... preferences," James tells me. "Relationships have ended for far more picayune reasons. This is *Paris*, for God's sake."

James and I see each other daily, though we have not yet spent a full night together. I meet him most mornings for a *café au lait*, and yes, we have sex quite often, and it is delightful.

He has invited me numerous times to come and live with him. Once, he took me to a charming vacant apartment on the Rue Joseph Bara and said it was ours for the asking. I behaved badly that morning, encouraging his expectations by not dismissing the notion out of hand. Since then, I've told him that when I leave Frederick, I shall have to be on my own for a time. I am not sure James understands this, but it is important to me, and I insist upon it.

According to the editors of the *Chicago Tribune*, there is an unquenchable thirst in America for articles on France, particularly featuring Paris, Montmartre, Montparnasse, and their denizens. I have been asked to consider writing a regular column for the newspaper! The salary is minimal, but it is in dollars. It won't require much work and James encourages me; he is certain such articles could benefit our artist friends. I have made one attempt so far; my first foray was sordid and repulsive.

Two days ago, Modi came to see James about the sale of additional paintings to the New York gallery. While Modi was there, James mentioned my interest in drafting a series of articles for the American public on the lives of artists in Paris. Modi laughed, saying there was no lack of material. All artists, he said, himself included, were characters worthy of entire novels. He then asked if I was interested in meeting one of the more *outré* personalities; a man, he said, who would fascinate U.S. readers.

"His name," Modi told us, "is Chaïm Soutine. I know him well; we shared a studio for some time. He paints…" There he paused. I suppose I should have been forewarned by his careful choice of words. "He paints odd things. Chaïm is one of the Russians, born in Minsk. Jewish, like me. He came to Paris in 1913 and has been here since. If you write something about him, it may help his career."

James was listening to this description and added, "He *is* an unusual man. It might make a good tale."

When their business was concluded, Modi left James's apartment, promising to return the next day with his mysterious friend.

The following morning was rainy and dark. I was late getting to James's and, when I arrived, I found Modi, James, and a curiously disheveled little man wearing far-too-large trousers and a workman's shirt plastered to his ribs. Modi introduced me—it was indeed his Russian friend Chaïm Soutine—and the man seemed to shrink further into himself. At this point, Modi's features darkened, and he grabbed the smaller man and dragged him to an adjoining room. I heard muffled threats and muffled responses.

James shrugged his shoulders and whispered, "Soutine does not like publicity. He's a loner, but he's also broke and homeless, and a squatter in Modi's studio."

A moment later, the two returned. Modi said, "Chaïm is going to find a model. Would you like to go with him? You can ask him questions along the way."

I looked at James who once again shrugged. "I'll be busy most of the morning, darling. Why don't you go?"

We did. Soutine led the way to the Metro, and for a small man he walked very quickly. I bought tokens for the both of us, and we rode a train bound for La Villette, a section of the capital that I was not familiar with. I asked him a number of questions about his background, his family, his childhood years in Russia. His responses were hardly worth noting. He was born in 1893, studied at the Fine Arts School of Minsk, and has never had a studio of his own. His paintings have not sold well, though some weeks ago, he told me with a sad smile barely creasing his drooping features, he managed to sell one of his pieces "for the third time." When I asked him to explain this odd statement, he shook his head and fell silent again. I have since learned that this strange way of doing business is common among local artists, who see no harm in promising—and selling—any given work to several people at once. I am still not sure whether I have properly grasped the concept, but it has something to do with the work itself not being a creation *per se* but merely the physical representation of the intended idea, or something to that effect. I'm not sure what to make of this notion. When James made a duplicate of his portrait of me, he simply said he wanted a copy to keep after selling the original.

We reached our Metro stop in a half-hour's time, and Soutine again led the way. La Villette is an undistinguished working-class borough of gray homes and shops. There are very few trees, and if any parks exist there, I did not see them.

The area had a nasty smell to it, like meat and vegetables gone bad. My guide did not seem to notice the odor that grew ever stronger. Indeed, as the vile aroma became a stench, Soutine appeared more and more animated. He walked bent forward as if battling heavy winds, and his nondescript coat flapped behind him.

Soon, I had to hold a handkerchief to my mouth in order to breathe. Soutine took no notice. Then I heard sounds I recognized from childhood: the lowing of cows, the whinny of horses, and I was seized by a dreadful suspicion. I noticed the street's gutters were running red and infested by flies. The sound of animals came louder. Soutine came to a stop before a massive oaken door. He pushed it open to a scene from hell. He had taken me to a slaughterhouse.

There was a large courtyard, its cobblestones wet from a constant stream of water flowing from a fire hose manned by two adolescents. Two big men in bloody aprons and trousers led an elderly blindfolded horse forward. The animal must have smelled imminent death, for it bucked in spite of its age, but its efforts were no match for the two muscular handlers When the horse was stilled, a third man approached, bearing a massive sledgehammer. He stood in front of the blindfolded animal, raised the sledge above his head and brought it down with a grunt. The horse, struck once between the ears, dropped to its knees and keeled to its side. There was a moment's stillness. The man with the sledge unsheathed a small knife and deftly sliced a vein in the doomed animal's neck. Blood spurted, then pulsed. The fire hoses came into play. Then two other men wearing leather aprons used a block and tackle to wrestle the horse's carcass onto a gurney driven by a butcher.

The men spoke briefly to one another, and then the gurney rolled past us into the street.

Soutine looked at me oddly, as if he were judging my reactions to the horrific tableau. I refused to give him satisfaction and averted my eyes, still clutching my handkerchief to my nose.

Soon, a steer was led to the killing place. Soutine tugged at my coat sleeve and motioned me to follow him. The butchers were staring openly at us, their fat, mustached faces creased with leering grins. What to do? Should I follow the demented artist or bear the lewd attentions of the slaughter crew? I followed Soutine, and promised myself that I would have a few choice words for both James and Modi. I turned my head as the sledge swung down, tried not to hear the dull thud of death, the steer's final desperate exhalation.

Soutine led me to the cold room, where hundreds of flayed carcasses hung from hooks set in the ceiling. The floor was slick with blood. The buzzing of flies and a cacophony of chopping and hacking sounds deafened me. Here men with hatchets, cleavers, and monstrous knives dismembered the animal remains. I stood as close as I could to the door; it was vital that a patch of open sky remain visible. I was sure I would faint if the door were to close and seal me in this hellish place. Once again, I heard the thud of the sledge, the grunt of a slain beast. When I turned around, Soutine had vanished.

I must have remained rooted there for a very long time, trapped between two nightmares. Twice, men with red, dripping hands approached and attempted to make conversation, but I was mute.

When Soutine returned, there was excitement in his eyes. Again, he tugged at my sleeve and I heard him say, "This one. Over there. What do you think?"

I looked to where he was pointing, saw nothing but more carcasses. We wound our way, carefully stepping on raised planks of wood, until Soutine stopped.

"Here," he said. "This is it. It is not perfect, but given time, it will be."

It took me a moment to realize that the 'it' was the skinned and headless corpse of a steer. The animal's hind legs were spread apart obscenely. Sinews and fat glistened in the dim light. Soutine circled the carcass, slapping it, running his hands over bone, and squeezing flesh and tendon between his fingers, nodding his head. Soon, one of the butchers joined us. There was a bit of haggling, an exchange of bills.

Once mercifully outside and walking quickly away from the butchery, my revulsion turned to pity for this detestable little man. I wondered what kind of a tortured soul could lead one to paint such carnage. That, I now realize, is what Soutine does. His colors are deliberately ugly—blood, gore, offal—his compositions cruel and hard-hearted. The meat will hang in his atelier until it rots, and he will study its deterioration day by day, until it reaches the proper state of putrefaction. Then he will paint a portrait of it.

Soutine was cheerful now. He offered to buy me a glass of wine or a meal, but I claimed a prior commitment. He invited me to visit the borrowed place where he painted, and I promised I would though, of course, I have no intention of ever going there.

We parted company at the Metro entrance and Soutine surprised me by quickly kissing me on both cheeks and thanking me effusively for accompanying him. I watched him flap down the stairs to his train and was reminded of a small brown bat.

I wonder at his torment, and am glad it is not my own, for if a man chooses to depict such ugliness in a world where beauty is readily available, surely he is daily wrestling darkness.

Another event—far less unpleasant but just as odd—occurred recently. Jean Cocteau came to James's apartment. He asked me to work as his assistant for the time it takes to get *Le Boeuf sur le Toit* produced. His request took me so by surprise that I laughed. He misinterpreted my amusement.

"Is it because of Frederick? Is that why you mock me?"

I was surprisingly unoffended by his offer, or his presence in my home. I truly no longer care.

Cocteau was dressed nattily, in a very sharply cut suit and a lemon-yellow tie with light blue dots. He has small, almost womanish feet and is vain about them, telling others that small feet denote large intellects. His features are knife-like, and his hair erupts from his head in small tight curls. He was displeased, arms akimbo, impatiently tapping the toes of his expensive shoes.

"Because," he continued, "I had nothing to do with it, *rien du tout*. Frederick came to me, and—"

I cut him off. "Jean, what Frederick does is his own affair. I'm not involved. I worry about him, but I do not try to run his life. He seems to survive quite well without my ministrations."

Cocteau was silent for a moment then nodded. A somewhat feral look crept into his eyes.

"Then it is true? You and Frederick?" His hands moved like a magician's making a rabbit disappear. "*C'est fini?* And now, you and James..."

This time, James cut in. "...are the very best of friends, Jean. I would be grateful if we left it at that."

Cocteau nodded. "*Oui. Naturellement.*"

It was late in the afternoon. We walked to the Rotonde and sat at one of the minuscule round tables. Cocteau ordered a Ricard. James and I shared a pot of tea. Cocteau waved his hand, waited for a waiter to appear, and ordered some Madeleines. "*Comme Proust, n'est-ce pas?*" Then he smiled. We spoke of Proust for a while. I have never met the man, and am told he is a recluse. I confessed that I had never managed to read his work. "I get to page 35 and fall asleep," I said.

Cocteau found this hilarious. "Only an American would admit that! Such honesty! I envy it so much! Here in Paris, everyone claims to have read Marcel's work, but in truth, I do not know a single person who has. It makes me believe that if writers are sublime liars, readers are only slightly less dishonest. In truth, Marcel's great epic," he laughed, shook his head, "it is boring beyond comprehension, all this guilt and these meaningless memories. The *Chez Swann…Mon Dieu*! It is, how would you say, so very laborious! But a great *succès d'éstime*, that is certain."

Then he turned serious, lit a cigarette and inhaled deeply. "I am glad that neither of you bears me ill will," he said. "Especially you, Easter. Because, really, with Frederick…" He must have caught James's warning glance. He stopped, then added, "At any rate, Raymond and I…" I knew he was referring to Raymond Radiguet, a handsome young poet who has shared Jean's company for some time now. The joint subjects of my husband's dereliction and Cocteau's love life evanesced by mutual consent.

For some moments, we watched the pedestrian traffic pass. La Rotonde occupies an enviable location: the convergence of the Boulevards Raspail and Monparnasse, and the Rue de La Grande Chaumière and Rue Delambre. The American Girls' Club is nearby, and it's not unusual to see a bevy of U.S. beauties flit by, speaking rapid-fire English and eliciting admiring glances from the *boulevardiers*. Paul Cézanne lived here, as did August Strindberg and Paul Gauguin. Modi and his Jeanne are only a block away. Fujita maintains a studio close to here as well. Impoverished artists arrive at the Gare St. Lazare from European points unknown and head straight for this very intersection, safe in the knowledge that they will find others of their avocation and language.

Cocteau broke into my reveries. "So, Easter, will you accept my commission? I will pay you, of course. Your name will appear on the *billet de théâtre* for all to see. It could be a wonderful opportunity for you!"

Cocteau is nothing if not insistent. When I asked him why I should be so honored, he said. "Because I think that a *belle américaine* who has contacts with the Chicago Tribune would suit my purpose very well. There. I have been as honest as I can be. Now, do you accept?"

I thought about it a few moments. Surely there might be an article or two of interest there for American readers. Was this not what Montparnasse was all about?

I asked him one last question. "Will I have to work with Picasso?"

He shook his head. "*Non.*"

I looked at James, who shrugged his shoulders and gave me a wry look. In the end, I agreed.

I will undertake my first assignment—locating a proper rehearsal space—as soon as I learn a bit more about my new employer. This situation screams of irony. Here I am, about to work for the man who was and perhaps remains my husband's lover. Surely this could only happen in Paris.

As we walked back to his apartment, James must have read my mind.

"Welcome to the madhouse," he said. "I think you've now earned your full standing here."

Much has already been written about Jean Cocteau. He is one of the blessed few whose success came very early—deserved or not—and his excesses are legendary. Plus, of course, people love to talk. My, how they love to talk, and my, how Jean adores being talked about!

I met Kiki outside *Chez Rosalie*, and she told me this story; Cocteau fell in love with a woman when he was 17, an actress named Madeleine Carlier.

"But he never fock her," said Kiki. "He has never been with a woman. He has always focked men."

He may or may not have had an affair with the dancer Nijinsky. Radiguet, his present lover, delights in causing scenes of jealousy.

Treize tells me Cocteau is not very healthy and does not eat enough vegetables. His high forehead implies great but misused intelligence. He is addicted to opium (as if I did not know this), which accounts for the occasional yellowish tinge of his skin. He is irregular *sur la selle*. In other words, Treize believes he suffers from constipation.

From an interview in *Le Petit Parisien*: Cocteau was born in 1889 and his father committed suicide in 1899. He attended the *Grand Lycée Condorcet* and shortly thereafter went to Marseille. His first published work was in 1908. He has worked with the Russian impresario Serge Diaghilev, creating posters and drawings for the ballet, *Le Spectre de la Rose*. He also worked with Igor Stravinsky—all this by the time he was 24 years old!

A while back, Frederick confided that Cocteau lives with his mother but maintains an apartment in town. He does not like cemeteries (?) and has a sweet tooth. He is an unpleasant guest at restaurants and often returns the food to the kitchen. He never eats fish and likes to dip his bread in olive oil.

From an article in *l'Echo de Paris:* Cocteau was a volunteer in the ambulance corps that served on the Belgian front. He acquitted himself well. He was arrested shortly after being demobilized; it had to do with his involvement with a group of sailors, or so people say. He is a friend of *le tout Paris artistique*—Picasso (of course), Modi, Braque, Satie, Kisling, et cetera. He has traveled with Picasso to Italy and Spain, but, according to Kiki, Picasso has come to detest him for his homosexuality.

James says that Cocteau is a passable writer. His style is flowery; he seems to relish words at the expense of sentences. Nevertheless, he has published some well-received works of fiction and poetry. He was briefly involved with a young pianist by the name of Jacques Février (how the world is small. I mention this only because this person is the cousin of Yvonne, my seamstress in Chicago), who is reputed to be a favorite of the composers Maurice Ravel and Francis Poulenc.

This next Cocteau tidbit comes from a very secret source; so secret, in fact, that I cannot write it down, even in this most private journal. It is a sordid tale that, if true, speaks of an unusual cruelty.

As a child traveling in Switzerland with his mother, Cocteau persuaded her to purchase a box of cigars for a family servant, then bullied her into hiding the purchase beneath her petticoats so as to avoid paying customs duty. Mme. Cocteau did so with some reticence.

She was about to clear customs when Cocteau pointed to her and shouted: "This lady is hiding a box of cigars in her skirts!" The poor woman was stopped, forced to undress and searched, then fined! It is difficult to imagine such treachery in a child.

James told me, "Cocteau is very accomplished at several artistic pursuits. He says he will produce films before long." Was there a note of jealousy in my lover's voice?

Cocteau has promised James and me "an extraordinary surprise" in the very near future—his way of saying thank you, I suppose. He refused to even hint at what this marvel may be.

CHAPTER 44

George Remus, the Michigan pharmacist, was well on his way to his first half-million dollars. The alcohol he imported from Europe found its way to speakeasies, private clubs, and individuals willing to pay a higher price than normal for top quality stuff. Among these buyers was Charlie DiMarco, a mid-level gangster who deeply loved his mother and was looking forward to her birthday celebration.

Charlie's mother would be 82 years old, was almost blind and toothless, generally irascible, and apt to forget most things. Charlie lived with her just outside Lansing, and he'd invited his brother Joey to the celebration dinner. There was an array of cold and warm antipasto, four pasta dishes with gravy, two cakes, her favorite ice cream, garlic bread, wine, and, doctors be damned, a bottle of absinthe recently arrived from France. Charlie's mother loved absinthe and was on her fourth small glass when she gasped, clutched her chest and doubled over into the *carbonara* on her plate.

Both Joey and Charlie stood at the same time, knocking over their chairs.

Joey had been a medic in France. He tried to find a pulse and couldn't. He and Charlie carried the old lady to the sofa, and Joey put an ear to her chest. She opened her eyes once, coughed, shuddered, and died.

After five minutes of trying to revive her, Joey looked up and asked Charlie, "Jesus Christ! What the hell was she drinking?" He took the bottle, which was now a third empty, and smelled it. "This ain't right, Charles. Where'd you get it?" He called Charlie "Charles" only when he was really upset.

Charlie took a small mouthful of the liquid, spat it out. "Fuckin' Remus is where I got it! Fat little kike!"

In death, Mrs. DiMarco looked no happier than she had for most of her life. Her eyes were open and glaring, so Joey closed them gently.

"Jesus."

Joey said, "Remus ain't Jewish. Lutheran or something..."

Charlie shrugged. "Lutheran, Jewish, I don't give a fuck. He's one dead asshole."

CHAPTER 45

If James Johnson had thought at one time that Easter might need a white knight, he now stood corrected. The closer they became, the more he learned her ways and saw into her mind, and the more he was impressed by the steel in her soul. Nothing fazed her.

He'd been concerned about her return to the apartment, about her feelings towards Frederick and, of course, about her feelings towards he himself. He feared she might go back to the States. Easter may have needed no white knight, but it turned out James required reassurance. She had to comfort him and assuage his fears several times.

The uneasy notion that Easter might choose Frederick over him was James›s constant anxiety. Easter told him he was ridiculous, that his fears were unfounded, but James could not let it go.

Frederick was now traveling, and James and Easter were together most of the time. They would even be working together on Cocteau's new production. The nature of their relationship had become unusual, in James›s experience, even for Montparnasse.

She had not moved in with him despite his repeated invitations. She needed time, she said, and he had no choice but to respect her decision.

That morning, M. Lefebvre came by and stayed longer than usual. He smiled when he saw Easter, doffed his cap, bowed and kissed her hand. If Easter was taken aback by the mailman's gallantry, she did not show it. She offered him coffee and, after a few moments of small talk, left the room, indicating with a gesture that the two men should go about their business without her.

The mailman had news. M. Lefebvre and Mme. Colombini had indeed consummated their relationship, as James had suspected. *"Trois fois en une nuit!"* The fact that he performed the act three times in one single night astounded M. Lefebvre, whose only prior experiences, he admitted with some embarrassment, were hurried couplings with working class *putains.*

Mme. Colombini, he thought, found him satisfactory, but for now coyly rejected his marriage advances. She, too, needed more time. James sympathized with M. Lefebvre's plight, and said so. Mme. Colombini had apparently told her Corsican suitor to get lost, much to M. Lefebvre's relief. Still, the mailman was not totally at ease, the victim of an age-old conundrum: He did not fully trust Mme. Colombini, reasoning that since she did The Act with him, could she not just as easily do It with another? The mailman brightened up when Johnson suggested that Mme. Colombini might be thinking the very same thing about M. Lefebvre.

Little was new on the Landru front. The accused murderer maintained his innocence, according to M. Lefebvre's cousin, but refused to present alibis, claiming a gentleman's discretion for affairs of the heart. Still, M. Lefebvre said postal employees were betting five to one that Landru would get the guillotine, and Inspector Gaspard Belin—the mailman's country cousin from Dijon—claimed Monsieur de Paris was preparing the widow-maker.

Monsieur de Paris was France's leading executioner. He had dispatched some 200 hardened criminals in three years.

Would he behead Landru? There had been so much death in France that a movement was afoot to ban the guillotine and the death sentence altogether.

Johnson and Lefebvre spoke a while longer; M. Lefebvre brought James up to date on neighborhood events. As he did so, Johnson noticed for the first time that the mailman used the term *petit*—which means little, or small—with great regularity, and it struck him later during the day that *petit* was a mainstay of French vocabulary.

A girlfriend was a *petite amie.* A poor soul, a *pauvre petit,* while *mon petit* was a somewhat endearing term. The word could also be used to patronize; being referred to as *mon petit* by anyone could be seen as condescending.

One woke up in the morning to a *petit déjeuner* with a *petit pain* and a *petit café* and downed a *petit coup de cognac* before bedtime. At lunch, there were *petits fours* for dessert and a *petit Beaujolais* to drink. The latter implied the wine was good but had no pretension to greatness.

A *petit Parisien* was less than a bourgeois but more than a worker. A *petit enfant* was a grandchild; *une petite aventure,* a fling. Most striking, perhaps, was *la petite mort,* the orgasm, the little death.

There were endless examples of this diminutive's hold on French consciousness, and Johnson could not find an English or American equivalent. He thought of suggesting to Easter that she devote a mention of this in her next article for the *Tribune.*

He had received his quarterly check from the family trust. The railroads were doing well. It was odd, knowing his funds came from a farseeing grandfather he had never met.

There were times he felt guilty about the money—he'd done nothing to deserve it, but lacked the wherewithal to give it up. When he first came to Paris, he was intent on spending it as quickly as possible. If he could have bankrupted himself, he thought, then he could truly have become one among his peers: a famished artist, living in an unheated garret, eking out an existence like Modi or Soutine.

One difficult Parisian winter taught him he did not have his friends' fortitude. He didn't like being cold, and he feared hunger. He enjoyed the warmth of his apartment and the ability to work as he pleased rather than as he must. Perhaps this would change soon. The portraits of Easter he had painted had been well received, but he sensed that he'd given his all—there was no more water in that well, and there were no other Easters. Yet how many times had Modi painted Jeanne, and before that, Béatrice? Fujita had Fernande Barrey and never tired of portraying her. Pers had Lucy. Mendjisky, Kiki. Surely Easter deserved more brushstrokes. James would purchase some canvases today and stretch them. Thank God for the railroads! Soutine was so poor he often painted over the same canvas a half-dozen times, since few buyers were taken by the esthetics of his carcasses.

Money allowed Johnson to indulge in whims and, in this case, the leisure to be with Easter.

Both had become assistants to the great and illustrious Jean Cocteau. Johnson had by now grudgingly admitted that the man did have a certain flair.

That Sunday, Cocteau called Easter at her apartment early in the morning and arranged to pick her up. Shortly after, they were both at Johnson's door. They ate a *petit déjeuner*, Cocteau checking his watch often and urging them to finish quickly. When they were done, he hailed a cab that took them to the Rue Vaugirard. During the ride, he kept up a stream of largely meaningless conversation on the weather, on Dadaism, and on Picabia's latest magazine. The car stopped before a turn-of-the-century apartment building.

Cocteau paid the driver and, snickering like a ten year old, led them up a flight of stairs. He knocked twice on a tall oaken door, which was opened by a large woman wearing a nurse's uniform.

Now thoroughly mystified, Easter and Johnson stood in the ante-chamber of a remarkably sunny space as Cocteau bussed the woman on both cheeks. She smiled, shook hands without introducing herself, then said, in French, "One moment. Let me make sure he is ready to greet you."

The three sat on a banquette.

Cocteau said, in a whisper, "Prepare to meet God," and a moment later the nurse beckoned them into the main room. Next to a huge window, ensconced in a wheelchair and swaddled in a pale blue blanket was an ancient man.

Cocteau hurried forward, bowed and said, *"Maître, je vous présente mes amies, Mme. Easter Cowles, une jeune américaine très douée, et son compagnon, Monsieur James Johnson, un américain également."*

Easter and Johnson approached. She peered at the ancient being and caught her breath.

It was Renoir.

Johnson was speechless; Easter looked light-headed. Cocteau wore the satisfied and gleeful expression of a boy whose prank has succeeded.

In the aftermath of the war and amidst the modern artists' raucous cries for attention, Pierre Renoir's works were still revered as the best Impressionism had to offer, but the man himself, almost completely paralyzed for the past twenty years, had been all but forgotten. In fact, Johnson had thought him long dead. Now, here he was, quite lucid, eyes twinkling and focused with great interest on Easter's bosom. She noticed and blushed.

The nurse wheeled him toward a quartet of easy chairs and bade them sit down. She brought tea and cookies on a silver tray and served from a delicate Limoges pot.

All around were small, framed paintings of a single lemon, a single rose, a single peony. Some shone with rare luminance, the colors leaping from the canvas, while others were shadowed, muted, faded recreations of an overcast day.

Cocteau said, *"Le Maître* will be going to Cagnes in a few days. I wanted to pay my respects before his departure, and thought you might benefit from meeting each other."

Le Maître was still staring at Easter's *poitrine* and occasionally throwing a glance over her shoulder. Johnson followed his gaze and saw, hanging on the wall, a magnificent nude with rounded breasts, pearly skin, and lustrous hips—his *Bathers*. The old artist was comparing Easter's figure to that of his creations. Easter noticed this as well. A look of defiance crept into her eyes. She stood, walked boldly to the painting and inspected it closely. Then, smiling, she unbuttoned her blouse and exposed her slip. She cupped her breasts with her two hands, turned to Renoir and said, *"Mes seins sont plus petits, mais tout aussi ronds."* "My breasts may be smaller, but they are just as round."

Cocteau gasped in delight. Johnson turned scarlet and closed his eyes. The nurse hiccupped.

Renoir's eyes opened slightly wider. There was a long, expectant silence broken by the clip-clop of a horse-drawn cart passing beneath the window.

Then he nodded, raised an arthritic arm and said, in heavily accented English, "You are very right, my dear. Yours *are* smaller. Maybe rounder as well. That I cannot tell." He drew a raspy breath, motioned her closer until she stood next to him. The arm snaked out and a withered hand came to rest on her thigh. It stayed there only an instant and moved away. "But you are too thin. There is no meat on your legs. I would make you fatter before I paint you."

The old man's compliment pleased Easter hugely. She pulled a chair close to him and said in French: "I am honored that you would consider me a worthy model, Maître."

Renoir reached out his bony hand and once again let it drop onto her thigh. He nodded once or twice as if falling asleep, but suddenly his fingers closed on the fabric of Easter's skirt. He whispered, "A painting is finished when you can feel its ass." Then he cackled. Easter found the statement outrageously funny.

He motioned the nurse to come forward and spoke a few words. She vanished, reappeared in a moment with the master's teeth, which she inserted into his mouth. He grimaced without the least self-consciousness and moved his jaws around until the plates were set. Then he ate a cookie and sipped at his tea. His eyes never left Easter's face.

"When I was young," he told her, "I went with Claude Monet and Alphonse Daudet on a long walking trip in the Creuse. We chased all the girls. Alphonse enticed them. Claude excited them. I screwed them." He winked at Easter, and then addressed the rest of the group. "Have you had lunch?"

Johnson was about to demure, but the old painter insisted. "Please stay. I seldom get company these days. People always sense when a life is about to end, and they stay away. It's understandable. I have never liked to be around the dying."

The nurse clucked, shook her head. *"Ah, Maître..."*

A woman servant set the table and, when the meal was ready, the nurse picked Renoir up like a child, one arm beneath his knees and one about his neck. She deposited him gently into a dining room chair. His joints were fused by the arthritis; he told the group that he slept sitting up.

It was a cold lunch. There were artichoke hearts, breads, fruit, cheese, *saucisson,* and ham cut into very tiny pieces. Renoir ate none of these, but slurped at a bowl of vegetable soup into which he dipped his bread. He kept a running commentary throughout the meal—the weather, Cubism, the miracle of motion pictures, Germany's state, France's future, his distaste for the Dada movement and his understanding of its necessity. He was particularly fascinated by Landru, and Johnson silently blessed M. Lefebvre for giving him information on the murderer, which kept the conversation lively.

During a lull, Renoir noticed Cocteau eyeing the many paintings of lemons and roses.

He asked, "Tell me, Jean, do you write every single day?"

When Cocteau answered that he did not, Renoir reproached him with a click of the tongue.

"Tsk. You should, you know. I never let a day go by without painting *something*—though in my present state, Marie Ange," he motioned to the nurse, "has to strap a brush to my arm. The lemons—every day I do a lemon. There are lemons in every closet, in every nook and cranny of this apartment. The roses I paint when I take the train to Cagnes. Same train on the same day, same hour, every year. It stops in a little town where the stationmaster has a trellis full of flowers. Ten years ago I began sketching the roses there, and I still do it, year after year."

Then, suddenly his eyes closed, his mouth dropped open and his teeth slipped partially out.

The nurse stood. *"Il dort. C'est l'heure de sa sieste."*

They left quietly, tip-toed down the stairs, and stayed hushed during most of the ride home. Cocteau was noticeably sad. "It's probably the last time I'll see him. His operation is scheduled to take place very soon. I doubt he'll survive. If he doesn't, it will be the end of an era."

Johnson thought that, though he often found Jean Cocteau tedious, he would never forget that it was Cocteau who took them to meet God.

That same night, after Easter had left, there came a frantic knocking on Johnson's door. When he answered it, he was amazed to find Fujita, scarlet-faced and obviously drunk. The little Japanese painter swept past him into the room and without so much as a greeting, extended his hand. Johnson looked at it and Fujita said, "Shake it! Go! Shake my hand!"

Johnson complied.

"Well?" Fujita looked at him expectantly.

Johnson did not know Fujita well, though the man's reputation was growing.

"Well?" repeated Fujita impatiently.

"Well what?"

"Is it like a fish?"

"Like a what?"

"Like a fish, a fish!" Fujita withdrew his hand, peered at it with a drunk's concentration. "Kiki says shaking my hand is like handling a dead fish. She said I should come and see you, because everyone knows Americans know how to shake hands. So, I am here. Teach me."

For half-an-hour, Johnson did. By the time Fujita left, his handshake was as firm as any mid-Westerner's. He clapped the American on the back once, twice, said, *"Arigato desu"* several times, which he explained meant thank you in his language, and promised to buy Johnson a drink the next time they met. Johnson wondered whether, in the morning, Fujita would remember anything of their peculiar encounter.

CHAPTER 46

Just outside Lansing, Michigan, things progressed quickly. Joey and Charlie DiMarco buried their mother, then went to visit George Remus in Dearborn Heights. They didn't kill him, but they blackened both his eyes, loosened his front teeth, and broke his right leg and both index fingers. George, without hesitation, gave up the name and address in Paris of the man who'd sold him the absinthe. He also thought it worth mentioning that the man liked opium. He knew this because he, George Remus, was an observant pharmacist and had smelled the drug on the man's breath.

Once back home, Charlie called Salvatore Calderone, head of Pittsburgh's Sicilian Mafia, and requested a favor. Could the family arrange for something to happen to someone in Paris, France? Money was no object, and Charlie would owe Sal a big one.

Calderone sent a coded telegram to his cousin Vincente Ferrugio in Palermo. Ferrugio seized the opportunity to be owed something by the Americans, and sent word out to the Union Corse in Marseille, the seat of organized crime in France. The Union, he knew, rarely trafficked in violence outside of its immediate purview, preferring more lucrative crimes: smuggling, prostitution and theft. Still, the Union had its contacts with various other groups, including the Chinese triad that ran the opium trade in Paris, and for a price, the Triads would do almost anything.

All in all, it took two weeks to arrange the DiMarco's business, and it cost Charlie and Joey just under a thousand dollars, which, both agreed was money well spent.

George Remus considered himself a tough little guy. He'd gotten beaten up before; in his line of business, things like that happened, although this time had been the worst. Still, he was pretty sure no internal damage had occurred. Bones knit, black eyes heal.

As soon as he was back from the hospital, he placed a call to Frederick Cowles' father in Chicago. This was not a selfless gesture—he needed a buyer in Europe, and if his source came to harm, the Remus pharmacy empire would suffer.

When he reached Mr. Cowles Senior, the connection was bad and it took a while to explain what had happened. Remus did leave out certain particular details that Senior did not need to know.

Senior, who might have had a drink or two, kept saying, "What? What?" and George repeated himself until, finally, he said, a bit louder than normal, "Tell your son to watch his ass! Some bad people are after him!" Senior said, "What? What? Oh. Thank you."

Remus hung up. He had gotten through, he hoped, though honestly, he wasn't sure.

Chapter 47

"Frederick!" Cocteau clapped his hands with delight. "How wonderful! You brought me Monsieur Bébé!"

Frederick had spent the better part of the morning in Radiguet's hotel bed. They had ordered breakfast in the room (Frederick had paid), bathed together, and gone shopping for shoes, shirts, and suits. Radiguet came from a poor family—his father was a political cartoonist—and wore a collection of cast-offs: brown shoes, blue socks, trousers of an indeterminate color, shirts made gray by too many washings. His only vanity was an incongruous pink tie stolen from his brother. They were in Montmartre having an early supper when Cocteau appeared at their table as if by magic. Cocteau leaned down and planted a loud kiss on Radiguet's left cheek.

"How wonderful you look in your new clothes," he said to the young man. Then he turned to Frederick, "Don't look so surprised, Frederick! Do you think you discovered this bad boy?" He tousled Radiguet's hair. Radiguet made a face. "Monsieur Bébé has been in more Parisian beds than…" He paused to think, "than even Kiki…*N'est-ce pas, mon chéri? C'est une véritable petite pute!*"

If Radiguet minded being called a little whore, he didn't let on. He buttered his bread, crushed and spread a chunk of Camembert on it, closed his eyes, and chewed. After swallowing, he gulped a mouthful of red wine and belched slightly.

Finally, he said, "*Salut, Jean…*"

Cocteau ignored him.

"He is interesting, this one," Cocteau told Frederick. "He sleeps with men, women, children, maybe even an animal or two. *Complètement amoral.* But he writes poetry worthy of Baudelaire. And then he runs away," he waved his hands like a magician, "only to reappear when least expected, and in the strangest company. Ah, Frederick, it's a good thing I found the both of you. I'll take him off your hands before he gets a chance to corrupt yet another gentleman." He leaned closer and stage whispered: "Monsieur Bébé and I have some, how do you Americans say it? Unfinished business."

Cocteau took one of the younger man's arms and with surprising strength lifted him out of his chair. Radiguet did not struggle and allowed himself to be thrust through the café door and onto the sidewalk, still working on a mouthful of bread and cheese. A cab appeared and both men vanished.

After a while, Frederick paid the bill, not quite sure of what had happened. Radiguet had left the bag holding his old clothes under the table. Frederick debated for a moment what to do with it. He drank a quick Cointreau at a café down the street and walked home. On the way, he dumped the bag into a trashcan.

Easter was not at the apartment, which did not surprise him. She seemed to spend more and more time away, with James Johnson, he was sure, and their ragged, impoverished friends. He went into the bathroom, reached under the claw foot bathtub and retrieved the small stash of opium he kept there. Soon, he had left Cocteau, Radiguet, Easter, and all of Paris behind.

Chapter 48

Paris, Monday, September 8, 1919

So the old master is a lecher. An amiable lecher, to be sure, and far too slow to compete with some of the others I have met (Picasso comes to mind, naturally). I would have thought that when a man reached Renoir's age, the sap would have stopped flowing, but on our way back from the Maître's home, Cocteau reminded me that thousand-year-old olive trees still flourish in the Holy Land and produce the most coveted fruit.

I shouldn't be surprised. Everything I have read, everything I have heard, would support the theory that great artists have great sexual appetites. Victor Hugo at age 70 seduced the daughter of Théophile Gauthier. The girl was in her twenties and married to the poet Catulle Mendès, who left her in protest. Barely a year later, Hugo bedded Sarah Bernhardt. The list of his conquests goes on and on: all young women who succumbed to his demands. I understand that Alexandre Dumas was no better. Closer to home, James tells me, Fujita's reputation as a ladies' man is unparalleled. People find his exotic features quite alluring. I found out recently that he was indeed Jeanne's first lover. Personally, I find the idea of a man wearing an earring repulsive, and have told James that he has nothing to fear as far as Fujita and I are concerned. I said this in jest, of course, but poor James looked aghast. He rarely knows when I am joking.

One lesson I have learned from Paris and Montparnasse is this: do not back down, do not allow yourself to be diminished by the actions of others. I'm certain comparing my breasts to those of the old man's model embarrassed James, even as it delighted Cocteau. James blushed; he is such a conventional man! His rectitude is a perfect counter for Cocteau's perversity. The truth is that my breasts *are* far rounder, if somewhat less bountiful than those of Renoir's model.

I saw the beggar again. I *know* he is not blind.

He was sitting on the sidewalk at the corner of Rue Bonaparte and Rue des Beaux Arts, and I went all the way around the block so I might take him by surprise. At one point, when I feared he'd spotted me, I hid behind a tree, feeling very foolish, and I'm sure a couple of walkers looked at me oddly.

He broke a piece of bread and chewed on it, then took a swig of wine from an uncorked bottle. I edged closer, trying to stay away from his peripheral vision. He was wearing the same disheveled clothes, and his shoes had no laces. His ankles were wrapped in newspapers. He took a small bag from a pocket, dumped some cigarette butts on the ground before him and tore the paper off these sad remnants—I have heard that referred to as 'field stripping.' Then he gathered tobacco and rolled a cigarette of his own. He lit it with a brass lighter such as I have seen used by former soldiers, which makes me believe that he was once in the military. He smoked for a while, chewed more bread, drank more wine, then drank again, deeply this time. He was asleep in a moment. I edged closer and noticed he wore woolen gloves with the fingers cut off. His fingernails were very dirty, chewed to the quick. When I looked closer still, it struck me that most of the vagabonds I have seen in Paris have faces blackened by the soot that permeates the city. Not so my man. Beneath the overlong hair and straggly beard and mustache was very white, well-scrubbed skin.

There was a *boulangerie* a few steps away, so I went there and asked the young woman behind the counter if she knew who my *clochard* was. She did not; he has recently appeared in the neighborhood, it seems. She did admit to giving him a loaf of yesterday's bread, and he had thanked her. I asked if he had an accent like mine. She thought for a moment, then nodded her head. "*Peut-être un petit peu... Vous êtes Anglaise? Canadienne du Québec?*" I said, no, I was American. She, nodded. "*Oui, comme vous.*" It would seem I am right—the man is, indeed, from the States. What is he doing here?

Chapter 49

Mme. Bertrand, the concierge, ushered William Thaw through Johnson's door with all the deference of a princess introducing her very own prince.

Thaw, a former RAF flyer, was an elegant young man with stylishly cut clothes *à l'américaine* and a stiff, waxed mustache. He limped slightly, not the result of a wartime injury, he said, but rather from a rugby game against some British expatriates a week earlier. He'd been raised in Pittsburgh and educated at Yale and preferred to be called Bill.

Thaw had left Yale in 1911 to learn how to fly. His wanderlust soon led him to the *Légion Etrangère*. When that was not exciting enough, he became one of the original Lafayette flyers. He was 23 at the time and quickly became an ace, bringing down 5 planes in 22 months of service. Only three other flyers surpassed that number of kills.

Johnson offered to make coffee, but Thaw said he never drank stimulants of any kind. They spoke briefly of the weather, of being expatriates, of the French whom they both admired and found amusing. Johnson made brief mention his days with the ambulance corps.

They walked to a nearby brasserie and, once seated, Thaw handed Johnson a manila folder. Johnson opened it gingerly. In it were Daniel's passport and military identity card, a wallet with a hundred francs and some odd change, a picture of a young girl with blonde hair and thick ankles, and a letter. Johnson immediately recognized his brother's handwriting.

Thaw said, "These are his papers. I guess Daniel forgot to take them, or he planned to come back. Perhaps, he left them behind on purpose.

Didn't want to be identified in case he was shot down. The letter is more recent."

Johnson stared at the envelope, turned it over in his hands. It was addressed to Thaw. The stamp was the standard *Trois Centimes* issued by the republic. The envelope itself could be found in any *papeterie*.

After a long moment, Thaw smiled, reached across the table to touch Johnson's shoulder, "This is not bad news, you know."

Johnson nodded and began reading:

My dear Bill,

I wish to report that your treasured Nieuport is unharmed. One guy wire snapped during flight, but I fixed it. I have also cleaned the fuel filters and tuned the engine quite well, so that it runs as smoothly as a Nieuport can, which you know is not very. I adjusted the trim and ailerons, repaired the cockpit, and recalibrated the instruments which, unfortunately, shattered upon contact with my legs (thereby breaking them both) at the moment of landing.

I hope you will forgive me. I am not a gifted flyer. In fact, as we both know, I am not a flyer at all. The little I learned of flying, I learned by watching you, Norman and Elliott, and of course Raoul. Quite obviously, it was not enough.

I took your airplane because I had to, and this I am sure you will understand. I <u>had</u> to fly, if only one time. Once aloft, I did not want to come down. My crime is explained as simply as that.

I did not contact you earlier because it took some time for my legs to heal. I refused to be arrested, or to turn myself in and be brought to court ignominiously. I had the very good fortune of landing in the oat field of M. Jacques Lupin, a gracious man of the earth whose family took me in and nursed me back to health. They think I am a member of the Escadrille and are quite impressed. I chose not to

*disabuse them of this notion. They believe they have brushed great-
ness. It would be petty of me to tell them they have not.*

*Your plane is in their barn. Their farm is three clicks east of the
village of Cunlhat, in southern Auvergne, and anyone in the village
can guide you to the place. I have told them that they will soon meet
a real hero—you—and their anticipation is bubbling.*

*Having returned your plane to you, I seek a favor. In a month or
two, please contact my brother, James Johnson, who lives in the
Montparnasse neighborhood in Paris. He is a painter, and I am
certain you will have no difficulty locating him. Please tell him I am
fine, and that he may inform our father that I will soon return to
the States. I ask that you delay speaking with him as I am certain he
will launch an immediate search for me (at my father's behest) and I
plan to do a bit of touristing around France first. You and I spoke of
traveling together after the war, but my present embarrassment forces
me to go alone at this time. I have money to last a few months and
my legs are now useable—though I will never play rugby with you.*

*Once again, friend Bill, I beg your forgiveness even as I know you, of
all people, could understand my actions.*

I trust we will meet again.

Your devoted friend and mechanic,

Daniel Johnson

James Johnson reread the letter. He felt a sense of relief, but no
gladness. His father would be thrilled. Johnson thought it typical of his
brother to be more impressed with himself and his deeds than he should
be, asking for forgiveness without a trace of remorse.

They returned to the apartment, and Johnson sat down in the big easy chair to reread the letter. Thaw pretended to show interest in the portraits of Easter. After a while, he said, "Beautiful woman! Is she a friend of yours?"

Johnson told him that yes, she was, and they returned to respective silences.

Thaw said, "I plan to retrieve my plane next week. If you were willing to come with me, it would be extremely helpful. If the plane is flyable, you could come back to Paris with the car. If it isn't, then I would simply enjoy your company." With a shrug he added, "You could meet Monsieur Lupin, the farmer who took Daniel in. He may have an idea as to where your brother went."

That same evening, Johnson sent a note to M. Lupin. Two days later, the farmer called from the local café to say he and his wife would be honored to meet with him any weekday, as Saturday was devoted to market while Sunday was church and *boules*. M. Lupin informed him that he was captain of the village team, that the team was regional champion, and that if Sunday was, indeed, the only day the American could come, he would gladly take Johnson to a match where he could meet his team mates, who had never before had the pleasure of speaking firsthand with *un américain*.

After checking with Thaw, Johnson sent a second note to M. Lupin saying he and Thaw would be arriving in Cunlhat the coming Wednesday.

Then Johnson drafted a note to his father, announcing the miraculous news.

CHAPTER 50

Henri Désiré Landru did not like the heads. They were hard, burned poorly, and seemed to create a blacker and more pungent smoke than the rest of the body parts he incinerated. He particularly disliked the necessity of searching through the ashes in the oven for teeth and jawbones. He had once read that while the rest of the flesh and bones might be consumed by a hot fire within an hour or two, a head might take as much as four hours to burn, and would never entirely disappear.

Whenever possible, he would take his victims' heads to a large pond near the village of Le Boulay a few miles from Gambais, wrap them in burlap sacks weighed down with stones, and fling them as far as he could into the water. This almost had disastrous results when the decapitated head of a young woman was snagged by a young boy who was fishing for carp in the pond.

Landru had met André Anne Babelay in January 1917, on the platform of a *station de metro*. The nineteen-year-old servant girl was crying, and when Landru asked if he could be of assistance, the girl explained she had been fighting with her employer and was to be let go the next day. She did not have a *sou* to her name. Landru offered her his room on the Rue Mauberge and there the young woman stayed for more than a month. Shortly before vanishing, she went to her mother's house and announced she was to marry.

The boy whose fishing line had snagged the grisly bundle was the son of Le Boulay's senior *gendarme*, and when he saw what he had caught, he carefully wrapped the sodden mess in his jacket, well aware that his mother would be furious while his father would commend him for good police work.

He put the bundle in the basket of his bicycle and pedaled furiously to the village and, breathless, went straight to the café where his father, he knew, was having a *petit coup de rouge* to start the day. He dumped the leaking sack onto a table, stepped back and said, *"Papa! Regarde ce que j'ai trouvé!"*

The head was sent to Rambouillet, where it was examined by a doctor who quickly determined it had belonged to a woman between the ages of 17 and 25, had been removed from the rest of the body with a butcher's saw, and had been in the water approximately three weeks. It was remarkably well preserved, perhaps because the pond was known to be fed by a frigid underground spring, and the burlap had protected the features from depredation. The pond was dragged in search of a body. None was found though the investigation produced the remains of a horse and saddle.

There was a brief flurry of interest by the Paris newspapers, one of which sent a writer to speak with the doctor, the gendarme, and the gendarme's son. The writer filed a brief story which made the bottom of the front page. "Head of Girl Found in Village Pond," read the headline. There was no follow-up.

Henri Désiré Landru, one of the story's readers, shook his own head at this close brush with the law and decided that from then on, he would go to the Forêt de Rambouillet to bury whatever remains resisted the flames of his oven.

CHAPTER 51

Paris, Thursday, September 11, 1919

James's brother, Daniel, is alive. It would appear to be a miracle, yet when James first told me this, it was in the tone of voice he would have used to say that the local *boucher* was once again offering lamb cutlets. Then he apologized as he added that he would have to leave Paris for a few days to accompany a former Lafayette pilot retrieve his plane and, oh, yes, perhaps locate his brother, a one-time mechanic for the Escadrille.

James does not care at all for his brother, but harbors a responsibility towards him and a deep guilt for this lack of sibling closeness. Essentially, James feels he *should* like Daniel, and that there is something wrong with him because he does not.

It was evident that even talking about his brother was painful. Daniel is a few years older and, apparently, was a bully from an early age. James suffered the brunt of his brother's malice, and Daniel was inventive in his nastiness. Daniel was the favorite who, in their father's eyes, could do no wrong. He once broke James's arm and was never taken to task for this by their parents.

Anyway, to make a long story short, just before the war's end, Daniel took an Escadrille plane for a spin without permission from the commanding officer. Daniel's whereabouts are unknown and James has decided to go search for him, with the help of a man named William Thaw, a former Escadrille pilot.

I met Mr. Thaw, who is a very handsome man in a Midwestern sort of way. I am sure Enid and company would go gaga over him. He strikes me as polite and understated. When we first met, he looked at me oddly for a moment, and then smiled. "You're the lady in James's portrait," he said. "Are you a model?"

I assured him I was not.

James and Mr. Thaw are heading out early next week in Thaw's automobile, a luxurious Simplex made in Great Britain, which he says he won from a wealthy British pilot in a card game. They should be quite the sight heading down the rural roads. I told James that he was not to seduce any village girl he might meet, and he looked abashed that I would even suggest such a thing.

CHAPTER 52

William Thaw did not drive his car, he piloted it with all the con-
centration and intensity of an ace shooting Germans out of the
sky. He did not make small talk or gaze at the scenery; he did not blink.
He hummed to himself, a rendition of *Hello, Central, Give Me No Man's
Land*. Sometimes he segued into *Inky Dinky Parlay Vous* or *Good Morning,
Mr. Zip*, a tune James Johnson found ridiculous and disliked. Luckily,
Thaw's humming could barely be heard over the roar of the car's engine.

Thaw would get his plane when they reached Monsieur Lupin's
farm, Johnson supposed, but what would he himself achieve? Peace of
mind, perhaps? Information regarding Daniel's whereabouts? Daniel,
said Thaw, had been quite popular with the men of the Escadrille. They
took him aloft many times, and he, in turn, made small design changes
to the planes allowing for greater pilot comfort. He machined a tea mug
holder out of old pistons. The device fastened directly to a plane's instru-
ment board and kept tea warm through a clever attachment to the plane's
exhaust system. Every pilot wanted one. Daniel also devised a compass
that would work no matter the position of the plane—vertical, diving
or upside down—and a triggering system, enabling the pilot to fire the
automatic machine gun fastened to the top wing without taking his
hands off the steering yoke. The system was so effective, Thaw said, that
soon after Daniel installed one, the Germans devised a copy of it and
fitted it on *their* planes.

Johnson found it amazing and difficult to think of Daniel being of
use to anyone. He failed to come up with a single instance of his brother
creating anything useful. Johnson could only recall Daniel ever making
bad practical jokes; setting afire a paper sack full of dog excrement on a

neighbor's stoop. The widowed woman had stomped on the sack with predictable and unfortunate results. James had been blamed, and his brother stood by mutely as their father whipped out his belt.

Johnson remembered that pointing at Daniel while pinching his nose shut as if overcome by a noxious odor infuriated his brother. For some reason, Daniel's blood boiled whenever James did this, so of course James had done it as often as possible.

They took their time reaching M. Lupin's village of Cunlhat. Thaw enjoyed testing the Simplex's agility on a variety of roads and conditions. At times, Johnson closed his eyes and held on for dear life.

The first night, they bedded down in Orléans. Thaw knew of a first-class restaurant owned by the parents of an Escadrille pilot, so they had an excellent meal without charge. The next night, they slept in Dijon, and Johnson remembered to purchase some of the local mustard for Easter.

In the afternoon, they drove into Cunlhat and asked for directions at the local café. A horde of children swarmed over the Simplex, leaving handprints on the hood and fenders. On their way out of the village, Thaw made sure to drive slowly enough down the main street so the children could run alongside the car.

When they pulled up to the farm's front door, the entire Lupin family, dressed in its Sunday best, was there to greet them. M. Lupin was an icon of the classic French *homme de la terre*—short, stout, generously mustachioed, topped by a jaunty cap. His wife, Madeleine, was slim, once beautiful but now old beyond her years, with brunette hair streaked gray. There was a son in his late teens—adopted, Johnson learned later—and a very pretty daughter, Lucienne, who eyed him appraisingly at first, and then with suspicion. Inside the farmhouse, a baby cried.

After introductions were made, Thaw headed for the barn where his beloved plane was stored. Within minutes there was a tremendous roar, followed by a cacophony of barks, squawks and panicked lowing. Thaw had started his plane amid a hurricane of straw, dust, and feathers. He reappeared, covered in a fine mist of engine oil, wearing a huge, toothy smile. He hugged M. Lupin, almost lifting him off his feet, and announced that Daniel had indeed done a fine job of fixing and storing the Nieuport. He would take a test flight in the morning and, if everything worked correctly, he would pilot it to an airfield outside of Paris.

It was a beautiful evening, and Mme. Lupin had set a feast of *charcuterie*, cheeses, butters, pâtés, and bread on a stout outdoor oak table that may have been hundreds of years old. The men sat around it in shirtsleeves and ate and drank as the sun set. M. Lupin was well-informed, keeping up with events; a reader of newspapers and magazines. He proudly showed Johnson his *bibliothèque;* a small room full of books, mostly on agricultural subjects, and his collection of inexpensive fountain pens.

M. Lupin's daughter, Lucienne, was in charge of refreshments and Johnson could not help but see that whenever she refilled his glass, she wore a dismayed expression. At one point, M. Lupin pulled her aside and, with a quick glance in Johnson's direction, angrily whispered something in her ear. After that, though Lucienne fulfilled her duties, she remained more aloof than before.

Little was said of Daniel at first. It was obvious that M. Lupin had found him endearing, and that Mme. Lupin had been charmed. After his broken legs had healed, Daniel had made himself invaluable around the farm. He had restored a tractor engine and used it to power a well pump, enabling the family to have an indoor tap for the very first time. Then he had installed a boiler in the cellar and given them hot water. He had mended fences, repaired leaks in the barn roof, chopped and stacked firewood, and removed plow-breaking stones from the fields. M. Lupin admitted that he had thought of Daniel as a second son until he had discovered that Lucienne was pregnant.

At that very moment, Lucienne went into the house and returned with an infant in her arms: Daniel's son. She handed him to Johnson. Johnson had never held a baby and stood rooted to the spot. He looked at the tiny, scrunched up face and saw nothing recognizable. All babies looked to him like little old men, and if there were traces of Daniel's features there, he could not find them.

Mme. Lupin took the baby from him; M. Lupin gently grasped Johnson's elbow and led him to a far room in the house where he offered a small glass of home-made *poire*. Johnson downed it, and Lupin refilled the glass.

He shrugged his shoulders exactly as M. Lefevbre would, and said, "*C'est une de ces choses qui arrivent...*" These things happen…

The boy's name was Jean Octave.

M. Lupin showed Johnson the best easy chair and explained that such unplanned occurrences were not rare *dans le pays*, and he was certain that Daniel would return and assume his responsibilities. No, M. Lupin did not know where Daniel was at the moment. Weeks ago, the family had received a single letter from him saying he had to take care of some urgent business matters, and promising he would come back and marry Lucienne. M. Lupin believed him. Daniel was an American, he said, and would be true to his word. The only thing that worried M. Lupin was that during Daniel's stay and recuperation, he developed a fondness for morphine to lessen the pain in the legs broken during the plane's landing. When the village doctor said there was no more drug to be found, Daniel began to drink. The farmer made the gesture—a fist twisting before his nose—that everyone in France associates with the *picoleur*, the habitual drunkard, and gave Johnson a sad smile and a pat on the back. "*Allons, Monsieur James…C'est pas sérieux. Daniel est simplement un peu alcoolique.*" Just a little alcoholic.

In the morning, Thaw took off in his airplane, leaving Johnson to drive the Simplex back to Paris. The entire village gathered to watch the Nieuport climb into the sky. Thaw grinned at the crowd as children jumped up and down, and the village women waved their handkerchiefs and aprons in the air. He did a barrel roll and a stall before vanishing over the horizon. Johnson left quietly while the town was mostly distracted, though a group of young men on motorcycles escorted him for several miles with exuberant thumbs up gestures.

Chapter 53

Xing Nian Zu was poisoning opium for a price. He planned to spend the 100 francs he was earning on a pair of new red satin shoes for his 14-year-old mistress and on a dress for his wife, or on a sumptuous meal at the Dragon Noir restaurant for himself and the three friends with whom he played endless games of tiu-u. Both options had merit, and Zu considered them carefully. Red shoes would bring his day to a happy ending, and the dress would guarantee household peace for at least a week. The meal, however, might provide the longer lasting pleasure.

He did not know who the opium was meant to kill, nor did he care. He had prepared more lethal doses than he could remember, and none had ever failed. Poisoned opium was a favorite way of dispatching addicts who did not pay, had become liabilities, or had somehow offended a power greater than themselves. It was a far more effective and elegant way of meting out death than was outright violence, and though any Chinese herbalist would immediately diagnose a victim's fate, Western doctors lacked the skill and knowledge to do so.

He kneaded the one-inch ball between gloved fingers, careful to ensure an even consistency. The powdered baneberry and ground fu-tzu changed the color of the opium slightly, so he added a drop of Indian ink to the mixture. He wrapped the opium ball in thin gold leaf and called for his assistant to deliver it to Yong Qing Shan, the assassin whose name meant Celebrating Goodness in the Western tongue.

Yong Qing Shan, who seldom celebrated anything, had been given the assignment by his Deputy Mountain Master. The Paris triad, though small in number, was remarkably well connected, and it took less than a day for Shan to discover that his target's distributor was a Chinese local.

Xiang Nian Zu was known as a man of skill and honor, and there was no reason to doubt the efficacy of his work. He was satisfied, although something about the job felt almost too easy.

CHAPTER 54

It delighted Henri Désiré Landru that the government based its case on eleven victims. People, regardless of intellect or origins, saw only what met their needs. The prosecution no doubt thought that eleven victims would more than merit the guillotine.

Eleven, thought Landru, was almost insulting in an amusing sort of way. If Gaspard Belin, the fool inspector, had properly led the investigation, the number of deaths would have tripled. Henri Désiré Landru had killed twenty-nine women, one man, three children—one boy and two girls—and two dogs. The dogs' deaths had caused him some real anguish. He liked animals and did not want them to suffer; he'd strangled them—the gentlest of demises, he believed.

The male victim had been inevitable, and Landru felt no pride there. He had been the jilted suitor of a woman who had responded to a Landru advertisement; the middle-aged whatever-he'd-been-in-life had followed Landru to Gambais, thinking the woman who had spurned his advances might be there. She was, though in several different pieces that Landru was in the process of feeding into his oven. When the man charged through the open front door, Landru, in his bloody apron and gloves, had been throwing a left foot and calf into the fire. The man had screamed in horror. Landru, caught by surprise, had grabbed a cleaver and swung wildly in the direction of the scream. The cleaver bit into the man's neck and sliced through the jugular. There was an arc of blood. The man grabbed his neck as if trying to seal the wound with his hands. He dropped to his knees, and Landru swung the cleaver straight down. The heavy butcher's knife sliced cleanly through skull and brain, stopping just above the topmost vertebra.

Landru was hardly aware of what had occurred. The man's blood was now flowing in small spurts, and abruptly stopped. He was still on his knees and did not topple. Landru pushed him over with one booted foot.

Before attending to the new corpse, Landru finished getting rid of the woman, a Mademoiselle Adrienne Lefoucault. She had been worth some 8,000 francs, not counting her furniture. Then he fed more hardwood into the oven until the fire roared. He went through the dead man's pockets, found a billfold with 40 francs and identity papers. Apparently, he was Jean Robert Gallimard, a *réparateur de cuisinières et de machines à laver*. He was a repairman of household appliances; Landru was unimpressed.

Landru briefly wondered what had prompted Gallimard to stampede into the house in such a reckless manner. He dismembered him—he was a rather small person with thin bones—and fed him into the oven so that his ashes and that of Mlle. Lefoucault would be forever one. Landru enjoyed this small joke and worked through the evening wearing a tight smile.

He regretted killing the children but there had been no choice. Their mother, Ernestine Boucher, was to come to Gambais by herself, bearing all the financial papers she needed to sign over to Landru prior to their being wed and stationed in Australia. She had never told him about the children, Albert and Katherine, fearing Landru might find them a burden. She had planned, she told Landru, not to introduce the children until after the nuptials, but had decided that Landru's marriage proposal was promise enough.

She had taken the train from Paris with her son and daughter, no doubt trying to instill some excitement for going to Australia, and failing. Her children *liked* Paris, she confided later to Landru. They loved their *lycée* and their friends, and had no desire to ship out to the bottom of the world where cannibalistic Aborigines hid behind bushes waiting to gnaw on the legs of white children. Albert liked the idea of kangaroos but not enough to be swayed. Katherine was intractable. "*Non!*" she had wailed. "*Je resterai avec Papa!*"

Papa had paid a small fortune to be rid of Albert, Katherine and their mother. The divorce had been mean, costly, and vituperative. Papa had not seen the children since the final divorce decree had been signed and was now keeping company with an 18-year-old coat check girl.

Ernestine had brought the children to Gambais hoping the fiancé she knew as Paul Edouard Guillet would talk sense into them. Paul Edouard was so credible, she flattered him, so persuasive. He could paint the landscape of Australia, and include in it the sound of birds and water rushing. He would describe the ample adventures available to the children, the opportunities in the land Down Under, and make them see that Fate had chosen them, that such an opportunity simply could not be overlooked.

If Landru was surprised to see Ernestine appear *avec enfants*, he did not show it. His smile was all encompassing. He kissed her on the cheek, patted the children on the head and, like a proud and fond father, draped an arm about Albert's shoulders. He tried to take Katherine by the hand but the girl avoided his grasp, so instead he took Ernestine by the elbow and led the three of them into the house's chilly vestibule.

It was not much of a place for children. Landru amused them for a little while by singing, twisting his body this way and that as a contortionist would, and finally he tied a piece of red cloth to a string and suggested they go to the pond near the house and hunt for frogs.

When the children were outdoors, he and Ernestine cooked a simple meal of boiled potatoes and beef. For dessert, all had cocoa with *crème fouettée,* whipped by Landru himself. He added a few drops of chloral hydrate to three of the cups, and watched the Bouchers, mother and children, fall into a dreamless sleep from which they never awoke.

CHAPTER 55

"What shall we do about the telegram?" asked Stabler.

The telegram from Mr. Cowles, Sr., made no sense at all. Frederick and Stabler were sitting in the office Frederick had set up in his new apartment on the Rue de la Terrasse near the Parc Monceau. The cable had arrived a few days earlier when Frederick was in a room at the Hôtel des Chevaliers entertaining Gerald Michelson, a new American friend. The one night had turned into two, then into three. Frederick had really *liked* this nineteen-year-old, who was visibly awed, couldn't do enough and, when on his knees, looked up with such visible adoration in his eyes that Frederick glowed.

Wonderfully, Michelson was not an artist! He did not pretend to write, paint, sculpt, act, sing, dance, or compose. He was a law clerk with Hobson & Turner, an American firm with overseas offices. He was delightfully free of pretense, and on the same page as Frederick in his opinions of the French.

"Love the city, can't stand the people," Michelson said to Frederick when they first met. "You?"

Frederick and Michelson were roughly the same height and coloring, so much so that Frederick could look at the other man and see himself. It felt peculiar, yet pleasing.

"What shall we do about your father's wire?" Stabler asked again.

Frederick shrugged, still thinking of his new interest. "Send my father a letter. Ask for clarifications."

Around three that day, Stabler paused from working on the company's books to answer a knock at Frederick's door. He found a smiling

Oriental man bearing a box wrapped in red crepe paper. The Oriental bowed, "Mistah Cowles?"

Stabler said, "Just a minute," and called into the apartment. "Frederick! You have a visitor!"

Chapter 56

Paris, Wednesday, September 17, 1919

How amazing! James has a French nephew, an infant by the name of Jean Octave, named after the baby's grandfather-in-law. James called yesterday from Auvergne to tell me the news. He sounded out of breath, and when I asked why he was panting, he said he had run a mile to get to a telephone in the village's *café*. I asked why he hadn't simply driven Thaw's car, and he said he hadn't thought of it.

He was very upset.

"They think he's going to act *honorably*!" He was shouting and I told him to restrain himself. He continued, a bit more softly but with just as much vehemence. "Daniel does not know what the word *honorably* means. That poor girl can't be more than sixteen years old! They should be trying to have him arrested, for God's sake!"

I asked what he was planning to do.

"I don't have a clue! What *should* I be doing? Shall I give them money? That seems so…so insulting, as if I'm trying to buy their forgiveness. And how much money, anyway?" He laughed, bitterly. "How much does a half-French, half-American baby cost nowadays?"

I suggested he do nothing until morning and then that he consider opening a small account at the local bank which would be made available to the Lupin family. James's parents could contribute funds to the upbringing of their only grandson.

James snorted when I first mentioned this. "My parents are highly unlikely to accept Daniel's bastard son, I'm afraid. This is just another perfect example of Daniel's total disregard for others…"

James was in such a fine fury that I decided to let him speak his piece. He did and, after a while, apologized for his anger. "It's just that he is so irresponsible! And on top of it all, according to M. Lupin, now he's become a drunk!"

I'm certain Mr. Johnson *père* will not react as James fears. The baby, be he French, American, or anything else, is his only grandchild. Surely this will have an effect on the older man's reasoning.

I will take James shopping for baby things. That may help settle his mind, even as it unsettles mine.

CHAPTER 57

A telegram from Johnson's father read:

Do everything for grandson stop arrange for English nanny stop communicate any need as soon as possible stop check forthcoming stop.

James Johnson was amazed. Monsieur Lupin had made it clear that his family was willing to assume all responsibilities for bringing up the child. Would they even accept having an English nanny in their home?

Two days earlier, Easter had taken Johnson to the Galeries Lafayette, where they'd spent a fortune on clothing and toys for Johnson's new nephew. They also bought items for the Lupin family. This included a baby carriage with an attached parasol, diapers with clever snaps that held the cloth together, bonnets, shoes that looked as if they would fit a doll, stout boots for M. Lupin and his sons, and four pairs of elegant kid gloves Easter thought the women might like for church days. Easter had a grand time.

On that same day, the impossible happened. Landru, the murderer, escaped.

Parisians—and the rest of the country—were agog and aghast. The largest manhunt in France's history began, and the city was awash in a sea of blue *gendarmes'* uniforms. It was thought the actual escape had occurred forty-eight hours earlier but that the authorities, hoping to avoid a scandal, had not alerted the police and instead sent only a few men after the fugitive. This French posse failed to find its man, persuaded Landru could not have gone far, and indeed might still be hiding in the Prison Saint-Lazare. This was the same place, where, two years earlier, Mata Hari had been jailed before facing the firing squad.

Much time was wasted, it seemed, as authorities turned the prison inside out and questioned other prisoners, jailers, nurses, and turnkeys. Landru was not there; he was gone.

Monsieur Lefebvre did not bother to deliver his letters and parcels, so eager was he to relate the news.

He had spent the better part of the night before plying his Dijonnais cousin, Inspector Gaspard Belin, with drink and *pot-au-feux*.

The postman told Johnson and the concierge that Landru had been a model inmate, though he had adamantly refused to answer questions regarding the women he was accused of killing. He had always been polite to a fault with all who approached his cell, particularly the prison staff to whom he gave cigarettes and other gifts received from female admirers.

"Zat," said M. Lefebvre in English, "is anozer story in ze altogezer."

No special consideration had been given Landru. The warden considered him *"un simple prisonnier, comme les autres."* He was fed three times a day—very simple fare, according to the Inspector—which he ate with finicky precision. He did not have a knife or any other sharp implement, so he sawed at his food with the wooden spoon provided. He was allowed to walk the corridors adjoining his cell fifteen minutes each day. He performed calisthenics after his breakfast, and took care of bodily functions once in the morning and once in the afternoon.

He changed clothes every two days, and was given a weekly fresh set of sheets for his cot, which was where the escape began.

Yvette-Marie Mercier was the laundress responsible for washing and pressing Landru's things. She apparently took ill early in the morning of the fateful day and went home. Yvette-Marie's duties were assumed by another woman who, shortly after Landru's breakfast, pushed her linen hamper into the prisoner's cell. This, of course, was forbidden and should have been stopped by the guard on duty, but that man was down the hallway smoking a cigarette and arguing with another prisoner who may or may not have been involved in the escape plot.

Landru, a small man, climbed into the cart after placing a dummy made of pillows beneath the sheets on the cot. The head of the dummy, brought in by the laundress, was—and this did not evoke even the hint of a smile from M. Lefebvre—a medium-sized melon upon which some hair had been pasted.

As she left, the laundress told the guard that Monsieur Landru was not feeling well and was asleep. The guard, still involved in his argument, paid no attention. In a moment, the woman was gone, and so was the murderer.

How both left the prison, M. Lefebvre continued, was a mystery, but not a very deep one. There was a constant flow of people to and from the prison grounds—visiting families, attorneys, gendarmes, witnesses—and no one noticed anything amiss. More than likely, the woman had some form of transportation waiting.

As soon as the subterfuge was discovered, Yvette-Marie, the original laundress, was dragged from her small maid's apartment to the warden's office and severely questioned. Under threat of imprisonment and worse, she confessed that, a week before, she had stopped for a *petit coup de rouge* after her work at the Café de L'Ile Blanche where she was befriended by a very nice middle-aged woman who called herself Berthe Beaufils. Mme. Beaufils—she wore a wedding ring, the laundress remembered—was quite well dressed and free with her money. They had one bottle of wine, then two. Mme. Beaufils bought Yvette-Marie an *assiette de crudités,* a rare treat the young woman ate with unrestrained appetite.

Mme. Beaufils was at the Café the following day and the day after that, always friendly, always willing to buy. Yvette came to recount the details of her day, and noted that the infamous M. Landru was actually a very nice gentleman, and certainly a polite one. Mme. Beaufils did not seem interested in Landru, but professed amazement when Yvette-Marie told her that one of Landru's guards was a Monsieur Anatole Lebuisson, a former corporal from Trifouilly-les-Oies who had suffered minor wounds in the war.

"Anatole Lebuisson?" Mme. Beaufils paled! They had been raised in the same village! She had thought him lost during the Battle of Liège!

They drank to Anatole Lebuisson's health, and before long Mme. Beaufils mused about the possibility of seeing Anatole again. That would indeed be something! Mme. Beaufils's face then turned melancholy, and with minimal prodding from Yvette-Marie, she admitted that as a younger woman, she had borne a long and fruitless love for Anatole. She had married another, a bicycle salesman who had died of influenza a year earlier, but deep in her heart, it was Anatole she longed for.

To Yvette-Marie, who had read Victor Hugo as a child and saved her *sous* to see his plays at the Théâtre National Populaire, the tale of Anatole, the prison guard, and Mme. Beaufils, the bereaved widow, was the stuff of unvarnished romance. There and then, between two mouthfuls of herring filet *avec moutarde* and *oeufs mayonnaise*, she decided she would be the one to reunite the pair.

Mme. Beaufils was reluctant at first. What if Anatole was married? He wasn't, Yvette-Marie assured her. He wore no wedding ring—she had noticed that because her mother had told her this was the first thing to look for on a man.

Mme. Beaufils hemmed and hawed, but Yvette-Marie was insistent. Soon they had worked out a basic plan that would allow Mme. Beaufils to see her Anatole again.

Here, said M. Lefebvre, the story became a bit more complex. Mme. Beaufils spirited Landru from the prison, and both vanished. Her true name, the police believe, was Brigitte Bonjean, a sometimes *comédienne* with a few arrests and convictions for theft and prostitution. Brigitte Bonjean was one of Landru's many conquests who did not end up being cremated in his oven. She loved the man. This impressed M. Lefebvre. "*Vous vous imaginez? Quel amour! Mon Dieu! Quelle passion!*"

Chapter 58

Paris, Monday, October 6, 1919

Frederick has returned from his latest jaunt looking very pleased with himself. He has moved out and is now renting an elegant apartment in the 17th arrondissement. I am not unhappy with his decision. He will continue to pay the rent on the place we had together and will contribute to bills and upkeep. I will have a home of my own. We exchange telephone calls every three or four days. Alan Stabler, the young man working for him, appears smart and industrious. I do not believe he shares Frederick's proclivities, but these days, who knows?

Frederick's move signals the end of our marriage. I search within myself for traces of anger or resentment and find none. Neither of us made the best choice in selecting a mate, and that is all there is to that.

There is a new café, Le Retrait des Peintres, where the food is placed on tables and one helps oneself, buffet style. You eat all you want, and return for more if still hungry, all for a very reasonable fee. Jean Cocteau has baptized it a *café-teria*—a café, he says, for the *proletariat*. James and I visited the place yesterday. Picasso was there—that man is *everywhere*—and were I the suspicious type, I would swear he is stalking me. He grabbed my bottom as we waited in line, so I stabbed the offending hand with a fish fork. He howled that I had destroyed the brush hand of the greatest artist who had ever lived. I said, "Sorry," and kicked him sharply in the ankle. I have never liked the man, and he brings out the worst in me.

I did embarrass James, who believes there are better ways of handling the Spaniard. I got quite upset. My emotions tend to rise to the surface very quickly just before menstration, and I accused poor James of being an unfeeling boor who would stand by like an Italian *carabinieri* as I was ravished. I immediately regretted my words, apologized, and we spent the better part of the afternoon making love in his apartment.

I almost forgot *the* news of the day. The murderer Landru has escaped! We women have been instructed by the authorities (the same ones who somehow let Landru wander off) to be wary of whom we befriend. James has promised to tell me all he learns from his mailman.

Chapter 59

Landru wore an ill-fitting wig, as did many former soldiers to conceal head wounds. If anything, passers-by averted their eyes. It was not polite to stare at someone who had suffered so.

He had a pebble in his right boot. It was uncomfortable and forced a limp. He was clean-shaven, wore a pair of spectacles, and carried a cane.

He would not remain free, of course; he knew this. He had simply wanted to demonstrate his superiority and had done so with success; more than 10,000 gendarmes and *flics* were looking for him throughout the land and in the colonies.

He was tired. The months spent in prison had weakened him. A year earlier, he could single-handedly wheel a barrow full of ponderous furniture up a hill without drawing a difficult breath. Now, climbing the stairs exhausted him, and he felt as weak as a sickly child.

He had money. Brigitte Bonjean, the woman who had rescued him, the woman he had recently killed and whose body was now hidden in a coal cellar, did not trust banks and so secreted small wads of bank notes throughout her apartment. He had found most of them.

He adjusted a strand of the wig. He had glued the thing in place and now his head itched and he couldn't scratch it.

Landru had wanted to see his children, but the authorities had spirited the family away to parts unknown, possibly for its own safety. Certainly, poor Maurice, his elder child, would not be resilient enough to cope with being Landru's son. Maurice, Landru liked to joke, had not invented the butter knife. The boy was slow and prone to smoldering angers, but he had been a good son and Landru missed him.

He sat on a bench on the left bank of the Seine, unwrapped a work-man's *casse-croûte* of bread, *saucisson* and cheese. He bit into the bread, watched the ubiquitous Parisian sparrows fight over crumbs dropped between his feet. He unscrewed the top of a battered Thermos jug and poured a cup of tea. In the slats of the bench was a folded newspaper. Landru opened it and smoothed it across his lap. The headline was enor-mous, flat black. *Le Monstre Echappé.* The Monster At Large.

It was not a good photo of him, taken when formal charges were lodged. Still, his chin jutted forward and his eyes glowed defiant. This was not a conquered man. The writer had misspelled Brigitte Bonjean's name and described her as a cabaret dancer, an error. The number eleven was once more cited as the toll he'd taken, which mildly annoyed him.

He read that he'd been spotted sitting on a bench at the Jardin Zoologique, feeding the pigeons. Also, on the Champs de Mars playing *pétanque* with a team of men from Nice. An *épicier* reported to the police that the fugitive had bought five hundred grams of *boudin* and a jar of pickles from his shop. A nursemaid said she'd seen him sailing a model ship at the Tuileries, and later that same day, he'd been witnessed wearing red pantaloons and a fez while riding an elephant at the Cirque Médrano. Reports of Landru sightings came from Brussels, Geneva, Antwerp, Nice, Algiers, Cannes, Madrid, Montpellier, Oran, Tunis, Dakar, and Dusseldorf. Landru laughed as he read, until he saw the next passage, the only piece of evidence uncovered so far that had any chance of leading to his capture.

The dismembered body of a woman believed to be Brigitte Bonjean, also known as Berthe Beaufils, was found in the coal cellar of a ram-shackle Clichy hotel. Her various parts had been wrapped in butcher paper and found by the hotel's dog. The obese animal had waddled into the establishment's sitting room with one of Mme. Bonjean's forearms clamped in its jaw.

Landru turned the page and read with interest that in the United States of America, the government had two months earlier forbidden the sale of liquor to its citizenry. This struck him as so ludicrous that he started laughing again and almost choked on his tea.

CHAPTER 60

M. Lefebvre reported to Johnson, *"Landru haz keelled agan."*
The mailman added that the chief warden of the Prison St.
Lazare had been ignominiously stripped of his rank and fired, as were
several lower-level functionaries. The police were no closer to finding
the escapee than they had been seventy hours earlier. Neither Landru
nor his victim had stayed at the hotel. The killer had simply chosen that
establishment to dump the poor woman's remains. Monsieur Lefebvre's
inspector cousin thought Landru would assume an identity with which
he was familiar—either a bicycle mechanic or a merchant of used furniture. The postman was taking a few days off to help the search. A vast
reward was posted. Monsieur Lefebvre thought he might use this to get
to America with his intended.

Jean Cocteau gave James Johnson his script for *Le Boeuf sur le Toit,*
and the American saw that the production's format had changed once
again. It was no longer a play but a ballet of sorts, set in a bar that may
or may not have been in the United States. There were to be men in
women's clothing. Clowns and dwarves were involved as well, as was
a beheading by an overhead fan, and a resurrection, all this set to raucous music from South America, with Cocteau himself playing a variety
of percussion instruments. This promised to be an evening designed to
destroy the reputation of all involved.

Cocteau was ecstatic, citing his work as an amazing display of artistic
cooperation. In one breath, he mentioned Satie, Coco Chanel, Darius
Milhaud, Raoul Dufy, and Charlie Chaplin. Johnson felt a nadir had
been reached in his career; he was relegated to translating for midgets,
freaks, transvestites and for all he knew a Hottentot. Easter found it

vastly amusing; Johnson did not and swore to avoid the play's opening night at the Théâtre des Champs-Élyseés.

He could not stay angry at Easter for long. Their most recent physical encounter had astounded him. It had never struck him that a woman could derive joy from the physical act of sex. Certainly, his former fiancée never had; twice, when they were engaged, she had raised the hem of her nightgown above her waist, then turned her head into a pillow and so maintained a dreadful silence. Both times Johnson had felt guilty after the act, as if he had somehow violated her. She, in turn, did nothing to make him feel otherwise.

Easter, on the other hand, genuinely liked sex. She moved about and twisted and turned and guided him into doing what she wanted, something he'd never experienced before and could scarcely have imagined by himself. When he resisted, she insisted. He sometimes wondered where she'd learned what she practiced. The outcome was as intensely pleasurable as it was embarrassing, to him at least.

CHAPTER 61

O n the last Thursday in November, Easter and James hosted a small party for *Le Jour de Merci Donnant*. It was James's idea; a number of expatriates were in town with no place to celebrate their Thanksgiving.

Jean Cocteau located two turkeys. He was inordinately proud of this and named them Eloise and Abelard. "You don't know the hardship I had to go through for these animals, my dear Easter. We call them *dindes,* and they don't exist in France. I had to send an extravagant check to a farmer in Nantes."

The two birds were delivered by the local butcher, who had never dressed such large fowls. He asked Easter if he might have a taste of left-overs, *"juste pour goûter."*

They found most of the makings for a traditional meal, save for the yams. Easter's bilingual Larousse didn't even list the word. Nor was there any cranberry sauce, so they settled on *confiture d'airelles* from the Vosges. Despite the unavailable American ingredients, all agreed the meal was splendid.

At the far side of the table, Johnson sat next to a visiting American businessman and his wife. The woman, a tall brunette who had once played a bit part in a Hal Roach movie, was smoking a cigarette in a long holder and complaining that Paris was dark, sooty, dirty, and depressing.

"Paris has gone through a lot," Johnson said. "It's still recuperating. Imagine—there were almost six million people either killed, wounded, or missing. The French have a right to look sad."

The woman shrugged, tapped her cigarette into an ashtray.

"Maybe so. But there's dog poop absolutely *everywhere!* Just because people die doesn't mean they can't keep their streets clean."

Johnson caught the embarrassed businessman's eye.

"Well," the woman continued, "it's true! We'd never let Baltimore look like this…"

Gertrude Stein and Alice Toklas, sitting side by side and holding hands, held forth to an impressed circle of English-language writers. James did not know all their names, only that one or two had recently been published, and that Easter had brought back autographed copies of their books.

At one point, he overheard Stein say, "Yes, Mr. Pound, we all agree that war is immoral. Tell it to the Germans. They're the ones who insist on pouring across the borders every fifty years or so."

After the meal, Modigliani and his Jeanne sat on a divan in the corner of the living room. The artist was speaking with his new agent, Leo Zborowski, while Jeanne looked both bored and tired. She was four months pregnant with their second child, and Easter had heard that Jeanne was having a difficult time. Much to Jeanne's distress, Modi was planning on spending several months without her in the south of France. Modi and Jeanne had spent summer months in Nice on the advice of the agent, in the hope of selling some works to the wealthy Brits summering there. This time, Modi would go alone during the winter season, and she would bear their newest child not knowing when its father would return.

Easter approached her. "Jeanne? *Ça va?* Can I get you something?"

Jeanne looked up, stood with difficulty. *"Une tasse d'eau chaude, s'il te plaît."*

Jeanne rarely drank anything other than hot water occasionally flavored with a lemon drop. She leaned close to Easter, whispered, in English, "Can we go somewhere and talk? I need your advice."

Jeanne Hébuterne, when she spoke at all, spoke English well. The product of a French middle-class education, she had studied languages at her *lycée* and spent time in London to improve her skills, though she seldom spoke English in public.

They moved to the kitchen. Jeanne leaned close to Easter and said, "He is very sick, Modi. I know. He won't tell me, but he coughs all the time, day and night. And he drinks all the time, too." She sipped at her water. "It is not good, this going to Nice by himself. When we are together, I watch out for him, make sure he eats, he gets sleep. But if he goes alone…" Jeanne shrugged her shoulders. She put the cup down, held her large stomach with both hands and gave a tired smile. "This one will be big, much bigger than *la petite Jeanne*."

She had given birth twenty months earlier to their first child, a beautiful six-pound baby, also named Jeanne.

"So, Easter," she said, pronouncing the name Eestair, "I would be happy if you could get your friend James to talk to Modi? Maybe tell him this is a bad idea, going to Nice now. Modi listens to James, he thinks James is very smart, very…" she struggled for the word, "you know, *futé*."

Easter nodded, smiled. "Of course. James is indeed *très futé*. In English, you would say 'clever.' I'll see to it that James catches Modi tonight, before the both of you leave."

Frederick, though invited, had chosen not to come. He was planning his next booze trip, as Alan Stabler referred to them. He was now a very rich man. His new friend, Gerald Michelson, was traveling to England for a week, and Frederick anxiously awaited the young man's return.

Frederick had told Easter of an unexpected visitor. A Chinaman, a day earlier, had bowed deeply at Frederick's door and introduced himself in remarkably good English.

"Mr. Cowles, I am Yong Qing Shan. I have been asked to give you this," and here he handed Frederick the box wrapped in red silk paper, then glanced quickly at Alan Stabler, who excused himself from the room.

"This is a new product we are offering to our most esteemed customers, of which you are one, of course. It is purer and only slightly more expensive. This gift, we hope, will speak for itself. Please enjoy it, and when you need more, I trust you will contact me, night or day." He pointed to the box which Frederick said carried an elaborately etched calling card, bearing two telephone numbers.

"Night or day," the Chinaman repeated. He bowed once, did a sharp about-face, and vanished down the stairs without a sound.

CHAPTER 62

The search for Landru continued. On five separate occasions, men bearing an uncanny resemblance to the escapee were arrested, then released. No more bodies were found. Inspector Gaspard Belin, now fully in charge of the investigation, kept his men close-mouthed. In public, he would only say that the police were following a number of promising leads both in France and abroad.

This unleashed a flurry of conjectures; one was that Landru had been seen in Madagascar, just outside Tananarive, running a bicycle repair shop. *L'Humanité*, the French communist newspaper, ran a long article explaining why Landru's crimes, though hateful, were committed by a man betrayed by the materialistic, war-loving society that raised him. Inspector Belin, in a rare and angry comment, said he found the article *"stupide et idiotique."*

Monsieur Lefebvre now spent less time gossiping and more time with his *enamorada*, Marcelle Colombini. The union was tempestuous. Mme. Colombini was sharp-tongued and heavy-handed. She used both appendages with gusto. When she and M. Lefebvre set up housekeeping in a street-level apartment in the Marais district, the postman discovered the price of quasi-marital bliss. Mme. Colombini, fierce in bed, aggressive and insistent on being granted her own satisfaction, refused to wed; she would lose her widow's pension if she became Mme. Lefebvre and was not about to give up the state stipend. This troubled M. Lefebvre, who had not entirely put out of his mind the swarthy Corsican suitor he had battled for Mme. Colombini's heart and thighs. On occasion, they had fierce fights and cursed at each other in English. That had been

Mme. Colombini's idea—that they speak English whenever they were together—and their progress was noticeable.

M. Lefebvre relied increasingly on James Johnson for words, phrases, and American idioms. Mme. Colombini did not have an available American source. On occasion—but not too often, as Mme. Colombini's sense of humor was limited—he teased her with new words his friend M. Johnson had taught him, refusing to translate until some small bargain had been made. This would send Mme. Colombini clomping to thumb her English/French Larousse with a moistened finger as M. Lefebvre laboriously spelled the word, using the American alphabet.

Johnson and Easter forged an easy relationship. They painted during the day, and Easter continued to write stories about the Paris of artists for English-language newspapers. She was commissioned to present a series of lectures and returned for two weeks to the U.S. to tour major cities. She spent time in New York, Chicago, Washington, Boston, and Philadelphia. The only difficult time was at Chicago's Art Institute Museum, where Frederick's mother assailed her during an appearance. The older woman was distraught and seemingly under the influence of alcohol. She insisted Easter return her son to her, believing him to be sequestered in Easter's hotel room. The ruckus was quickly dispelled and Easter never heard another word from either Frederick's father or mother.

Back in Europe, she again began dealing with the minutia of putting together Cocteau's play, *Le Boeuf sur le Toit*. There had been endless delays with every aspect of the production. The Théâtre des Champs Élysées, hearing rumors of the play's absurdities and refusing to become the laughing stock of Paris, twice cancelled the show. It was only when Cocteau pulled strings with an older "good friend" who served in the *Ministère de la Culture* that the theater relented and agreed to rent space for the performance at twice the normal rate.

Chapter 63

The little ball wrapped in gold foil was in the side pocket of his new tweed jacket. Frederick's hand rested on it gently. He scanned up and down the street, sipped his martini. Gerald would be there any moment, back from his week in London, and Frederick had plans. Despite the coolness of the day, he was sitting outside the restaurant Maillabuau on Rue Ste-Anne. The place—some had called it shabby—was known for superb food and prices that made the rich blink. Frederick knew this and had selected the restaurant to impress Gerald, who lately maintained an air of bored diffidence when they were together in public.

When Gerald arrived, Frederick kissed him gently on both cheeks, received a hug, and whispered, "I hope you have the afternoon off..." He led him inside, and they ordered a *fricassée* and salads. They spoke of London, America, the weather, the French, the economy. After dessert, they had coffee and anisette, then walked to Frederick's car.

As they drove to the Cimetière du Montparnasse near the train station, Frederick reached under the dashboard of the car to a secret compartment he'd had installed there. He pulled out a suede pouch and handed it to Michelson. "Go on, open it."

Michelson did so gingerly.

"The long stem piece attaches to this shorter one, and the meerschaum bowl screws on top." He watched Michelson assemble the opium pipe, added, "It's an antique. From China. I hope you like it."

Michelson smiled and shrugged.

Minutes later Frederick was leading him past graves and mausoleums to his favorite bench beneath the oak tree. "I love this place; I come here as often as I can. My friend Cocteau dislikes it, says he doesn't like the sense of walking on bones, but I never feel that way. It's quiet, and there's almost never anyone here."

They both sat.

"Now, you've told me you've never smoked opium before. You're in for a rare treat. Opium is the one thing the French have taught me that I consider worthwhile," Frederick said. "Of course, they didn't come up with it themselves, but I'm relatively sure that if I'd stayed in Chicago..." He assembled his own pipe, took the gold leaf-covered ball from his pocket. "This is a gift from my Chinese associate. I want to share it with you."

Michelson was unsure. "I've heard bad things about opium, Frederick. People get addicted; once they start they can't stop. I'm not sure this is a good idea."

Frederick smiled. "Do I look like an addict to you, Gerald? Do I look like a man in the throes of cravings? No," he shook his head. "There's no danger. For lesser men, perhaps, or lesser races. But not for the likes of us. We are Americans and we guide our own destinies... Now, here is what you do."

Frederick peeled the gold leaf from the opium, took a large pinch, kneaded it until it was malleable. "Opium's been around a very long time. My friend Cocteau thinks it dates from before Christianity—imagine that! For all we know they were smoking opium at the last supper!

He placed the brown ball in the bowl of Michelson's pipe, "When I light it, you're going to inhale deeply, like this..." He made a deep sucking sound to demonstrate. "And hold it in your lungs for as long as you can, at least for the first puff." He handed the pipe to Michelson, who looked uncertain. Frederick peered at him closely. "You know I wouldn't dream of harming you, Gerald. I've done this hundreds of times. I promise: This will change your life!"

Frederick lit the opium with his gold lighter; Michelson inhaled deeply, held his breath and coughed violently. Frederick laughed, said, "That's normal, do it again!" Michelson did, and suddenly stopped moving. His eyes grew wide, wider, alarm furrowing his brow. He wheezed once, made a choking noise. Still smiling, Frederick slapped him on the back. Michelson, struggling for breath, coughed once, very hard, and a mist of blood erupted from his mouth. He wiped his lips with the back of his hand, looked at the blood curiously, then at Frederick, who frowned and said, "That's not supposed to happen."

Michelson's legs buckled when he tried to stand. He collapsed back down on the bench, spewed more blood from his mouth and nose. Frozen, Frederick looked down on his friend, then without thinking tried to staunch the flow with his linen handkerchief. It turned red in his hand. The stream suddenly stopped and Michelson said, "Oh! Oh!" very softly. He fell against Frederick and exhaled a mouthful of blood and vomit on Frederick's shoulder and neck. Aghast, Frederick watched Michelson collapse on the bench and roll to the ground. His eyes were open, pleading; a last tremor surged through him, and he was still.

Frederick nudged the body with the toe of his shoe.

"Gerald? Gerald, are you alright?" He stepped back, looked around. No one in sight, no help to be found. He thought of yelling for assistance but something stopped him. Gerald, he knew with ghastly certainty, was dead. Frederick retched, felt the very fine food from Maillabuau come up and tickle his throat. It took all his strength to swallow, breathe, and breathe again.

He knelt next to Michelson's body and smoothed his friend's disheveled hair. He stroked his cheek, wept tears on his lips and neck. He held him as if a child. After a time, he reached into the man's breast pocket, removed a wallet, a comb, a capped fountain pen, and a ticket stub for the Toulon-to-Paris train. Gerald's other pockets yielded a pack of Chesterfield cigarettes, three books of matches, a set of house keys, a folded six-page legal brief and a silver-plated business card case. Frederick took it all.

With effort, he lifted Gerald's body and sat it on the bench. From afar, it would look as if a *clochard* had fallen asleep there.

Frederick walked back to his car, disembodied, as if watching his own actions from a hidden place. The words "poison meant for me" bounced about in his mind.

Almost audibly, he whispered, "Why me? I'm a nice person; I've never hurt anyone. Who would want to hurt me?"

He sat in the car and shuddered uncontrollably. He started crying, anger, sorrow and fear melding into one horrendous and uncontrollable emotion. He let it wash over him, shoulders shaking. A pedestrian walked past the car, crossed himself. Mourners in tears were common near the cemetery.

It took Frederick a fierce effort of will to drive his car home. Every passer-by, motorist, idle walker and street-crosser was staring at him. He knew this and weathered their stares with a scowl of his own. His hands trembled, and when the car was finally in front of the apartment on Rue de la Terrasse, he stayed in it, trying to breathe deeply to control his panic. Someone had tried to kill him.

When he felt strong enough, he opened the car door and scuttled to the entrance of his building. He did not wait for the elevator but took the stairs two at a time. He entered the apartment, locked himself inside and braced a chair against the door.

On his desk, a note from Alan Stabler read:

Frederick: Could your father have meant "absinthe" and not "absence"?

Chapter 64

Paris, Monday, December 1, 1919

Frederick is leaving Paris, apparently for good. He came by my apartment yesterday evening flustered and wild-eyed. He is persuaded that some Chinese people are trying to kill him. He says they killed his new friend Gerald by mistake or perhaps on purpose, and that he is next, and here I completely lost track of his tale.

Frederick has become a wealthy man in mere months. I know something of the business he is involved with—essentially supplying American bootleggers with French alcohol—and he told me a month or so ago that he had concluded a deal that had reaped a small fortune. He was planning to buy a new car, and I wonder if the pressures of newfound wealth and his increasing use of opium were too much for him.

I suggested he talk with Cocteau or James, but he was adamant. He says he will go to Holland or Belgium and will be in touch later. I don't know what to think.

I called his assistant, Alan Stabler, a nice man with whom Frederick has traveled, and was told Frederick had received a strange telegram from his father and that a Chinese man had indeed visited his apartment some days ago bearing a gift! Young Alan also said that up until very recently, Frederick's demeanor had not changed, but that two days ago *something* occurred, though he does not know what.

In spite of his agitation, Frederick made it a point to say that our financial arrangement would remain in place. He will continue to pay rent and contribute to expenses.

I wonder what happened. There was an item in the newspaper about a body being found at the Cimetière du Montparnasse which, come to think of it, should not be considered strange at all. Bodies and cemeteries often share space.

James thinks it must have had something to do with Frederick's smuggling—for that is what it was—spirits to the States. "It's not exactly a savory trade," he said. "Some very nasty people are involved in this. Gangsters and such. Maybe Frederick made some enemies there..." This is as good a theory as any, but the idea of Frederick crossing paths with gangster seems far-fetched.

I have not spoken with Jean Cocteau; he and Frederick have been estranged of late. The last time I saw Jean, he told me Frederick has a new friend, a young American working in Paris. Jean said it was odd—the two even look alike.

CHAPTER 65

Johnson learned of Fredericks' move. He was surprised, hopeful, and quietly elated, but Easter dashed his expectations within minutes.

"I know what you're going to ask, James, and the answer is no."

He didn't protest.

She added, "I have to be alone a little while, just long enough to make sure that I am not simply flitting from one relationship to another. I know you understand."

He didn't and sulked for the rest of the day. Easter was having none of it.

"It's silly to be angry, James."

He thought about it, answered, "I'm not angry, just disappointed."

She looked at him, held one of his hands in both of hers. "My James! You never do get angry, do you? How is that?"

He thought for a moment.

"I don't know. Honestly, I think after having seen some things during the war, being part of them, I just don't have the capacity for anger any more. I'm alive. I have all my limbs. I live well. I do what I like. I'm in love," He looked at her and smiled. "There's nothing to be angry about."

She pressed him. "Even the things you saw? That didn't make you angry?"

He shrugged again; his eyes misted.

She said, "Tell me, James."

So, he did. He spoke of Felker, with whom he drove the ambulances, and of bodies made rigid by both death and cold. He told her everything in a quiet, even voice, patting at his eyes with a folded handkerchief.

CHAPTER 66

Paris, Tuesday, January 29, 1920

M odi is dead. He died in my arms, five days ago. I can scarcely hold a pen and write; my hands are still shaking. He died as Jeanne looked on, her pregnancy almost full term. Her eyes were blank and as dead as his.

I must try to make sense of this for my own peace of mind. I have a dreadful feeling of *déja vu*. It has been more than two years since Mother died in my presence, that I heard her last breath and saw her eyes close. Now, death has come again. I held Modi's head in my lap. Jeanne was there—but not really—as were Leo Zborowski and Ortiz de Zarate, an Italian painter living one floor below. It was a horrible scene, a dismal setting not worthy of such a genius.

Last month, Modi and Jeanne moved to their new apartment on Rue de la Grande Chaumière. Five days ago, Jeanne, uncharacteristically, invited me over, saying she wanted decorating advice. She had told me in the past how much she liked the place on Rue Vercingétorix.

I took the small elevator to the third floor and found the front door of their apartment open. I could hear a commotion, then de Zarate rushed past me, saying something in his heavy accent about getting a doctor. I hurried through their living room into the small bedroom to the left and witnessed a scene of absolute despair. Modi was in the disheveled bed, delirious, surrounded by empty wine bottles, and opened tins of sardines. There were oil stains on the sheets and the remnants of a half-eaten sandwich on his pillow. He was holding his head and complaining of a terrible migraine.

Jeanne sat on the edge of the bed, holding her stomach and swaying from side to side. I tried to calm Modi, and suddenly he was very still, his breath coming out in loud rasps. I took Jeanne by the shoulders and shook her slightly, but she did not respond. Modi let out a heavy moan, so I turned my attention back to him and supported his head on my lap. He looked up at me, but he did not recognize who I was. He said, *"Mamma, la domanda? Qual è la domanda?"*

Zborowski ran into the room at that very moment. He had been waiting downstairs for Modi when de Zarate almost bowled him over. Behind him was a man I took to be a doctor. He knelt by us, took Modi's wrist, and tried to find a pulse. Then he raised Modi to a sitting position while I still supported him, and looked into his eyes. He tried for a pulse again, slapped Modi lightly on both cheeks. There was no response.

Jeanne was still swaying from side to side, keening low and gently. She leaned over, took Modi's face into her hands, and kissed him violently, her mouth on his, as if to force her breath into his chest. Then, with surprising strength, she wrested him from me, took hold of his shoulders and stretched him out over the bed. She tried to lay on him, but her stomach got in the way and she only managed to drape her legs over his, and this upended an open can of sardines that began leaking oil onto the coverlet. Finally, she kneeled over him and started hitting his chest with her small fists, whispering, "Non! Non! Non!"

I saw the doctor fumble with his bag and remove a hypodermic syringe. In one smooth move, he raised Jeanne's left sleeves and slid the needle into the flesh of her upper arm. Jeanne looked up, made a coughing sound, and collapsed on top of Modi. The doctor and de Zarate pulled her gently off, and sat her on a chair. I noticed she was not wearing any undergarments. Her legs were splayed, so I stood and closed her knees. Modi's eyes were wide open as if focusing on a spot on the ceiling. The doctor closed them. He looked first at de Zarate, then at me, and finally at Zborowski, who had moved off to a corner of the room and was holding his hands up to his mouth.

"C'est fini. Il est mort."

No one reacted. De Zarate's eyes brimmed with tears. Jeanne was immobile on the chair. The moment lasted an infinity. Finally, the doctor picked up his bag and shut it. He asked if there was a telephone in the room, and Zborowski shook his head "no." He asked, very softly, if I would be so kind as to go downstairs to the concierge's *loge* and to call the *hospitaliers*. I did this and, within fifty minutes, two stocky men in white uniforms were at the door with a stretcher. They took Modi away.

I don't remember clearly what followed. Jeanne woke and I decided to take her to my home. Her parents—stolid middle-class citizens—had disowned her when she was pregnant with Modi's first child. Bringing her with me in this terrible hour was all I could think to do.

Zborowski had a key to the apartment and promised to lock up after he and de Zarate cleaned the bedroom of sardine cans, cigarette butts and empty bottles. I gathered up a few of Jeanne's clothes and put them in a leather bag I found near their armoire.

When we were on the sidewalk waiting for a taxi, the doctor gave me a vial with a dozen pills in it, and a small bottle of serum to facilitate sleep. "*Pour la jeune femme*," he said. For Jeanne.

On the way home in the cab, I changed my mind and asked the driver to take us to James's apartment instead of mine. I needed to be with him; he would be a calming influence on Jeanne. Also, I thought, his studio could become a makeshift bedroom. Truthfully, at this tragic moment, I did not want to be with her alone.

James was not home. Mme. Bertrand let us in and fixed tea, all the while cooing at Jeanne, who was indifferent to her surroundings.

I settled Jeanne in the spare bed, moving her as if she were a marionette with no will of her own. I gave her a pill and two teaspoons of the sleeping potion.

James returned an hour or so later. He had been buying tomatoes at Les Halles. When I told him what had happened, he dropped the sack of tomatoes and the fruits rolled about the floor. He regained his composure, and while we were both on our knees picking the tomatoes up and placing them in his kitchen sink, I said that Jeanne was sleeping and would need our help. I told him I would also stay until morning. It would be the first time we spent a night under one roof in Paris.

CHAPTER 67

Modigliani's death stunned James Johnson.

Tragedy came in threes. Not long after, they lost Jeanne and her unborn child.

Jeanne spent the last night of her life in Johnson's studio, huddled beneath blankets on the sofa where his models normally posed. Easter slept next to her in a *chaise longue*.

The morning after Modi's death, Jeanne's parents, M. and Mme. Hébuterne, came for her. Monsieur Hébuterne worked as an accountant for *Le Bon Marché*, the giant department store. They were dressed somberly, spoke in whispers and treated their daughter like a broken doll. When Jeanne left, she hugged Easter, and then barely touched Johnson's cheek with her lips. He had the impression a ghost had passed.

The next morning, she threw herself from a window of her parents' fifth floor apartment. She died instantly, and the unborn baby was crushed in her womb. Little Jeanne, the one-year-old daughter she had with Modi, was sent off to live with relatives in the country.

Jeanne was not buried next to Modi at Père Lachaise; her parents forbade it. The funeral was a brief affair. None of her friends were invited, but most showed up anyway at the Cimetière de Bagneux where she was interred. They stood at the periphery of the ceremony, and not once did the Hébuternes look in their direction.

It rained.

Fujita, her first lover, cried like an infant.

Many wondered how the Hébuternes obtained a full Catholic funeral for their daughter, since suicide is a mortal sin and against the Church. Johnson supposed money changed hands, as it always did.

Modi's agent, Zborowski, made an effort to catalog Modi's works, as well as Jeanne's, since they shared the same studio space. Modi apparently had staggering debts, and the sale of his art would eventually help settle some of these. Some works were missing. Modi had apparently been working on two commissioned portraits, and these were nowhere to be found. Of course, it was possible that Modi had painted over them to save canvas since he did that often.

Jeanne's works went to her family. She lived so deeply in Modi's shadow that people forgot she was very much an artist in her own right. Johnson had always liked her work, and while they were at the beach, she had given him a sketch of Easter that was both whimsical and revealing.

There was an unofficial get-together at La Rotonde to celebrate their lives. A number of people spoke, including Picasso who, between puffs on his stinking pipe, managed to turn the subject to his own creative visions and talent. Easter glared at him; Picasso never noticed.

Modi's old friend Brancusi was there. He sat by himself in a corner of the room and accepted condolences, nodding his head and muttering in a thick Romanian accent. It was to Modi that Brancusi had once said, "Create like a god, command like a king, work like a slave." The next day Modi painted those words on the ceiling above his bed.

Kiki, Treize, and a covey of other young women—some models, some not—made a relatively discreet entrance, all dressed in black by Coco Chanel, who took the opportunity to make a fashion statement. Kiki kissed Johnson on the cheek and gave him a light hug while whispering, "*Je suis désole, chéri...*" Rumors had it that long ago, shortly after she first appeared at La Rotonde looking like country girl, Modi had taken her to this studio where the two had spent a frenzied week together.

Most of Montparnasse's people came to La Rotonde, for once not solely to eat. The pickings were slim. La Rotonde's *patron* had not wanted a horde of drunken louts to degrade the evening. Modi, he said later with a wan smile, already owed him for more than a dozen meals.

According to the attending doctor, Modigliani died of meningitis, an inflammation of membranes that cover the brain and spinal cord. He was already so ravaged by alcohol and drugs that the illness easily took a mortal hold on him. He had no chance of survival.

But Jeanne… Johnson could not fathom Modi's hold over the young woman. He had never understood Jeanne's depth of feeling. He remembered seeing Modi drunk and vicious to her on occasion, and the softness of her demeanor never wavered. She'd accepted his poverty, his drunkenness, his abuse of hashish, the incredible selfish streak he wore almost with pride. Her one wish—to meet his family, to be legitimized—had never been granted.

Jeanne's brother, André, also came. It was he who had introduced Jeanne to this *beau monde*, had taken her to La Rotonde for the very first time. André had not amounted to much as an artist; he'd never shaken the mantle of Catholic sternness, nor escaped his bourgeois upbringing. He was shattered; it was visible in the paleness of his skin and the haunted quality of his eyes. Guilt, earned or not, was etched across his face.

In the days following the funeral of Amedeo Modigliani, life in Montparnasse took on a slower, more reflective pace. Those who knew him well reminded each other of the times they'd admonished him on his use of drugs and alcohol. But Modi had been proud, headstrong, in some ways irresistible, and, if only in his own mind, invincible as well.

The newspapers and magazines made more of his and Jeanne's death than they ever had made of their lives. The artists of Montparnasse and Montmartre were once again described as a raffish and immoral lot; their neighborhood a modern Sodom where sin and iniquity shared a bed. A long story in *France-Dimanche* on Kiki and her friends drew irate letters from readers who complained about the photos of Kiki wearing a very short dress and baring a shoulder and three-quarters of a breast.

Tsuguharu Fujita was given a show at the *Galerie Nouvelle*. His subtle use of colors was praised by everyone who attended, including the critics of *Le Monde* and *L'Echo*. He sold 23 pieces, prompting him to host a small gathering of friends, which turned into a somber affair; many spent the evening thinking of Jeanne.

Cocteau had gone to Cagnes in the Midi to attend a memorial for Renoir, who at age 78 died in his sleep in the early hours of December 3. Henri Matisse, studying under the older painter, was inconsolable and thinking of moving back to Paris. On November 30, Cocteau reported, the master was still painting a still life of two apples, using a brush taped to his thumb and forefinger. He weighed less than 40 kilograms and had to be carried everywhere.

Cocteau stayed and spent a week with Matisse and his companion and helped sort and catalog the master's works. When he returned to Paris, he was much subdued and, when he spoke to Easter, told her he could hardly cope with *la mort d'un dieu*, the death of a god.

CHAPTER 68

Paris, Monday, February 2, 1920

Things are very quiet here. I have heard from Frederick several times. His assistant, Alan Stabler, journeys every two weeks to Vienna where, thanks to the weakness of the currency there, Frederick lives like a king. I still do not know the details of his flight and probably never will. In a strange way, I miss him. When we were first together, Frederick was a bright young man full of good humor and eager to please. There are times I still feel guilty for having brought him here, and being responsible for who and what he has become. Alan has told me Frederick says he now abstains from opium, but a letter I received last week leads me to believe otherwise. Perhaps one day I will travel to Vienna and see him, but I'll wait until I am invited.

The deaths of Modi, Jeanne and the baby, and of Renoir in Cagnes last December, have stripped Montparnasse of its vitality.

James has at last stopped agonizing about his newfound nephew and his brother's whereabouts, knowing Daniel is alive somewhere.

I had a pleasant encounter worth recalling since it was made possible by The Detestable PP (Pablo Picasso, of course). I met Edith Wharton!

She is legendary, and for months I have heard of her exploits. The wife of a powerful New York banker, she had a life of ease but discovered her spouse was having endless affairs. For three years, and while still married, *she* had a passionate love affair with another writer, a Morton Fullerton who, like Frederick, was capable of loving both men and women. She and her husband came to Paris in 1909, and she established herself as a very successful writer. Of course, she had already been published and, as a matter of fact, I remember looking through her book, *The Decoration of Houses*. Mother had it in her modest library and referred to it often.

Here is how it happened. The Detestable PP was pontificating at *La Closerie des Lilas*, a brasserie where James and I enjoy excellent grilled ham and cheese sandwiches called *croque monsieurs*. PP was seated close to our table and holding court as he generally does, noting that the number of Americans in Paris is growing at an alarming pace (there are more than 6,000 of us today, with hundreds arriving every month.) At any rate, PP, who has not forgiven me for the fish fork incident, looked at me with that deprecating sneer I have grown to hate and said something to the effect that soon, the better restaurants would be serving American cheese and iced tea rather than *charcuterie* and Beaujolais. As he was speaking, a rather petite and not very elegant woman came up and whacked him sharply behind the head with her gloves. PP jumped out of his chair, furious, but when he saw her face, he slid into a most ingratiatingly false smile.

The woman said, "*Comme d'habitude, Pablo, vous racontez des conneries…*" Loosely translated, "As usual, Pablo, you speak nonsense," except that one would have to substitute a rude word for "nonsense."

I liked her immediately. James, seated next to me, had risen and bowed slightly.

"Easter Cowles, this is Edith Wharton. Edith, this is my friend, Mrs. Cowles, formerly of Chicago but now a resident here."

She took my hand in hers, shook it slightly, smiled, and asked if she could join us. James pulled out a chair. She leaned forward and whispered, "Are you the one who stabbed that silly man with a fish fork?" When I nodded, she gave me an extraordinarily bright smile. "Well then, we're going to be great friends!"

And that is exactly what has happened! In the last two weeks, I have met her at the Hôtel Crillon three times for tea. She moved from Paris some years ago and now lives in a glorious villa, Pavilion Colombe in Saint-Brice-Sous-Forêt, some 30 kilometers north of here. She has invited me to visit her next week.

We had a late lunch yesterday, and she astounded me when she said she had read my columns in the European edition of the *Trib* and found them interesting. She, herself, is awaiting publication of her latest work, titled *The Age of Innocence*. I was careful not to question her too much about the book, and she told me only that it deals with the lives of New York socialites over a 35-year period. She has promised me an autographed advance copy.

We were eating dessert when she mentioned Jean Cocteau and Frederick. I must have reacted awkwardly, because she dabbed her lips with her napkin, then reached across the table and took my hand in hers.

"Easter, my charming companion, surely you never expected Cocteau to keep a secret! *Everyone* in Paris knew about him and your husband, and not a single person cared! Frederick, right? Where is he? In Austria or Switzerland? Will you divorce him? You know, in New York, divorce is in itself a diploma of virtue. I wrote that in one of my books, or perhaps an article in Scribner's. At any rate, it's one of my favorite quotes of myself!"

She laughed, delighted at her own wit. I'm sure that I continued to look discomfited, because she added, "Really, Easter… You have a lovely companion, and I am so happy that James has found someone. He was so lonely, so guilty over his brother's disappearance. He's decorated, James is. You knew that didn't you? Apparently drove his ambulance with great bravery and fortitude." She reached onto my dessert plate, spooned the last of the profiterole into her mouth. "And that fling with Kiki, well, it may have done him the same immediate good," she paused, waved her fork in the air, "as a mouthful of dessert!" She sipped her tea, looked at me with a glorious smile and added, "In Paris, sleeping with Kiki is a rite of passage. They've all done it—Fujita, Picasso; that writer Ernest tried but it didn't go well, I am told… Even that unfortunate Soutine has had his time with her…"

Well, I managed not to react, because I *did* know; James had told me. Still, hearing it between one mouthful of profiteroles and the next, that did set me back a bit. I took a long swallow of wine before responding.

"Frederick, my husband, has found a new side to himself since he's been here. As have I. I think we're both the better for it."

She nodded. "Well, of course you are. *That* is one of the best aspects of Paris. You can come here and be who you really are, or who you really are not. And you know, when I divorced my husband, I discovered that I loved the company of women as well as of men. Now I like to refer to myself as a 'vagitarian.'"

I choked on the profiterole. Edith laughed so hard I thought she might faint. Then she added, "And that was not a pass. So please do not take it as such."

CHAPTER 69

Edith Wharton hovered like a dragonfly over Parisian society. She knew everyone and everything, and few events escaped her attention. If a play opened, Wharton was there, often leaving before the end if she did not like it. At the opera, she had a private box habitually occupied by traveling luminaries. She was on a first-name basis with the composers of the day—Satie adored her and had once knelt at her feet in a pastiche of homage. Francis Poulenc, barely 20 years old, sat at her piano and unleashed a fury of notes. Maurice Ravel essayed the first few bars of a piece for violin and cello in her drawing room, then went home and wrote a sonata that took Paris by storm. He credited Wharton with its creation.

Easter and Wharton were sitting in a tea room near the Trocadéro when Wharton learned Easter was to work with Coco Chanel. She put down her pastry, carefully centered her cup on its saucer and said, "I have *never* liked that woman."

Easter, surprised by the small rush of anger in Wharton's voice, took a bite of her scone and said, "Ah."

Wharton repeated, "*Never.*"

They sipped in silence. Wharton appeared deep in thought, then said, "I detest gossip, although I love to hear it and pass it on, as long as it isn't about me or the people I like." She smiled, "So let me tell you a thing or two you should know about Mademoiselle Coco since you're going to be working with her."

Easter leaned closer.

"She's a *coucheuse*," Wharton said. "Do you know what that is?"

Easter did. The word described a woman who slept with men not for money, but for social or business advancement.

"When I came to Paris the first time," Wharton went on, "it was with Teddy, my husband—we split up several years after that—and one evening we were invited to dinner, I forget where and for whom, some passing-through American what-not. In any case, Mademoiselle Coco was there, and she seemed very polite, very charming. Pretty, too, I have to admit. That little upturned nose is quite appealing when it's not pointed towards the heavens as if it were the only way of getting there." She took a breath, a sip. "Anyway. When it was time to leave, I couldn't find Teddy, so I searched through the house and began to wonder if perhaps he'd left, because he would do that, you know. If he was bored, he would just take off and leave me to fend for myself. So then I heard some noise down a hallway and, yes, you guessed it, my dear husband was entertaining Mademoiselle Chanel in the *toilettes*." She paused, poured more tea, stirred in a trace of milk and a sugar cube.

"It was a ridiculous sight! He was sitting on the *bidet* huffing and puffing and *La Chanel* was astride him, her little skinny bottom bouncing like...like..."

Easter hand flew to her open mouth.

"Like some sort of plucked *chicken*. Yes, that's what it reminded me of. Skinny and bony and chicken-colored. *So* unattractive." She raised the china cup to her lips but did not sip.

Easter, eyes wide, asked, "What did you do?"

Wharton shrugged. "Closed the door, went back to the dinner party and had stiff drink. When Teddy came out, I suggested we go home. On the way out, we crossed Mademoiselle Coco and she gave the most glowing grimace..."

"She hadn't seen you?"

Edith Wharton smiled sadly. "Why, yes. Yes, of course she had."

Within days of meeting Chanel and working with her on Cocteau's production, Easter had good cause to wonder whether the diminutive designer was from the same litter as Picasso.

In Johnson's studio, she fumed. "Edith warned me, and she was right. That Chanel woman is utterly dislikeable and insanely demanding. And it doesn't matter what anyone thinks, she simply talks faster and louder. Plus, you know, it's very strange, but she seems to *lie* a lot. I don't know what to make of it."

Johnson looked up from the paint he was mixing. "What does she lie about…"

"Well," Easter paused, remembering. "Last week she said she'd been raised on a thoroughbred horse farm by her uncle. This week she said it was by impoverished maiden aunts. And her age. She told me she was 29. But I remember Cocteau once told me he knew for fact she was 36, and that she used to sing at the *café-concert*, and that's where she got her name. She sounded like a rooster, so people would go *cocorico* whenever she got on stage."

"As opposed to cock-a-doodle-doo?" Johnson smiled, added a dollop of orange to the mix. "This all sounds pretty benign."

"I know. And I'm not trying to be petty. But there are some things about her that truly bother me. During a rehearsal, she accused one of the helpers of having lost or stolen some fabric, and it created a nasty scene. Then she remembered that she'd never brought the fabric to the theater in the first place. That kind of thing has happened two or three times already, and it's not good for morale." She paused, sighed, "I must admit, though, she is a genius. She can take a bolt of cloth and turn it into anything."

Easter was now the go-between for several entities involved in producing Cocteau's *Le Boeuf sur le Toit*. Johnson, having translated the minimal stage directions for an eventual show in London, had politely declined to become further involved in what he called "the disaster."

Le Boeuf sur le Toit, Easter soon realized, had not been written by Cocteau, though the playwright liked to take credit for its conception. In fact, it was the composer Darius Milhaud who, returning from Brazil, had dreamt of the piece as a ballet scored for two flutes, woods, brass, strings, and percussion, and the work had been named after an existing Parisian restaurant that featured South American music.

"I suppose it is the nature of artists to invent realities about themselves," Easter said. "One would think Cocteau has enough accomplishments without taking credit for those of others."

Johnson shook his head. "No. Men like Jean are never happy with what they've done. That's what keeps them moving, a day-to-day dissatisfaction with their achievements. I think that also accounts for the addiction, at least partly, whether it's opium or alcohol or hashish. There's always a desire to see what's farther beyond, to try to grasp something unattainable."

Later that week Coco Chanel, in a fit of pique, quit the production. Though Cocteau used all his charms to prevent her departure, she stormed out, her two assistants juggling swatches and bolts of fabrics as they hurried after her. Easter saw her off with a cheerful American smile, a hug, and kisses inches away from both cheeks. Within half-a-day, Cocteau had enlisted the help of Guy-Pierre Fauconnet, a watercolorist and amateur dress-maker who arrived with *his* two assistants. In a matter of minutes, Fauconnet reduced all of Chanel's work to a colorful pile of discarded textiles. Then, he directed his assistants to stitch, cut and baste. In forty-eight hours, they completed the costuming. Fauconnet also handled much of the scenery.

The Fratellini brothers, Paul, François, and Albert, clowns and star members of Paris' Cirque Médrano, arrived at rehearsal in tailored suits of British worsted wool which they carefully draped on wooden hangers in one of the changing rooms. Cocteau thought them royalty and fawned, ordering a case of inexpensive champagne to celebrate their advent. The Fratellinis did not drink, so stagehands shared the bottles.

Picasso, Cocteau's great friend, had volunteered to assist Fauconnet create the scene settings for the play. Remembering Cocteau's promise that the painter would not be involved, Easter absented herself when he arrived. She returned to the theater two days later to discover the Spaniard had created an amazing backdrop of muted colors and violent blacks and whites. She was impressed, even as she avoided him, and mentioned it to Cocteau. When Picasso next saw Easter, he made a show of bowing and kissing her hand sloppily. Reeking of cheap pipe tobacco, he announced to the cast and crew, *"Madame. l'américaine aime mon Travail. Je suis humblement touché."* Easter was quite sure Picasso was neither moved nor humbled.

CHAPTER 70

Easter returned from a run-through of *Le Boeuf* exhausted, frustrated, and concerned. The apartment felt empty of life, almost as it had been the first time she'd seen it. She took off her coat and hat, propped the wet umbrella in the kitchen sink. Mathilde, the Bretonne maid, now came only once a week to clean. The place was too big for one person. Johnson desperately wanted to set up household with her, but Easter had demurred. Perhaps soon.

She went to the kitchen and boiled water for tea, carried pot and cup on a tray to the study, opened the large desk where she kept her writing and withdrew the diary.

*****

Paris, Tuesday, February 10, 1920

Frederick's departure still affects me. I don't know why. Recently, he sent me a will drafted in English by an Austrian lawyer. It was totally unexpected. He leaves me everything, should he pass on, and it is obvious that he is a savvy businessman. His holdings surprised me. Just before leaving, he gave our maid a bonus so large that she purchased a used Renault automobile for her son. She smiles ceaselessly now, though her cleaning skills still leave something to be desired. Whatever his faults, whatever his secrets, Frederick has become a generous man.

Our play will open on February 21 with a *répétition générale* for guests, mostly those who have put money into the production. Guy Fauconnet is a welcome addition to our crew. He is even-tempered and keeps an amused demeanor in the worst of times, and we have had some challenging afternoons.

The giant heads the performers are supposed to wear did not look right, so Picasso redesigned them. For all my dislike of the man, he did an amazing job. The actor portraying a policeman who is to be decapitated by a ceiling fan—and then recapitated—could not get his head to stay on. By the third rehearsal, the clay and *papier mâché* was so damaged that a new one had to be made. The Fratellini brothers threatened to walk out if they were not treated with more respect, and even Darius Milhaud, whose creation this *really* is, lost his patience when Cocteau, for the hundredth time, changed lines, sets, costumes, and order of presentation. Jean is treating this as if it were a groundbreaking event, rather than a 20-minute farce of doubtful taste. No matter. He has sponsors, a theater, and an audience. We are to travel to England in a few weeks, where the play will be performed at the Coliseum in London. James suggested the English version be named *The Nothing-Doing Bar* and Cocteau liked that immediately. James remarked that in the future, this will be the one thing he will be remembered for. I joked that he would be remembered for being my lover, after I became rich and famous. I am not sure he found this humorous.

Edith asked what I planned to have on at the opening, and when I told her I had not given it much thought, she dragged me to her *couturière* and the woman whipped up a very elegant dress in less than two days. The following afternoon, Edith surprised me by bringing to my apartment a collection of magnificent jewelry for me to wear. I was aghast at the very thought, but she insisted, so on opening night I will be wearing an array of diamonds and rubies.

Last night, Cocteau took the cast and crew to dinner—a rare event since he is notably close to his *sous*—and we went to the *Petit Bessonneau*, a tiny restaurant on Rue Blanche. Darius Milhaud introduced me to his composer friends who call themselves *Les Six*. I fear I remain somewhat of a Philistine, as I had heard of only two of them, Francis Poulenc and Arthur Honneger. I do not even remember the names of the other three. At any rate, we filled the small room, and, though the food was marginal, everyone had a wonderful time. After the meal, we all piled into three automobiles and drove to the Montmartre fair, where Cocteau demonstrated his shooting skills at one of the stands, and James knocked over milk bottles with tennis balls. He won me a small plush orangutan, and everyone applauded. We ended up in Milhaud's house sometime around 2 a.m. Francis Poulenc played his composition, *Cocarde*, and Darius let us listen to his original score for *Le Boeuf*. James and I got back to his apartment at four in the morning and we slept until noon the next day.

I saw my *clochard* again! He looked different—cleaner and freshly barbered—but I recognized him. He was sitting on a bench, and when I approached he walked away quickly. There is something very odd about the man.

CHAPTER 71

The *clochard* had been watching his brother for a long time. In Paris, so many men like himself were homeless, drunk, or addicted to morphine for their war wounds, that they ceased to exist in the public eye. Passers-by dropped a coin or two in the beggars' cups, and volunteers from the Salvation Army daily offered solace and a bed in return for prayers and church attendance. Most *clochards* rebuffed these advances. The American had spent two nights with the Sallies, arising at dawn for a breakfast of mush, pale coffee, and redemption. Two nights was all he could tolerate.

A week before, he had gone to a free veterans' clinic, and the doctor had shaken his head. "*Vous buvez, vous allez mourir. C'est simple.*" You drink, you die. He felt near death now; the excesses of alcohol had dulled his senses and maimed his stomach, tongue, and throat. There was a constant pain in his chest and he suffered from perpetual diarrhea. He knew he smelled—stank, actually—and for inexplicable reasons he had begun to care about this. He vomited daily, staggering into the *pissoires* and voiding his guts. Sometimes there was blood.

It was time to make a choice—life or oblivion—and if every fiber of him yearned for some sort of disappearance, still, minute parts of who he had been clung to life with tenacity and hope.

One morning when the last bottle of *gros rouge* was empty, he took begged francs to a rag man and bought a frayed but clean shirt and a worn jacket with patches at the elbows. He begged a little more and had his hair cut and stubble shaved by a barber in a *bas quartier.*

The next morning, he presented himself at the American Embassy on the Place de la Concorde. He had met the ambassador, William Graves

Sharp, when the latter had visited the escadrille during the war, and he'd shaken the diplomat's hand with enthusiasm. Sharp had invited all the boys to visit the embassy, but the *clochard* never quite got there.

The marine guards turned him away at the chancellery gate, as they had three earlier times when he had presented himself without any identity papers to prove his citizenship. The consular staff had asked if anyone could vouch for him, and he'd said no. He would not depend upon his brother or family, nor could he seek the aid of his former colleagues whose trust he'd betrayed. France, after the war, was a country dependent on and steeped in paperwork; a man without a passport or *carte d'identité* simply did not exist. He had foolishly left his papers behind when he'd stolen the airplane.

For weeks he had lurked about his brother's neighborhood, spied on the man as he went about his business. He knew the concierge by sight and sensed her wariness anytime he was near. She did not like *clochards* and stared them down with hooded eyes.

Never once did Daniel Johnson approach his brother James. He could not, would not, allow himself to be seen in such a sorry state. He had always considered himself James's protector, had rescued his younger sibling from countless situations involving parents, teachers, neighbors, and adults in general. He had taught James how to be tough, how to survive, and if his brother had on occasion felt more abused than aided, so be it. Life was harsh, Daniel knew, as his present situation confirmed.

James had been first to go to Europe at the beginning of the great conflict. He hadn't gone there to fight, as one might expect, but to drive an ambulance, a meat wagon. Daniel, on the other hand, sought to fly, to dominate the skies and rain harm upon the enemy. He had arrived in France ready to pass tests and master tactics, but his eyes had betrayed him. Nevertheless, he had *served*, had been there when the pilots limped home in broken planes, had fixed the Blériots and Nieuports, had celebrated the victories and mourned the fallen. The men had liked him, encouraged him, rewarded his enthusiasm with respect and admiration, and when the commanding officers were not around, they'd somewhat taught him how to fly. Had it not been for a drunken bet with another airman, he would not have stolen a plane, not crashed it in a farmer's field and broken his legs, not made such a mess of his life.

He spoke French passably well now, though he often pretended to be mute. Occasionally he slipped, as he had a few months earlier when a pretty young woman had dropped some change at his feet. He'd thanked her in English, which would not have mattered except that she was American, and, worse, a friend of James. Daniel had seen them together at least three times. After that, he was careful to stay away from that particular street corner. She'd spotted him a few days later and he'd made a quick getaway.

He was not sure of his own actions anymore. He simply sensed that in time something would happen, and that he should be there when it did.

So, 72 hours after being turned away from the embassy, Daniel Johnson was sitting on a bench in the Parc Monceau, eating a dry sandwich of yesterday's bread, last week's butter, and a sliver of ham bought at an *épicerie*. The *épicier,* an unkind man, had sliced the meat to wafer thin shavings, and Daniel saw the man's thumb on the scale when the ham was weighed.

Daniel had ended his drinking four days ago, and he was devoid of sense or reason. A deep anger rankled without settling on any single incident; he wanted to drink but his resolve, at least today, was steady in spite of the cravings, even as he felt the madness creeping over him. He was broke, having spent all but a few *sous,* and he had not begged for three days. He was almost clean-shaven; reddish stubbles spiked his face. His hair was cut neatly and parted on the right side. He wore a second-hand shirt and pants, and a battered *casquette* pulled down low over his eyes.

Twice in two days he had seen James escorting the woman who had almost unmasked him. They held hands, and Daniel assumed they were lovers, but thought she was far too attractive to be with someone like his brother. James, Daniel knew, had always been shy around women, stuttering like a squirrel whenever a girl spoke to him or looked his way. Daniel remembered that James had once had a monstrous crush on Marie Anne Wharple, who lived two houses down the street. Daniel had told Marie Anne that his brother was simple-minded and that their Father was going to be sending James to a special school for backward children. For weeks, Daniel had guffawed at his brother's bewilderment when Marie Anne ignored him or worse, made strange faces and ran away. Then, one day, James had cornered Marie Anne in the school hallway. She had confessed what Daniel had told her. Furious, James had flailed at his brother and been rewarded with a split lip and black eye. Later, Daniel told their father that James had gotten into a fight with a bigger boy and that he, Daniel, had saved him from a savage beating. James was sent to his room without supper; Daniel was given an extra portion of dessert. Marie Anne Wharple never spoke to either boy again.

It angered Daniel that James was now the taller of the two. His brother's posture was erect but not rigid, and he walked with confidence, the woman's hand moving to rest lightly on the crook of his elbow. They were talking, laughing over something that did not include him.

Daniel fought valiantly against the temptation to leap out, shout who he was and watch the astonishment on James's face, but it no longer seemed so appealing when Daniel looked down at his scuffed shoes and ragged pants. The woman would be repulsed, and James, so dapper now, would he hold his nose in disgust as he had as a child? He might. So, when Easter and James passed close to Daniel, he pulled the hat tight down over his forehead and pretended to be asleep on the park bench.

It bothered him, this strange situation. *He* was the war hero. *He* had given his youth to the effort. *He,* rightly, should have been the one rewarded by the attention of a pretty young woman. His brother had been a transporter of bodies, nothing more than the driver of a hearse.

The day was warmer than usual. He had the shakes and was sweating, a revolting set of withdrawal symptoms. He rolled a cigarette using a small square of discarded newspaper, then inhaled, felt the acid flow of tobacco, ink, and newsprint sear his lungs. He flicked off the ember with an index finger and stowed the butt in a pocket. His head fell forward. He slept.

CHAPTER 72

On opening night, it rained with unusual ferocity. Fat drops splattered on the streets into instant floods, cars stalled in traffic amid horrific jams and a din of horns. Inside the theater, Cocteau fretted, paced, whined, irritating an already tense cast and crew. It was not until the hall was two-thirds full that he began to calm down, informing Easter in all seriousness that it was his angst that had drawn spectators.

"My anguish spreads over Paris like an *édredon*, a quilt, I think that is the word. Strangers come to bask in it and friends to save me from perdition. That is always the case with my creations…"

Easter no longer paid much attention to the playwright's strange pronouncements. She admired Cocteau, found him amusing and entertaining, and envied his ability to get *le tout Paris* to attend one of his events. He had cajoled and enticed some of the city's brightest lights to come and see a marginal experiment that, she was sure, would not be remembered a year from now.

Cocteau himself appeared to agree and was quoted in an interview as saying, "In *Le Boeuf*, nothing happens. Look for no double meaning, no anachronism. It is an American farce, written by a Parisian who has never been in America."

Later, immensely pleased with himself, he would tell Easter, "I invented a word, *coctelian*. Isn't it wonderful? It describes me perfectly. I made a bet with Pablo that it will be in the *Dictionnaire Larousse* within five years!"

The first two rows of orchestra seats were filled by friends of the Comte de Beaumont, a nobleman interested in promoting *nouveaux spectacles*. The Count had reserved the theater's boxes as well and these held an assortment of women models, members of the *beau monde*, politicians, and musicians from John Philip Sousa's marching band on a six-month post-war tour of Europe.

Backstage, Easter helped the actors with their costumes. The giant *papier-mâché* heads were still troublesome. They were held in place by a complicated set of harnesses that were tight and uncomfortable to the wearer, but when loosened enough allowed the heads to slip sideways.

The policeman's head, which was to be lopped off on stage by a ceiling fan, was proving particularly difficult. Easter struggled with it as its wearer, one of the Fratellini brothers, cursed under his breath in French and Italian while sweating garlic and tomato fumes.

Guy-Pierre Fauconnet had died of a heart attack shortly after a particularly demanding rehearsal, and Cocteau had persuaded the Fauvist painter Raoul Dufy to take over the costumes and final details of the set production. Dufy exhibited no urgency. A superstitious man, he thought the production might be ill-favored, but agreed to the project, he admitted to Easter, so he could become better acquainted with the Comte de Beaumont. He hoped the count, who appeared to have unending funds, might show interest in subsidizing a mural Dufy was planning for an exposition on St. Germain.

Easter, who'd liked Fauconnet and bought one of his paintings, attended the funeral service but had no time to mourn properly. In the last days before the opening, the rehearsals had become frenzied gatherings that taxed each and every participant. Nor had she managed to get a complete grasp of the play's plot, such as it was.

Cocteau had refused to elucidate." *C'est ce que tu veux, chère Easter.* It is whatever you would like it to be."

As far as she could tell, the pantomime took place in the present time—that was to say, during the prohibition—in an unnamed bar of an anonymous American city. A Negro boxer smoked a large cigar, a Negro dwarf capered about the stage, the decapitated policeman searched for his head while being tickled by the barman. A red-haired woman gymnast walked on her hands as the bar customers danced, flirted, drank, and gestured at one another, all in slow motion. In rehearsal, the piece took fifteen minutes from opening to closing curtain, but Cocteau and Milhaud promised to draw out the performance by repeating musical phrases.

That people would pay good money to see this defied logic, and both Easter and James thought the play would close after one show.

CHAPTER 73

Later that afternoon Daniel Johnson started drinking again, using his last *centimes* to buy a *demi* of wine. After only twenty minutes with the bottle of *gros rouge*, he had forgotten what anger had so consumed him that alcohol was the sole option left. It had something to do with James, and something to do with James's woman, but that was all he could recall. He was hungry and his stomach rumbled, and now it was James's well-fed demeanor that infuriated him.

He had no real plan. He followed the couple, trying to be discreet, to blend in, but he bumped into pedestrians at least twice. James and the woman were so engrossed in each other that they never noticed him.

They stopped once, and the woman turned to face James and kissed him long on the lips. Daniel stopped as well and pretended to light a cigarette.

She was wearing a coat that hugged her hips, and he could see the swell of her rear against the fabric. She displayed a pair of earrings with red stones—rubies?—set in gold, and a matching bracelet. When she turned to kiss James, Daniel saw a necklace loosely looping her nape. He wondered if the stones were real, then let the thought fritter away.

When they reached the Avenue Montaigne near the Théâtre des Champs Élysées, they paused and were soon joined by a dapper man whom Daniel had seen before coming in and out of James's building. The man hugged Easter, kissed James on both cheeks. Daniel snorted, muttered "Faggot."

CHAPTER 74

Landru had an aisle seat on the tenth row, not too far from an exit, not too close to the stage. He wished he were more properly attired for an evening at the théâtre, but many men and women in the audience wore proletarian garb, with the exception of the first two rows. The latter were elegantly attired, busty women in organdy dresses and too much jewelry, upright men in evening tuxedos. Landru assumed they were *bourgeoisie* or lower nobility, or friends of the playwright and composer.

He had always loved theater, great or small. He knew every *café concert* in Paris and attended the opera regularly. In fact, the day after his arrest, newspapers throughout the country had made much of his singing *Adieu Petite Table,* the farewell aria from Massenet's *Manon Lescaut,* when the police led him away from his mistress's apartment.

He'd seen *Le Boeuf sur le Toit* advertised in *Le Petit Parisien* and thought it might be interesting. The price of a ticket was well within his means, and, somewhat depressed over the death of Brigitte Bonjean, Landru had decided to treat himself.

He had genuinely liked Brigitte, found her humorous and pleasant. The decision to rid himself of her after his escape was sad but necessary. She died quickly, quietly; this was the only gift he could offer. He'd waited until she was nude, exhausted from lovemaking and wine, then finished sedating her with chloroform. He'd lifted her with difficulty into the bathtub full of warm water, wrapped her neck in a thick towel and opened the carotid artery with the blade of his razor. She did not make a sound, her breathing merely stopped, one whisper gone within the noise of the city. He dismembered her with regretful and practiced strokes, lost her body in various neighborhoods.

He missed her. He hadn't spoken to anyone in days save to buy food and drink.

The man on his left smelled poorly. Landru thought of changing seats, but the theater was filling quickly so instead he took a scented handkerchief from his pocket and held it to his nose. The square of cloth imbued with lavender reminded him of Brigitte. It had been hers.

She had pleased him; her retelling of maneuvering the laundry cart during his escape, almost overturning it in the street fronting the prison, made him laugh uproariously, harder than he had in years. He missed her hips, the trimmed cleft at the center of her body and the warmth of her legs around him, the way she could perfectly imitate a police whistle being blown by an out-of-breath *gendarme*, how she enjoyed small cigars without taking the smoke into her lungs. He missed her perfume, something expensive by Guerlain that she had stolen from the Galeries Lafayette and wore, she said, only when she was to see him. Just a few days earlier, he had been caressed by the scent while walking near Montparnasse and it had so taken him that he'd followed the unknown woman wearing it several blocks, feeling like an enamored schoolboy. He had purposefully stayed a few meters behind her, unwilling to chance coming closer, and he'd noticed the woman was roughly the same size and height as Brigitte. He had felt his heart pause in his chest, forced himself to turn and walk the other way.

Landru shook his head, used his handkerchief to dab at a tear.

He looked at the program. There were several performances scheduled, all of which Brigitte would have found amusing. He dabbed at his eyes again and muscled his way out of his seat and back into the aisle, headed for the concession stand in the lobby. Brigitte, too, had adored the *café-concert* and on occasion performed there. She could read music, had a more than acceptable singing voice, and knew most tunes of the day by heart. Landru had a particular fondness for the singer Yvette Gilbert—he liked her long and lean nose—and was delighted when Brigitte sang the star's tunes.

He bought a bar of chocolate and a lemonade from one of the theater girls, ate and drank standing up, then returned to his seat.

He was used to the stone in his right shoe and the limp it caused was by now second nature. What he had not managed to accept gracefully was the wig, which, since it had never been fitted professionally, was a constant reminder of his fugitive state. Still, he could not go without it. His face, bearded and mustachioed, was in every Post Office, *Commissariat*, *mairie,* and public hall in the country. Now clean shaven, bewigged and limping, he was unrecognizable. He did not wear his *pince-nez* glasses in public, was careful to limit his conversations to a minimum lest he let something slip. He had fooled them all, the police, the prosecutors, all who sought to imprison him. He was free and undeniably miserable.

CHAPTER 75

Cocteau beamed. Milhaud glared—the musicians had massacred his composition. Picasso smiled superciliously. The Fratellini brothers were gathering their overcoats as the Comte Etienne de Beaumont shook hands with Raoul Dufy, agreeing to underwrite the painter's next project.

The critics had hastily written their pieces and sent them to their papers via taxicabs, a good sign that the reviews would be favorable. Easter, exhausted, found James engrossed in conversation with Leo Zborowski. James put an arm around her shoulder and said, "Leo wants to handle my work! He says he believes he can set up a show at the Papillon Gallery. Isn't that wonderful?"

Easter hugged them both, chatted for a minute or two, then excused herself. "I am sweltering here, gentlemen. Please allow me to disappear and get a breath of fresh air."

She left them as Zborowski asked James how many canvases were ready for display.

On her way to the doors, Easter was intercepted by a resplendent Edith Wharton, swathed in sable and accompanied by a man of indeterminate origin sporting a canary yellow sport coat.

Wharton grabbed Easter's arm, shouted over the din: "Wonderful! Loved it!" She did not introduce her escort but added: "And Easter, you look *ravishing!*"

Easter smiled, pointed to the jewelry Wharton had lent her, but the writer made a face.

"Return them tomorrow, or the day after, or maybe next week will be fine for that." She shimmered away, trailing the yellow sport coat.

Easter squeezed through the crowd, retrieved her own coat from the check room, stepped out of the theater and into the night air. It was unseasonably warm and she stood on the sidewalk, suddenly very aware of her American-ness. Her thoughts flashed back to Chicago, then returned to Paris. An immediate and sudden joy coursed through her and she clapped her hands like a child.

Below her, cabs vied for customers, a few of whom opted for horse-drawn carriages. She reached into her pockets for her gloves, searched for a moment, then realized she had left them on a table backstage. She turned to re-enter the crowded theater, thought better of it and headed instead for the stage door behind the building.

CHAPTER 76

All told, Landru thought the spectacle embarrassingly sophomoric. He much preferred the opening acts to the main one, and thought whoever had put together *Le Boeuf sur le Toit* must have had the intellect of a 10-year-old boy. Why, his own son, Maurice, could have done better!

Still, Landru had always been a polite and appreciative theater-goer, so he applauded, though without much enthusiasm. That some in the audience were cheering left him cold; obviously, the playwright had friends.

His thoughts turned again to Brigitte. Had she been with him, they would have discussed the performance's shortcomings over a late-night meal. She would have made him laugh, and later they would have returned to the room she rented and...

A man jostled him, apologized, moved on. Landru immediately checked for his wallet, found it. He detested pickpockets, knew they frequented theaters and music halls. His wig felt askew, so he tugged at it slightly. He was jostled again, this time without apology. A florid man with an exasperated brow was pulling along a small woman, who resisted. Landru stepped back, though his sense of propriety was somewhat offended. The protesting woman threw him a desperate glance, but he ignored her. He straightened his coat, hiked up his trousers and stepped into the aisle.

The scent froze him; his breath caught in his throat, he gasped, took in another lungful, and almost fainted. The perfume was subtle, insistent, filling the theater, overriding the miasma of other aromas, deafening, blinding.

Five rows closer to the stage, he caught sight of her. Brigitte? Impossible! He breathed again, felt the fragrance diffuse through his body, knew without a doubt it was hers. The woman who was not Brigitte turned slightly, her face blurred by his failing eyes. Landru at that moment would have given his freedom for a pair of spectacles; he squinted, tried to get a better view but the woman moved off, heading for an exit with a retinue of well-dressed spectators. He followed.

CHAPTER 77

Daniel Johnson had trailed them to the theater's entrance and, unable to get past the ticket-taker at the door, slumped against wall, his now empty bottle rolling at his feet. He was in the shadows, half there, half not, his imagination endeavoring and failing to create scenarios of revenge.

The thought of his brother, whole and uninjured, no broken legs there, no dishonorable descent to the level of the streets, no war, either, or danger of any kind—the ignominy of it was shattering. That James might be enjoying the favors of a beautiful American woman was equally galling. Daniel's last experience, barely remembered, was of prickly hay in a farmer's barn with a crying girl scarcely into womanhood. It had been wholly unsatisfying, malodorous, scratchy, a one-time wrestle while the rest of the family was at church. Afterwards, the girl had spit into her hands and had tried to wipe him away with a rag. She had not spoken throughout.

He heard the woman approach before he saw her.

CHAPTER 78

Landru was 20 feet behind the not-Brigitte, enraptured by the woman's perfume. He dared come no closer, closed his eyes, felt rather than smelled her fragrance cutting through the city's acrid mélange of bus and car exhaust, wet sidewalks, and leafless trees.

He felt rather than saw the indistinct shape launch itself at the woman; he heard her scream, heard her muffled fall, heard the sharp intakes of two breaths, one predatory, one prey.

He ran forward and the stone in his boot cut the bottom of his foot. He didn't feel it. He grabbed the assailant by the shoulders, pulled back, and was rewarded with a backhanded fist that caught him just above the bridge of the nose and knocked off his wig. He heard the woman yelp in pain, saw something red and glinting in the aggressor's hand, saw blood on the woman's temple.

Landru, small but no stranger to street fighting, stepped back and launched a hard kick that landed on the man's lower back, then another, slightly higher. The man grunted, let the woman go, turned. Landru kicked him again, this time in the stomach. The man stopped his charge, doubled over and vomited. The woman was screaming, a high wordless keening sound and Landru straddled the man's back, wrapped an arm about the neck and squeezed. The man struggled, rose to his feet, slammed Landru against a wall, did it again but failed to dislodge the clinging demon on his back. And then there was a whistle, running feet, shouts. Landru let the man go, bent to look down at the woman's face. She was sobbing; a trickle of blood ran down her right cheek from the torn lobe of her ear.

Landru cradled her head, whispered, *"C'est fini, mademoiselle. Ne vous en faites pas; tout ira bien."* He found the earring on the ground where the man had dropped it, handed it to her. *"Tenez, mademoiselle. Prenez ça, c'est à vous."*

Hands grabbed him, held him immobile. He saw the attacker stagger a few steps, crouch, begin to run crablike into the shadows, turn a corner and disappear.

Landru was jerked upright by arms stronger than his, spun around to find himself face to face with a very large, very young policeman trying to look older than his years. They stared at each other for a moment and the uniformed youth's eyes widened. He whispered, *"Mon Dieu, c'est lui..."*

A staggering exhaustion settled on Henri Désiré Landru's shoulders. His knees trembled and he dropped to the ground next to the woman. She was cupping her ear with one hand and still shaking. Landru put two fingers on her forearm, stroked it gently once, whispered again.

"Ça ira, mademoiselle. Tout va bien maintenant. Tout va bien."

CHAPTER 79

Landru's capture caused a sensation. The young policeman, eighteen years old, blue-eyed and handsome, was on the cover of every major magazine in France, Holland, and Belgium. He quit the force and starred in a movie as himself. He continued to act until the advent of talking motion pictures.

For a month or so, young women took to wearing only a left earring. They painted their right lobes to appear torn and bloody, as Easter's had been following the attack.

Easter was asked if she wanted to press charges and declined to do so. It would be silly, and she was not sure of what had happened. For days she struggled with the feeling that Landru, in fact, had not assaulted her, had instead come to her rescue, but that seemed so far-fetched that in time and in recounting, the murderer and womanizer did indeed become the culprit. Still, when she learned Landru was to be executed, she felt a strange and unaccountable emptiness.

CHAPTER 80

Monsieur Lefebvre and Mme. Colombini were wed four weeks later at the St. Joseph Catholic Church on Avenue Hoche. The ceremony was in English. St. Joseph's had a long history of serving Paris's Anglophones, and its parish priests were known for ministering to the English-speaking soldiers of the Allied Forces. Monsieur Lefebvre and his bride wanted their union to mirror the seriousness of their intents. They were going to America.

M. Lefebvre's colleagues were on hand in full uniform, as was the Parisian postal service's brass band, which played a medley of French, British, and American tunes. Mme. Colombini, sporting a new bobbed hairstyle, was resplendent in a silk tulle cloche over a multi-layered, off-white taffeta dress that gently draped her ample proportions.

Easter and Johnson attended, as did M. Lefebvre's cousin, Inspector Gaspard Belin. Belin hugged Easter, congratulated her on the *sang-froid* she had demonstrated during the horrifying Landru attack. She smiled, nodded, and did not mention her doubts. James Johnson and Belin got along very well—the inspector, it turned out, was something of an artist himself, a weekend painter of Parisian monuments and bridges, and he was happy to talk about the Landru case.

Mme. Bertrand, Johnson's concierge, was also in attendance and whispered to Easter that Mme. Colombini, considering her non-virginal status, should not have worn white, particularly since she was pregnant. Mme. Bertrand had a gift, she assured Easter, for divining such things. Twin girls, she said, within seven months. Mme. Bertrand hoped they were indeed from M. Lefebvre's seed.

CHAPTER 81

The Chinaman crossed Gumpendorfer Strasse in the heart of Vienna. He pedaled the bicycle with short, powerful strokes from legs knotted with muscle. Though nothing in his face showed save exertion and a light sheen of sweat, he was feeling good and thanking the spirits of his ancestors.

The load of folded and boxed white people's laundry was strapped down securely in the bicycle's basket, and neatly hidden at the bottom of the basket lay seven little packages of medical grade opium destined for three customers. One man would get five packages, which explained the Chinaman's happiness. The American businessman, the one who spoke no language other than English, was cultivating expensive tastes, and this was a pleasant development for the Chinaman to consider. He was not highly placed in the family that governed the opium trade in Vienna, but a few more clients like this one would enhance his standing. Soon he would have the funds to send for his wife and two sons.

But until then, he would have to be careful the American didn't take too much opium and die, so he shortchanged the American every time, a few grams less than what he had ordered, and he made sure the mix was not too potent. After the wife and two sons, there were many nephews and cousins to bring over. The American would have to last a long while.

To be continued...

EPILOGUE

Henri Désiré Landru was executed February 25, 1922, in Versailles. His death by guillotine was witnessed by members of the press and by some survivors of his crimes. Easter Cowles was invited to attend and declined. Landru maintained his innocence to the end. His descendants were granted a change of name by the French government. Four great grand-children still live in Paris.

Monsieur Lefebvre and his wife, the former Mme. Colombini, and their twin daughters, sailed to New York on the Normandie a year to the day after their marriage. They eventually settled in New Orleans and opened the Café de la Croix in the French Quarter. The couple would have seven children.

Daniel Johnson was issued a passport and repatriated to the United States in January, 1922, following a program of detoxification in Bern, Switzerland. He never married and took his own life in December, 1931. His child by Lucienne Lupin learned to speak English from a tutor and often spent holidays in Paris with James Johnson and Easter. She never met her father.

Jean Cocteau, one of the 20th century's most prolific artists, left his mark in a variety of media including music, film, painting, poetry, lithographs, théâtre, fiction, and sculpture. He died in Milly-la-Forêt, on October 11, 1963.

ACKNOWLEDGMENTS

Books seldom write themselves. *Montparnasse* almost did. I have been fascinated with that neighborhood and era since childhood, and I suspect my subconscious was figuring out plot twists for a couple of decades before I put pen to paper.

This being said, many, many friends, acquaintances, and scholars pitched in. Paris is perhaps the most often written-about city in the world, so I thank the numerous authors whose works I relied upon for veracity. Many of the restaurants and cafés mentioned still exist, even if their names and ownerships have changed. The artists mentioned in the book all have copious biographies to their names. I've read hundreds and, on occasion, have taken some liberties with facts regarding their lives and deaths.

The book started out as a 600-page manuscript. Talented readers and editors helped me trim it to a manageable size. I have to thank Melanie Davis, Dani Williams, Patricia Buckley, Arielle Seidman, Paul Lavrakas, and all the writers in the various authors' groups I attend. Almost every word in *Montparnasse* was read and critiqued by a host of talented writers who gave me their thoughts and made the book better.

Finally, I have to thank my mother, Marie-Thérèse Henriette Hughette Février Sagnier, a talented artist in her own rights who regaled me with stories of the *Montparnasse* and Montmartre *quartiers* and their denizens.

Merci à tous!

Thierry Sagnier

About the Author

Thierry Sagnier is a writer whose works have been published both in the United States and abroad. He is the author of *The IFO Report* (Avon Books), *Bike! Motorcycles and the People who Ride Them* (Harper & Row), and *Washington by Night* (Washingtonian Books). He is also the author of *Thirst*, a thriller based in Washington, DC's, mean streets. *Writing about People, Places and Things* is a collection of essays chronicling Sagnier's thoughts on writing, family and friendships, and cancer.

In 2016 he wrote *The Fortunate Few*, recounting the memories of the men and women who served with the International Voluntary Services, the precursor of the Peace Corps. *L'Amérique*, the tale of a French family coming to America in the 50s, was published in 2018 by Apprentice House Press. He is currently working on sequels to *L'Amérique*, *Thirst*, and *Montparnasse*.

Sagnier was born in France and came to the United States in his early teens. He has worked and written for *The Washington Post* and several other newspapers and magazines, produced videos and short films for the Canadian Broadcasting Corporation, and was a columnist for Canada's *Le Devoir*. He was Senior Writer for the World Bank and traveled the world to write about that institution's projects in developing countries.

His plays have been produced both locally and by Tada Theater in New York, as well as featured by the East End Fringe Festival.

He currently lives in Virginia.

Apprentice
House Press
Loyola University Maryland

Apprentice House is the country's only campus-based, student-staffed book publishing company. Directed by professors and industry professionals, it is a nonprofit activity of the Communication Department at Loyola University Maryland.

Using state-of-the-art technology and an experiential learning model of education, Apprentice House publishes books in untraditional ways. This dual responsibility as publishers and educators creates an unprecedented collaborative environment among faculty and students, while teaching tomorrow's editors, designers, and marketers.

Outside of class, progress on book projects is carried forth by the AH Book Publishing Club, a co-curricular campus organization supported by Loyola University Maryland's Office of Student Activities.

Eclectic and provocative, Apprentice House titles intend to entertain as well as spark dialogue on a variety of topics. Financial contributions to sustain the press's work are welcomed. Contributions are tax deductible to the fullest extent allowed by the IRS.

To learn more about Apprentice House books or to obtain submission guidelines, please visit www.apprenticehouse.com.

Apprentice House
Communication Department
Loyola University Maryland
4501 N. Charles Street
Baltimore, MD 21210
Ph: 410-617-5265 • Fax: 410-617-2198
info@apprenticehouse.com • www.apprenticehouse.com